Bernie & Bertie

by

Mike Owens

Bernie & Bertie

Cover Art by *Jennifer Greeff*

The Wild Rose Press, Inc.
PO Box 708
Adams Basin, NY 14410-0708
Visit us at www.thewildrosepress.com

Publishing History
First Crimson Rose Edition, 2020
Trade Paperback ISBN 978-1-5092-3272-7
Digital ISBN 978-1-5092-3273-4

Published in the United States of America

He followed her inside past the hanging frozen carcasses, to the back of the truck, half expecting a bloodied, frigid Dr. Carruthers to leap out and grab him by the throat.

"Here we are," Bertie said. And there, between the carcasses of two pigs hanging from hooks, was the former Dr. Carruthers, wrapped in heavy plastic and hanging upright from a hook.

"Bertie, she's naked." The nausea came roaring back.

"Of course, I couldn't very well leave her in a dress. Anybody who came into the truck would have spotted that right off."

"But you took off everything." Of course, Bertie was right about the dress. Leaving Dr. Carruthers fully clothed would be silly at best, dangerous at worst. But the harsh fluorescent light left nothing to the imagination.

"Look around, Bernie, do you see any meat hanging in here wearing a bra and panties?"

Praise for Mike Owens

"Get ready for a book that will keep you guessing the whole way through, as you turn each page wanting more! In Michael Owens' thrilling *BERNIE & BERTIE*, you won't help laughing, even though you may be in shock—because you've never read characters like this before."

~*Michael Jon Khandelwal, Executive Director*
The Muse Writers Center (Norfolk, VA)

Dedication

To members of the Fiction Writers' Studio
at the Muse Writers Center,
with thanks for helping develop this project

Chapter One

It was a dark and stormy night…or not. Thirty-four-year-old Bernie Mitchell couldn't remember for sure. Lately, he couldn't remember what he'd had for breakfast, or if he'd even eaten breakfast. Those electroshock treatments—ECT, his therapist called them—blew bits of recent memory out of his brain like so much exhaust from a tailpipe, not necessarily a bad thing because many of his memories were best forgotten.

But one thing he knew for certain, she was dead, that woman stretched out motionless on his living room floor. It had happened so quickly, but that was usually the case. Sometimes, afterward, he felt as if he'd imagined the whole event, but no, there was a real body lying there, freshly deceased. He'd done it again. Now his evening was ruined, and it was all her fault, everything. If she weren't already dead, he would make her clean up the mess she'd made.

Just another quiet evening at the Mitchell house, at least, that's how it began. He'd just taken his pasta dinner out of the microwave and set the container on the table beside his beer when the doorbell rang. He ignored it. It rang again. Then again. Somebody wasn't giving up, and somebody would be sorry. A very pissed off Bernie stomped off toward the door, his heavy footsteps making the overhead lights flicker.

"Hi, my name is…" A petite blonde with an old-fashioned beehive hairdo and a briefcase, she wore a bright yellow blazer with a logo on the breast pocket. She breezed right past him at his front door without being invited in, then dropped that weighty briefcase on his coffee table where it landed with a thud.

She didn't even sit down before she started in on something about long-term care insurance. "Have you ever thought what would happen to you if you had a disabling illness, like a stroke? You know, where you don't actually die but you can't take care of yourself either. I mean, nobody likes to think about these things but it's better to be prepared, you know?"

What the hell was she talking about?

"Okay if I call you Bernie?" Where had she gotten his name? *Chirp, chirp, chirp.* She just wouldn't shut up. She walked around his living room like she owned it, all the while yapping about care facilities and not becoming a burden on his friends or family and other crap that meant nothing to him because he had neither friends nor family.

She touched his things, his framed citation for not missing a day of work at the Post Office for eight years running. She tapped on the glass case where his pet copperhead, Alvin, slept. When Alvin struck, banging his head on the glass, she jumped back. "Ohmigod. I didn't know it was alive."

"Please, be careful." Bernie clenched his fists, or rather, his fists clenched all by themselves, because a guy could only put up with so much, and beyond that, things just happened.

"What's this?" She walked over and stuck her nose close to the model Bernie had made, one of many.

"It's a model airplane, a P51 Mustang."

"You made this, all by yourself?" She ran her finger along the fuselage. The model wavered on its spindly stand. "How cute. Wow, the little propellers turn too."

She did a pirouette and smiled at him as if she was going to come over and pat him on the head for being such a clever boy. Then she said it, "Groovy."

Groovy? Did she really say groovy? That did it. He couldn't take any more. Nobody could have. Everything that happened after that, all her fault. Now she lay there on the floor, sightless eyes staring upward, a quizzical look as if she were confused, like she'd forgotten her place in her little presentation. He could almost hear her saying in that stupid singsong voice, "Oh, wow, I've got this axe stuck in my head, and I just can't figure out how it got there."

He expected, when he hit her, a quiet collapse to the floor, like the others, but no, she had to go all dramatic on him. She twirled around like a drunken ballerina who had been spinning in the same place for too long, all the while making a noise like a train whistle in a tunnel. She thrashed about, grabbed for the mantelpiece, missed, and fell headlong into the fireplace, then rolled out covered in a thick paste of blood and ashes and crawled across the floor. Appalling behavior, just appalling and so unnecessary.

The ordeal ended when she collided with the sofa. That spot must have been okay for her because she rolled over onto her back and didn't move again.

What a mess. Blood and ashes congealed into a sticky swath that marked her path from fireplace to sofa and was already beginning to smell like the bottom of a laundry hamper. The carpet was probably ruined, and he had just vacuumed earlier in the day. It would take the rest of the night to clean things up. Now his dinner was cold and his beer warm. He didn't deserve this.

Her open eyes bothered him, seemed to follow him around the room. He tried to close them with the toe of his slipper, but they wouldn't stay shut, so he draped the sports section of the morning newspaper over her face. He dropped to one knee when the headline caught his eye: *Cubs Lose Again.* Damn. Nothing was going right.

With all that floundering about, she'd managed to foul the axe handle now protruding from her head with the same blood-and-ashes paste that covered her face and shoulders. The axe was brand new—a Penn Model 32XX Climbing Axe with a titanium head, and Bernie wanted it back. He'd just bought it the week before and might need it again.

When Bernie had laid the axe on the desk beside the cash register, the skinny little clerk at Alpine Outfitters had looked him up and down, his gaze finally resting on the thick midsection that hung over Bernie's belt. "You don't look like a climber."

"It's a gift." Bernie focused on a spot just above where the clerk's raised eyebrows nearly touched. How he'd love to drive the axe point in there. *Do I look like a climber now, you think?*

Yeah, he wanted that axe back. For certain he'd need it again. Things just worked out that way. But to get it he'd have to touch her head, a sickening thought, touching dead things, ugh. He went into the garage, looking for work gloves, plastic wrap, anything that would spare him the revolting prospect of touching her with his bare hands.

Bitsy, his longhaired Persian cat, had been lurking in the garage and dashed between Bernie's legs as he headed back into the living room.

"Dammit, Bitsy," he said when he found the cat sitting on the woman's chest, kneading the goo that had dribbled down from her head. "You'll track that shit all over the house."

Bitsy flicked his tail in the air and jumped onto the sofa, his path marked by alternating black and red paw prints.

Bernie plopped into his leather recliner and laid back, his arm across his forehead. He grabbed a chocolate-covered mint from the box beside his chair and popped it into his mouth. It just wasn't fair. Why did things always go wrong for him?

He glanced at the body and groaned. Whatever would he do with this one?

****

Tuesday morning, nine a.m. sharp. Bernie was never late for his appointment. Most mornings he was early—not too early, not like some needy out-of-control type, just early enough to show he was serious about his sessions. Not so with his therapist, Dr. Bowman. She usually dashed through the door—Starbucks' latte in one hand, briefcase in the other—with about thirty seconds to spare. Once she'd even left a couple of curlers dangling in her hair like cheap holiday ornaments. Sometimes Bernie wondered who was really the crazy one here.

The inner office bore no traces of clinical activity or intent, nothing even vaguely medical in sight. It was also rather impersonal, no certificates or diplomas on the walls, only a few photos of Dr. Bowman and some other lady who, in each picture, had her arm around Dr. Bowman's shoulders. He'd never asked about the photo, and Dr. Bowman never volunteered any information about the mystery woman…family? Friend?

Only the sofa close by Dr. Bowman's desk looked out of place. Who'd put a sofa in the middle of the room? The sofa was obviously there for the truly crazy ones, of which Bernie definitely wasn't. Several times during their early sessions, she'd encourage him to lie back there, explaining that relaxation often helped open up the mind and let thoughts flow more freely. No way, Bernie didn't want his mind opened up and wasn't about to let his thoughts flow freely. So, he always took the armchair close by the desk where he kept close rein on any wayward thoughts and where he could observe the observer, his therapist.

Her routine was always the same. She'd pick up her notebook, lean back in her chair, take a couple of deep breaths, then make eye contact. Probably some sort of ritual they'd instilled during her training.

"How was your weekend, Bernie?"

"Fine."

"Any new problems?" She made quick notes on the writing pad she kept by her right hand, probably just checking items off so she wouldn't repeat herself.

"No."

"Anything in particular you'd like to discuss today?"

"Not really."

"How's your depression?"

"Okay." Their sessions were often like a game of

ping-pong, same questions, same answers, but that routine seemed to satisfy Dr. Bowman. Whatever kept her happy kept Bernie happy too, so long as she didn't get any bright ideas about changing his therapy. As long as he got what he needed—ECT—he would play along.

"Are you sleeping well?" Sometimes she threw in a sleep question, almost like an afterthought, sometimes she didn't.

"Yes." Now he could answer that question in the affirmative. But before the blessing of ECT, Bernie rarely slept because that was when those horrible, gory visions of people he'd had to kill, blood still oozing from the wounds he'd had to inflict, came to haunt him. They'd hover about his bed, sometimes one, sometimes many, but none of them wished him well. It was as if they couldn't wait for him to join them *on the other side*, where they could get at him. Only after his ECT treatment sessions erased his short-term memory, banishing those specters, could he sleep soundly. To Bernie, it was the wall between the living and the dead, and a non-negotiable part of his treatment.

Bernie always came prepared to his counseling sessions. Psychiatrists, or so he'd heard, could read your mind. He didn't care for that idea, not at all. So, it wasn't as much the answers he gave her—they were always the same—rather it was the way he gave them, the body language, and, over his months of therapy, he'd become quite the expert. Since a diagnosis of severe depression was what kept him in the game, he'd mastered the appearance of clinical despair, sitting for hours in front of his mirror, practicing listless, practicing hopeless, practicing dejected. In particular,

7

before his appointment time, he'd sit and recite his depression mantra:

"I am worthless, I have no future, my life isn't worth living."

He'd mumble the lines to himself again on the way to her office, then use the expression on Dr. Bowman's receptionist's face to gauge how effective his act was. After all, two could play the body language game. If the receptionist, a blonde woman who never left her seat behind the desk, said something like, "Oh, poor Bernie, are you having a bad day?" he knew he was right on target. Other times, when he felt he wasn't creating the dramatic impact he wanted, he'd squeeze out a few tears.

True enough, in the beginning things hadn't gone so well with his therapy. Sometimes things seemed to spin out of control. Months passed while Dr. Bowman simply tinkered with his medications, and little changed in his life. Whenever he heard one of those '60s clichés: "far out," "right on," or—worst of all—"groovy," somebody usually died. Not his fault, things just happened, all beyond his control. Needless to say, these events caused him no end of difficulty; bodies to dispose of, messy sites to clean up—blood stains were so hard to get out. Not like he didn't have other things to do.

But that wasn't the real problem. Doing in people who didn't have the good sense to stay out of his way was an inconvenience, like taking out the garbage, nothing more. The problem came after. Bernie called them the Dream People because that's when they tormented him most. No sooner would he drift off to sleep than his most recent kills would reappear, floating about the room, screaming silently. Even when he pulled the sheet over his head, he knew they were still there, complete with the gory wounds he'd inflicted. It was the most unkind cut of all: first they'd goaded him into killing them, then they lacked the decency to go away and stay away. Before the shock treatments, he worried constantly, chewed his nails, developed a nervous tic. It was all so unfair.

Only when Dr. Bowman began a trial of ECT did Bernie's life improve, but he wasn't sold on it, not at first. "No way," he'd said when she first mentioned it. "I saw that in a movie. It was awful. Barbaric." The memory of the victim, electrodes pasted to his head, bouncing around on the gurney when they turned on the current, was too much. Even though it was just a bunch of actors probably hamming it up for dramatic effect, he wanted no part of it.

"It's not like that now, Bernie, not like that at all."

"I'm not going into a hospital. I hate hospitals."

Dr. Bowman put her hand on his arm. Except for shaking his hand when they first met, she'd never touched him before. "I said it's not what you think. It's all done as an outpatient. You come in and leave on the same day."

"I won't have to stay in the hospital?"

She shook her head. "I'll give you a sedative through an IV. You won't even know when it happens, and you won't even remember it afterward. We'll keep you a short time for observation, then, off you go."

There had to be a catch. "What about—what do you call them—side effects?"

"You might have a little memory loss. It's usually not severe."

"Memory loss? You're gonna turn me into a vegetable?" Bernie gripped the arms of his chair, ready to bolt. Many years before, his mother had dragged him along to a long-term care facility to visit her aunt, an elderly woman tied to a chair, eyes like blank spaces, with green liquid dripping down her chin. That memory burned into his adolescent brain, becoming a permanent fixture. He never knew what happened to that unfortunate woman, how she came to be in a vegetative state, but he couldn't take the chance of becoming that way himself.

Dr. Bowman laughed. "No, no. You'll be able to do everything you're doing now. It mostly involves recent memories, and it usually isn't severe, so it won't cause you any problems."

Recent memories? He had a few of those he'd like to be rid of. "You promise it won't hurt?"

"Promise."

****

A very subdued and apprehensive Bernie reported to outpatient admitting at Bandon General Hospital on a sunny April morning that should have raised his mood but did not. He looked at the stack of forms the receptionist pushed across the desk to him. "I thought I wasn't going to be here very long."

"Oh, no, you're not. This is all routine, just insurance information, who we should call if something happens, things like that."

"What do you mean, if something happens?"

"Just routine information we have to keep on file. Dr. Bowman will explain it all to you."

He made up a name on the spot. If they ever checked, he could always say he forgot how to spell it correctly. Anyway, he was having second thoughts, third thoughts, even. Why did he ever agree to this?

At that moment Dr. Bowman arrived, which was fortunate, because Bernie was just about to bolt. The idea of having his brain microwaved was looking less and less attractive.

"As soon as you've finished your paperwork, one of the aides will bring you back, and we can get started. You won't need your bag. You'll be going home later this morning."

He searched her face for some hidden agenda; there had to be a catch. They were going to put him to sleep—conscious sedation, she'd called it—then zap his head like a bag of frozen spinach. How could that possibly do him any good? Beef cattle, he wondered, when they reached that final point just before they ceased to be cattle and became beef, did they know what was coming? Would he?

The aide who conducted him to the point of no return, a quiet room that, in spite of the bright floral wallpaper, was filled with gadgets and equipment that reminded him of the movie where Dr. Frankenstein blasted an electric current into his monster. What if, instead of making things better, they got worse? What if he became a monster? Would he be chased through the village by a mob waving torches and pitchforks?

The slender aide, who had identified herself as Sadie, while the same height as Bernie, couldn't weigh half as much, must have sensed his apprehension. If he decided to bolt, very much a possibility now, she must have known there was no way she could restrain him. "It's going to be just fine, Mr. Mitchell. I've seen this done lots of times. Don't worry."

"You've seen it?" he asked.

"Oh, sure. Dr. Bowman is very experienced. You're in good hands."

Later, when he tried to reconstruct the events that followed, everything after the time he climbed onto a gurney was very fuzzy. Then, "Mr. Mitchell, Mr. Mitchell." Someone rubbing his shoulder. It felt good. "Time to wake up." He didn't even know he'd been asleep.

****

Miracle of miracles! Dr. Bowman was spot on about the sedative effects, and the results of ECT were far better than he could have hoped. There may or may not have been some improvement in his depression, but that was never the problem to begin with, not for Bernie. What mattered most was that the images of those dreadful dream people who tortured his sleep were now muted, sometimes gone altogether. His slate of misdeeds was wiped clean, and he could go to bed without any fear of unwelcome visitors. Thanks to the recent-memory erasing effects of ECT, Bernie was a new man.

Not completely new, of course. Although the spectral visions from his past were less troubling, his future still had a few speed bumps in reserve, events beyond his control. Just as before, hearing any of those special '60s clichés still sent him into a tailspin, forcing him to add to an already lengthy list of victims, like the slightly-built Bible salesman who appeared at his door one Sunday afternoon and uttered, "Right on, brother," when Bernie told him he attended church regularly and had no need for an additional Bible.

The salesman could have walked away unharmed,

but he seemed determined to make a sale, and be a nuisance and no sooner had he turned his back to reach into his shabby valise for another Bible than Bernie's fingers had tightened around his chicken neck. After all the unnecessary wriggling, kicking and thrashing about, he managed to smash one of Bernie's dining room chairs. Bernie, rightfully so, became quite angry and did some truly dreadful things to the body before dumping it into the ravine just up the county road from his house.

The week after he'd dispatched the Bible salesman to find out for himself whether there really was a heaven or hell—not that he'd be able to report back, one way or the other—Bernie had another ECT treatment. His recent recollections, including the strangulation, vanished into the void, and, once again, his slate was wiped clean.

The only downside from his treatments was he sometimes forgot stuff he needed to remember, like whether he'd paid his utilities bill. So, he made himself a checklist to remember what he couldn't remember.

****

For the past twelve years or so, thirty-four-year-old Bernie Mitchell had lived in the same small house, fourteen hundred square feet, attached garage, on Mulberry Street, a dead end avenue close by the southern coast of Oregon, accompanied more recently by Bitsy, a temperamental Persian cat and Alvin, a three-foot-long copperhead that appeared to have no personality whatever.

A creature of habit, Bernie's daily routine remained unchanged. His trips outside the house included daily drives to his workplace at the Post Office in Bandon, twice-monthly visits to his therapist, weekly trips to the same market for the same selection of groceries, and the pet store for mice to feed to Alvin and cat food and litter for Bitsy. He saw no reason for running about the countryside except for those special occasions when it became absolutely necessary.

The few people who knew him, mostly work associates, would probably describe him as a "loner," not because he had a bad reputation—he had no reputation at all—but because those unfortunate enough to witness his peculiar foibles were never around to pass on that information to others. So, Bernie remained a mystery, not that anyone cared, usually.

****

"You sure you don't recognize me?" The stocky detective at Bernie's door that Saturday afternoon scowled like he'd just chewed into something bitter. "I was here last month."

"Nope." Bernie shook his head. "But I been really busy lately, might of forgot." In fact, he recalled the detective perfectly: a plodder, just going through the motions, no imagination, bad suit. This guy was no problem at all.

"Then maybe I ought to go over everything again." The detective pushed past and plopped down on his sofa. He pulled a manila envelope from his pocket and emptied a stack of photos onto Bernie's table. "Take a close look at these. Seen any of them?"

This was like one of Dr. Bowman's games—ask a question, then watch how he responded. Years in therapy taught Bernie a thing or two; the body language was always what they looked for. He had a little extra time on his hands. Maybe he should have some fun, string the guy along, toss out a few cues, then pull back. So, Bernie sat on the couch beside the detective, not meeting his gaze—the very image of someone with something to hide. Before he looked down at the photos, he took a deep breath, glanced down, then quickly looked away. "Nope."

"Look again." The detective leaned in closer, breathing more rapidly, disclosing that his lunch had been heavily seasoned with garlic.

This time Bernie picked up the stack, shuffled it like a deck of cards and pored over each one. He was careful to touch only the edges, mustn't leave any complete fingerprints. He turned them sideways, upside down, then, finally, "Nope."

The detective slumped and sighed. Probably, for a moment, he'd seen a flicker of light only to have it go out again. "Here's my card. You remember anything, call me."

"I'm curious." Bernie figured it would be suspicious if he didn't ask. "Why are you interested in these people? Did they do something bad?"

"They disappeared, some of them from right around here, in this neighborhood."

"Oh, really? How about that. You don't suppose...."

"Suppose what?" The detective's eyes grew hopeful again.

"Alien abduction." Bernie clenched his jaw, so he wouldn't laugh out loud. "Two weeks ago—I never told anybody about this—there was a big round light, it hung over the street. About eight o'clock. Then, last week it was back again."

"Huh?" The detective cocked his head like a puppy

hoping for a treat and looked sideways at Bernie.

"I wrote down the dates and times." Bernie leaned in closer, dropped his voice to a whisper. "Say, if you'll just tell me when these people disappeared, I can check it against my notes. Bet they match up."

"You're fucking crazy." The detective grabbed up his photos and edged away from Bernie like he was afraid he might catch something. "You oughta get help."

"Oh, I am, but I can't tell my therapist about this." Bernie put his hand on the detective's knee. "You're the only one who knows."

"Get your hands off me."

"Wait. Don't leave." Bernie grabbed half-heartedly at his coat, but the detective was up and running. "We can work together. Those people were abducted, for sure. Let me help."

The door that slammed behind the fleeing detective startled Bitsy, asleep in his usual spot in Bernie's favorite chair. The fluffy Persian leapt into his lap, fur all in cowlicks, and hissed at the door.

"Don't worry, Bitsy," he said. "We won't be seeing him again." No problem at all.

Chapter Two

Not long after he'd started therapy with Dr. Bowman, around the second or third interview, when she'd asked the standard questions about his childhood, he gave her exactly what he knew she wanted, all carefully prepared and rehearsed ahead of time. He told her stories about poverty and neglect, about the untimely accidental death of his parents, about being shuttled between a series of foster homes, about sexual abuse at the hands of uncles and cousins.

During a later session, when she asked the same questions, he gave the same answers. She was just checking up, of course, trying to catch him in a lie. But Bernie was far too clever for that. Just as he'd rehearsed his symptoms of depression, he'd repeated his fictitious life story until he knew it cold.

She must never know about his real childhood, about his hippie parents, gentle, loving, clueless people—children of the '60s. Bernie hated them both. He hated them more fiercely than if they'd abused him, when, in fact, he'd received their true, gentle affection from the day he was born.

The problem was they weren't normal. The world had moved on, gotten real jobs, life insurance policies, and second mortgages, while Bernie's parents were caught in a time warp of long hair, beards, beads, and sandals. His father, to the great amusement of Bernie's classmates, drove him to school in the "clown wagon," an aged VW bus adorned in flower and rainbow decals. Every school day Bernie disembarked from this vehicle to the howls and jeers of the other kids. "Freak family, freak family," they'd chant. And his father, so tenderhearted he'd walk out of his way to avoid stepping on a cockroach, simply smiled and waved at Bernie's tormentors.

His father's speech still featured dated phrases such as "groovy," and "far out," long after the rest of the world had adopted a new idiom. Those words, and the rage they evoked, were hard-wired into Bernie's brain. Finally, when he'd had all he could take, there was the accident, the fire that consumed the hated clown bus along with his parents, but it was just as well. Everything was over and done with at once.

For sure, the foster homes that followed weren't fun. Some were downright brutal. Through it all, Bernie's hatred for his parents and everything about them festered, then hardened like a scab. His plight was entirely their fault. Anything that reminded him of his earlier life acted like a switch. Anyone who uttered some '60s nonsense like, "Peace, brother," to Bernie likely caught a fist in the mouth, or worse.

****

You have to watch doctors all the time. Just when things were going well, they'd want to change, try something new. Bernie knew this, but Dr. Bowman's question still caught him off guard.

"If you could have your life exactly as you choose, what would that be like?"

"I don't understand." Bernie hadn't prepared for this one. He stalled. He coughed several times. "Could I have some water?"

"Just describe your ideal life. That can't be too hard."

"I want to be a good person." There, let her chew on that for a while.

"What does that mean to you, being a good person?"

What the hell was she up to? Bernie checked his watch; ten minutes to go, then his session would be over. "If I wasn't so depressed all the time maybe I'd take up some hobbies."

"But you said the ECT treatments were helping."

"Oh, yes. They make things better. I couldn't get along without them." He'd almost slipped up. He would have to be more careful.

"All right, then, if your depression went away completely, how would your life be different? A new job, perhaps? You've been with the Post Office now, what, twelve years?"

"I like my job fine." So long as people left him alone, he was relatively happy, and the isolation of the mailroom at the Post Office worked out well. It was probably the ideal job for someone like Bernie who shunned social interaction whenever possible. The very idea of trading small talk with co-workers made him break out in a cold sweat.

"How about friends, social activities? How would things be different if your depression was gone?"

"I don't want things to be different." Such bullshit. What if he just walked out? But he couldn't. Dr. Bowman held the key to his ECT treatment, something he couldn't do without.

"So, you're satisfied with your life just as it is?"

"Most of the time, yes." He sniffled. "Say, could we stop a little early today? I think I'm coming down with a cold."

She was writing so furiously on her notepad she didn't even look up when Bernie left. He made his return appointment with the receptionist and got away as fast as he could.

****

Yes, Bernie liked the solitude of his mail sorting room. He could work when he wanted, nap when he wanted and—best of all—he had no contact with the public. But this afternoon his sanctuary seemed to close in on him. The recollection of his last session with Dr. Bowman foiled his three o'clock nap. What was she up to? Why this new line of questions? The terrible and intolerable truth was she was probably going to change things, try to make his life better. He had to stay a step ahead of her, had to give her something to write in her notebook.

By the time he pulled into the Food Mart parking lot—Bitsy was out of milk—he had an idea. He'd make up a hobby. Fishing was the biggest waste of time he could think of, and it was easy to fake. He'd even throw in a few imaginary fishing buddies—Ralph, Charlie, whatever. Yeah. That oughta make her happy.

****

But some days, no matter how hard he tried, things went wrong, and Bernie leaned against his truck, trying to steady his nerves with a diet Coke and a cigarette. He seldom smoked but something unpleasant had just happened, and now he had to dispose of another body—more work, more inconvenience. Moments earlier, as Bernie carried out his groceries in two small bags, the apparently homeless man, tattered clothes and reeking, had followed him across the parking lot at the Food Mart asking for spare change.

"You oughta help a fella out." The vagrant smelled of stale beer. "Your luck might run out some day, just like mine did."

He followed Bernie right up to the back of his truck, a Ford 150 pickup with a black camper permanently bolted to the back. Bernie had made a number of small additions and alterations to meet his own particular needs. He had painted the small side windows black so no nosy busybodies could see inside. The floor of the truck bed was covered in several sheets of heavy-duty clear plastic cut from a roll that hung in brackets in the front right corner. Shelves inside contained several rolls of duct tape and a spool of parachute cord. He'd made a small bracket to hold a pair of shears and a small paring knife.

Two pine-scented air freshener wicks hung from the ceiling. He replaced them every month, not that he had a thing for pine scent—in fact, having to odor-proof his truck made Bernie angry—but some of the cargo he carried inside was downright rank. Once a passerby laughed and said his truck looked like a hearse...well.

"How about a little something to, you know, help me make it through the night, man." The vagrant kept after him, right up to the back bumper, still saying all the wrong things, and that's where he died. Bernie would help him make it through the night, oh yeah. He jerked him into the truck and smashed his skull with his axe. What else was he to do? He wrapped a plastic bag—*FOOD MART, We Appreciate Your Business!!*—around the man's head that caught most of the blood.

He shoved the body farther into the truck and covered it with a stained tarp. He would complete the wrapping up process later. Damn. Now he'd have to hurry to get home before Bitsy's milk spoiled.

****

Although the landscape features weren't the primary reason he'd chosen to settle along the southern coast of Oregon, it's rocky coastline with deep, inaccessible ravines filled a rather unique need for Bernie, sites for disposal of bodies no longer of use to their original owners. He'd always been careful to spread his activities among several different spots, those hidden from passing traffic by bushes with room enough to pull his truck off the road. He even had a little routine worked out should any curious passerby stop to question him: everybody had to pee sometime, right?

The spot he pulled into now, just off lightly traveled county road 14, wasn't his favorite, but it was closer to his house than the others, and the vagrant, who hadn't smelled particularly good when he was alive, had become positively rank overnight, overpowering the pine-scented air wicks in the truck camper. Bernie, always thinking ahead, had brought along a yellow paper protective body suit from a stock he kept in his garage, and heavy gloves. He wanted no direct physical contact with the loathsome thing in his truck.

The entire routine, donning the body suit and gloves, dragging the body over to the ravine then pushing it over, took only a few minutes; Bernie had had lots of practice. Then the gown went into a black plastic garbage bag, and he sprayed the inside of the camper with enough air freshener to produce a fog. He waited another fifteen minutes or so before he closed up the rear doors and prepared to drive off.

He'd just gotten back into his truck when the county sheriff's deputy pulled up behind him.

"Why are you stopped here, sir?" The deputy ambled over, hitched up his belt, and peered into the front seat at Bernie.

Bernie squeezed out a sheepish smile. "Had to take a leak. My doctor has me on a new medication for my blood pressure, and it makes me pee all the time."

"You work at the Post Office?" The deputy pointed to the patch on Bernie's sleeve.

"Yeah. Just on my way in."

"Okay, then. Drive carefully, sir." The deputy turned toward his cruiser, then came back. "Hey, you know you're headed the wrong way?"

"Huh?"

"The Post Office in Bandon's north of here. You're headed south."

"Yeah. I guess you're right. I'll just turn around."

The deputy pocketed his sunglasses and took a long look at Bernie, sniffed the air like a dog on the hunt. "Mind if I check out the back of your truck?"

"Why?" Bernie frowned before he could stop himself. "Nothing in there but junk." Junk and the smell of death only partially concealed by a heavy spray of air freshener. If the deputy ever got a strong whiff of that, it would be all over for Bernie.

"Step out of the truck, please." The deputy hooked his thumbs in his heavy belt, apparently expecting—or hoping—Bernie would refuse.

"Okay, okay. No problem." Damn. Of all the luck. Bernie slipped his climbing axe, still encrusted with dried blood, from under the towel on his seat then followed the deputy around back.

The deputy leaned over the rear bumper. "What's this here red smear?" He pointed to a swath over which Bernie had just dragged the body. "That ain't blood, is it?"

Bernie sighed. The man could have walked away, could have left him alone, but, no, he had to be pushy, ask questions. The deputy was a big man, XXL at least, so, when he knelt by the bumper to get a closer look, Bernie hit him twice with the axe, then rolled his body over until he could retrieve the keys to the cruiser from his pocket. He dragged the former deputy, still twitching, over to the embankment and shoved him into oblivion. He felt a rather ominous twinge in his back as he gave that final push, which made him even angrier than he might have been at having to do all the extra work with the bulky body.

Then he cranked up the cruiser and drove it to the edge of the precipice. He shifted it into neutral, jumped out and gave it a careful shove, sparing his back as best he could. First time he'd dumped a vehicle at the site, and he was surprised at the amount of noise as it crashed down the side of the ravine.

Still panting from the exertion—heavy guys were always trouble—he looked around the area. Didn't want to leave anything behind. Lightning flickered in the west, out over the open water. Good. Rain would wash away any tracks and any blood spatter on his truck. No worries about the two bodies or the car. The ravine was very deep. A search party would have to go halfway to hell to find them.

****

The fog began to lift and familiar shapes in the ECT lab became more distinct. His mouth was dry, and Bernie coughed several times. The overhead fluorescent light gave off an angry buzz. Dr. Bowman's hair seemed to flow around her head like a mousy brown cloud.

"Thought I was going to have to douse you with cold water to wake you up." Dr. Bowman held his wrist, checking his pulse like she always did while the sedative wore off. "You know, Bernie, we can't keep on doing this ECT thing indefinitely."

"What do you mean?" He tried to sit but a wave of dizziness engulfed him, and he lay back down on the gurney with a groan.

"I don't know how long it's safe to continue." She took a penlight from her pocket and directed the beam into his left eye, then his right. "I've never given one patient so many treatments."

"But I don't want to stop." Bernie grabbed her arm, something he would never do except under extreme circumstances. She had no idea of the hell she would bring down on him if she stopped the ECT treatments, and he had to make her see that. "It's the only thing that's helped me."

"We could try some other medications." She smiled and patted his hand. "There are several new ones out now. They work by an entirely different mechanism. Think how much easier it would be, just taking a pill, not having to get zapped every month."

He gripped the edges of the gurney, shaking his head. "But the shock treatment works. Even the sedation doesn't bother me, not really."

"We'll talk about this next Tuesday." Dr. Bowman

walked to the little desk in the corner and began writing in his chart.

No. This would not do. He couldn't face the memories, the dream people floating around his bed, shaking their gory heads at him. Not without ECT. Next Tuesday, huh? By then he would have his fishing fable polished and ready to deliver. Of course, if that didn't work, he'd have to escalate.

****

Somebody new at the door. She was almost as tall as Bernie, and a crooked scar ran from the bridge of her nose to underneath her left eye. "I'm Detective Molinaro. Investigating a series of disappearances in the area."

"There was another detective here before. He already talked to me," Bernie said. Why wouldn't they leave him alone?

"And I'm here now. Mind if I ask you a few more questions?" She didn't wait for an invitation but pushed right past and left him standing in the doorway while she stalked into his living room. Bernie had had just about enough of people barging into his home uninvited.

He didn't know what to make of this new cop. She didn't move around much. When she looked straight at him, which was most of the time, it was like she could see straight through him. This one could probably spot a liar a mile off. He'd have to be careful.

"New sofa?" she asked. "Nice."

"My cat." Bernie looked around for Bitsy, but the Persian was nowhere in sight. "He claws things up. That's why I left the plastic on it. You can sit over there if you want."

"You sit." She pulled a straight-backed chair into the center of the room. "I'll stand."

He sat.

"You're a pretty big boy," she said. "I reckon if you hit somebody you could do some real damage."

"Why would I do that?" Why the hell had he let her pick this chair? It was his house, goddamnit. He twisted around trying to follow as she circled him, probably just as she'd intended.

She stopped right behind him, close enough that he could hear her breathing. "How about if somebody made you really angry?"

"I don't get angry." A bead of sweat popped from his hairline and crept down the middle of his forehead.

She moved in front of him, fists on her hips like a street brawler. "You don't ever get pissed off? What are you, some kind of saint?"

Bernie shook his head. "Nah. I'm depressed."

It started off as a stifled snort. Then Detective Molinaro's bellow of laughter filled the room. "That's the funniest thing I've heard all week."

"It's true. I'm in therapy." He went into his depressed mode, a little visual demonstration for this detective who just couldn't seem to get the point.

"So maybe I should talk with your therapist."

"You can't." Bernie looked her up and down. For sure she had a gun, but where? "That's confidential, just between me and my doctor."

She nodded, as if he'd just confirmed something she suspected. "So, it is, so it is. I think you should come down to the station for a few tests."

"What kind of tests?" Bernie took a deep breath, more like a gasp. Now he knew what she had, where she was going. She was fishing. Sure, he'd play along, but now he was way ahead of her.

"A polygraph," she said.

"You mean a lie detector test?" He cringed just a bit, playing along, although the polygraph held no more fear for him than a spelling test.

"Some people call it that." She folded her arms across her chest, looking confident, like she had him backed into a corner.

"You think I'm lying to you?" He opened his eyes wider, trying for indignant.

"It might help me to help you."

"I don't need your help. I'm already in therapy, I told you."

"Maybe, maybe not. Will you come down voluntarily? I can make you do it, you know." She stood directly in front of him, taking on what must have been her *Go ahead, make my day*, pose, fists on her hips, feet spread apart, daring him to make trouble.

A lie detector test. What a joke. He could pass that standing on his head. But for now, he'd go along with her little game. Act frightened, anxious, let her think she was getting to him. Nothing for him to get excited about. After all, his recent memory bank was all cleaned out. God bless ECT. He hesitated just for effect, then said, "Fine. Let's go."

****

The polygraph room was much as he expected, half-filled coffee cups stacked all over, reams of paper held together by rubber bands scattered about, stale smell of a poorly ventilated area. If they were going to catch him, they'd have to be a damned sight more efficient than they appeared to be.

"That's too tight," Bernie plucked at the rubber strap around his chest.

"Don't touch it." The technician pulled his hand away. "It has to be snug."

"It's not snug. It's too fucking tight." Bernie continued to fidget, might as well have a little fun while he was there.

"Leave it alone."

Detective Molinaro sat beside the technician. "What about that tattoo?" She pointed to the faded monogram on Bernie's bare arm.

"What about it?"

"*Lay off.* What's that mean?" she asked.

"What it says." Let her figure it out, she thought she was so damned smart.

"Lay off," she said again. "You're a real tough guy, aren't you?"

"Don't antagonize him." The technician glared at her. "You'll mess up the test."

But Bernie knew this game. As the technician's questions progressed from general stuff about current events, the weather and such, to specific inquiries about killings and bodies—things that might give him away if he remembered them, which he didn't—he had no trouble staying calm. The queries rolled off him like rainwater off a newly waxed car. The farther along they got, the more comfortable Bernie became, until finally the technician said, "That's it," and turned off the machine.

"How'd I do?" he asked as the technician unhooked the straps on his arm.

"I'm not supposed to say anything until we study the results." The technician looked at him, raised an eyebrow, and grinned. "What the hell. You passed with flying colors."

Bernie rolled down his sleeves and stood up. As he walked out, he winked at Molinaro. He couldn't help himself. She glared like she wanted to rip his arms off.

****

Maybe he'd pissed her off or maybe she just didn't know when to quit, but there she was again the next morning, pounding on his front door.

"This is harassment." Bernie backed across his living room, away from the detective.

"What's the matter, tough guy? You got something to hide?" She followed, keeping a distance of a few feet between them. She wore a different suit, even more wrinkled than the one from the day before.

"I took your damned test, didn't I? And I passed it. You got no right to keep bugging me like this." Bernie edged farther away. Where was his axe when he needed it?

"You're dirty." She moved a few steps closer. "I know it. You smell like death."

"That's crazy talk. I'm calling my lawyer."

"Go ahead. But I'm gonna keep after you. I'm gonna nail you, and you know it."

"I'm under medical treatment. You're jeopardizing my health. I'll get a statement from my therapist. A restraining order from my lawyer."

Now she was so close he could see the wrinkles gathering at the corners of her eyes, the frayed lapels of her department-store suit.

"You can't shake me, Bernie. From now on, every time you turn around, I'll be there—pure coincidence, understand? You might have fooled the rest of them but you're not gonna fool me."

She had him cornered, caught between the wall and his lounge chair. Their wrangling woke Bitsy. The fat Persian jumped out of the chair with a yowl and streaked past the cop.

"What the hell?" Molinaro turned, just enough.

The fireplace poker was in easy reach. Thank God he'd left the plastic on the sofa.

Chapter Three

Bernie began to wonder whether there might not be some sort of detective magnet on his lawn that kept drawing them to his door. This latest version, so bulbous that he might have had a walrus link somewhere back in his family tree, said his name was Webster.

"Got a few questions about Detective Molinaro," the walrus said. "She came out to see you, let's see, last Tuesday, had you come in for a polygraph test, right?"

"Right," Bernie said. No need to deny it because the walrus would have all the information already. He remained standing while they did the question-answer thing, fearing that the walrus might crush any piece of furniture he chose to sit on.

"What was that all about?" the walrus asked, as if he didn't know.

"There was no problem," Bernie said. "I passed the test."

"So I see." The walrus thumbed through a couple of pages of a small notebook he'd taken from his pocket. "But why did Detective Molinaro want you to take it in the first place?"

"She said she was checking on a missing persons report. I never did find out who was missing, or why."

"More than one. Seems like an epidemic around here. Nobody goes missing for years, then cases start popping up all around." The walrus poked the tip of his pen around in his bushy mustache. An itch? Who knew what might be hiding in that growth of whiskers?

"I told Detective Molinaro I don't know anything about anybody going missing," Bernie said, the very picture of innocence; he knew this because he'd practiced it. Why, with his well-rehearsed role-playing skills, he might have even become a successful performer on stage, only he couldn't practice handsome, could he? No amount of time spent in front of a mirror would ever make him physically attractive. So, what the fuck? There were worse things. He could be like Detective Molinaro...dead.

The slow-moving walrus did not appear to be the kind of man who would put forth a lot of investigative effort, regardless of the situation, which was fine by Bernie. He handed Bernie his card. "You hear anything, you let me know, right?"

"Yes, sir. Thank you, Detective Webster. I will for sure."

Ironic, Bernie thought, after the detective had lumbered away, how Detective Molinaro had started out investigating missing persons only to become one herself. Only, she wasn't really missing, was she? Bernie knew exactly where she was. She'd been quite right when she guessed that Bernie could do significant damage when he was angry. The deep, bloody crevasse in the back of her head that he'd made with the fireplace poker showed that clearly enough.

So, she was gone, Detective Molinaro, but not forgotten, not yet. She still swooped in and out of his consciousness, making jerky movements like a marionette whose strings were controlled by someone having a seizure. And his next ECT session was still three days away.

ECT. He needed it, had to have it. Dr. Bowman's pill-and-capsule salads had been no help at all. Without ECT the dream people would continue to make his nights miserable, swarming all around him, filmy figures with holes in their heads. Sometimes his parents drifted among them, making peace signs. He tried to touch his mother once, but his hand went right through her, like touching smoke. How in the world was a guy supposed to sleep with all of that going on?

But just as he feared, the following Tuesday, Dr. Bowman started up again. "Bernie, we need to talk. I've said this before. I'm concerned about continuing this ECT indefinitely. I just don't know enough about the long-term effects."

No! If she stopped the treatments there wouldn't *be* any long-term effects to consider, because there wouldn't be any long term. He couldn't tolerate having those specters floating around. There would be no time today for the fishing story he'd prepared. This new threat called for immediate action.

Bernie fell to his knees in front of her. "Doc, I'm begging you. The shock treatment is the only thing keeping me alive. If you stop it, I won't be able to go on."

"Let's try something different. Maybe a short stay in an inpatient facility." She walked around her desk and knelt beside him. "We can try more intensive drug combinations, find out what works best for you."

By God, he'd show her. He rolled on the carpet, drummed on the floor with his fists and heels, sobbed loudly enough to attract the attention of the receptionist in the outer office who finally got out of her chair. "Everything okay in here, Dr. B.?" She stuck her head through the door but didn't enter the room. She looked at Bernie writhing on the floor. "Oh, you poor, poor man. Dr. Bowman, can't you do something for him?"

Dr. Bowman waved her away. "We're fine. Bernie, get up, please." She helped him into the chair. "Won't you at least consider inpatient care?"

He hit the floor again, still drumming, still sobbing noisily. Why quit when you're ahead?

"Okay, okay, we'll continue the shock treatments. For a while. Now, please, get up off the floor."

Bernie struggled to his knees, prepared to dive again if necessary. "Promise?"

Dr. Bowman held up her right hand as if taking an oath.

He stood and tucked in his shirt. "Okay, then. I guess I'll go now."

She leaned against the corner of her desk, rubbing her eyes as if she couldn't believe what she'd just seen. "Far out," she said softly.

Bernie spun on his heels. "What did you say?"

"I just said, far out."

****

Having to dispatch his own doctor right there in her office, proved very inconvenient, requiring Bernie to make any number of changes in his daily schedule, but it couldn't be helped. "Far out," indeed. How could she have been so insensitive?

The fuss they made afterward—an official inquest that dawdled along for several weeks, no less—seemed a bit over the top, particularly when they confined him in a locked ward at the state hospital like some deranged psychopath, which he certainly was not. After all, it wasn't his fault.

It took Bernie's best efforts, but he soon had the situation under control. The testimony by Bowman's receptionist—that she'd seen Bernie "rolling on the floor in extreme emotional distress"—made all the difference. When she described how she'd pleaded with Dr. Bowman to help him and yet her pleas went unanswered because poor Bernie continued rolling and moaning, the scales shifted in Bernie's favor. Her testimony, along with his show of remorse carried the day. He was so, so sorry. He knew he'd done wrong—he'd practiced contrition, complete with tears-on-demand, until he could do it in his sleep—but couldn't he please have another chance?

His little group of questioners, mostly advocates from the mental health field, seemed to hang on his every word, and Bernie warmed to the task. "Dr. Bowman pushed me too far," he whispered. "She threatened to discontinue ECT knowing that without it I couldn't go on, my life wouldn't be worth living." It was so unfair of her to back him into a corner like that. One might say—someone, not Bernie, certainly—she got what she deserved. Then he added in an inspired moment, "Could someone please take care of my cat?"

By the time Bernie was finished, most of those at the hearing probably felt Bowman's killing was, if not justified, at least understandable, because several of them spoke out against what they called her aggressive techniques. Besides, a man like Bernie couldn't possibly pose any ongoing threat to society. He was a broken man now, a hollow drum. He needed their support, not retribution.

Having carried the day, he felt justifiably proud of himself. But best of all, he had a new diagnosis…he was disabled. Now, in addition to owning the rights of the mentally ill, he could claim all the privileges that went along with his disability. This made the whole unpleasant affair seem worthwhile.

He got off with a stint in rehab at the state hospital. One member of the inquest, apparently caught up in Bernie's performance, apologized for the inconvenience. The state facility wasn't as nice as Dr. Bowman's private office; it smelled like a combination of disinfectant and human excrement. And he wouldn't give food they served there to his cat. But he'd been through worse, and soon enough, he'd be sleeping in his own bed again.

His new therapist, a member of the hospital staff, was perfect—a bearded young man with a passion for his work, a true advocate for the rights of the mentally ill. When Bernie, careful to keep his gaze directed down as any good depressed patient would, saw the doctor was wearing sandals he couldn't believe his good fortune. Here was someone who, with proper coaching, would do whatever he asked. As their sessions went on, Bernie heaped lavish praise upon the good doctor. "No one has ever helped me like you have, Dr. Peele. I'm so grateful."

When Dr. Peele pursued a less desirable course, so did Bernie. "I know you're trying to help me, and I'm trying so hard to be a good patient." He even squeezed out a few more tears.

"You're a wonderful patient, Bernie. I don't remember when I've ever had anyone as motivated as you."

Nauseating work, but it had to be done.

It took only a couple of weeks to train Peele; in short order Bernie had him cavorting about like a kid on Christmas morning. Then he was back on ECT, on his own schedule, just like he'd planned. At Bernie's urging Peele even kept the police at bay, after he explained how they terrified him. "I'm just afraid they might set back my treatment. All your hard work."

Dr. Peele had stood directly in front of the police officer shaking a skinny finger in his face. "If you must blame someone, blame the system that failed, not this poor man."

Best of all, with Dr. Peele's help, the Post Office had to take him back. After all, Bernie had a disability, not much different from the deaf guy who worked at the front desk.

When his required stay was completed, Bernie hugged and shook hands with Dr. Peele and left the foreboding walls of the state hospital a free man with a conscience freshly cleansed by his most recent ECT treatment. With his new entitlements—his new disability plus his pre-existing mental illness—he was practically untouchable. In his pocket he had an appointment slip with one of Dr. Peele's colleagues and a guarantee he could continue ECT as long as he wanted.

He walked out into a day of deep blue skies and high wispy clouds. His stride on the gravel path was brisk and confident. Here was a man who could handle whatever life threw at him. Here was a man who deserved the best, if only as compensation for all the trouble people had caused him over the years. It was time to set his sights higher, time to think about his future...law school, perhaps. His recent success at the inquest suggested he might have an aptitude for that line of work.

Bernie stopped and inhaled deeply, drawing in the subtle aroma of the lilacs that flanked the path. Ah, life was good. And for times when it wasn't, well, he still had his axe.

****

Early September, and the late morning fog had lifted, not that Bernie cared. Weather, unless it was severe, usually did not interest him. Since it was Saturday, one of his three days off each week, he'd driven to the nearby town of Bandon for gas and a pit stop at the rest room of the Texaco station. Tank filled, bladder empty, he ambled slowly back to his truck. No rush, his time was his own today, and most days, really. His mind wandered among a half dozen unrelated topics, when his progress was halted by a snuffling sound, like a pig rooting for acorns. When he crept around the corner of the building, he was confronted by a wide, white-clad posterior which belonged to the person—a female?—dragging a large limp body down the path toward the stream that gurgled along behind the building.

He must have made a sound, because she stood upright and whirled around facing him. "Hey, give us a hand here, will you? He's heavy." She spoke with an accent that sounded regional, but he couldn't be sure.

"But...there's an ice pick in his chest." Bernie pointed to the object in question, embedded up to the hilt just to the left of the man's sternum.

"Oh, yeah, thanks, I almost forgot." She pulled the ice pick from the man's chest, wiped the clinging blood onto his shirt, then slipped the lethal utensil into her pocket. "You take his feet, okay?"

Even with the two of them, progress was slow and labored, and by the time they reached the riverbank, both were panting. "I'm getting too old for this," she said. "Let's roll it into the river."

The body entered with a splash, then bumped along the bank for fifteen yards or so and seemed to be going nowhere fast.

"Now, watch this," she said, hands clasped together in front of her formidable chest. The body darted into the middle of the stream, caught up by an unseen current, swirled around a couple of times, then shot off downstream as if moved along by some interior propulsion mechanism.

"Is that cool, or what?" she asked, a grin spread almost the width of her face. "They always do that. By tomorrow it will be way out to sea, fish food, sort of like recycling."

Bernie marveled at her disposal system. Why couldn't he have thought of that? All those unnecessary holes he'd had to dig. "You've done this before," he said.

"Yeah, but don't get the wrong idea. I'm not some sort of mass murderer, one every few months at most, and usually not that much. And thanks for the help." She extended her hand. "I'm Bertie."

To Bernie it was like looking in a mirror and shaking hands with his own reflection, same plus-sized body, lank hair, questionable complexion. Everybody had a double, a doppelganger, he'd read, and his was staring right back at him.

"Bernie," he said, giving her hand a firm shake that

she returned even more firmly.

"Bertie and Bernie." She laughed. "What a coincidence. Have you had lunch?"

****

She directed him to a small garish green cinder-block building situated beside a vacant laundromat. The large plaster chicken, most of its paint peeling, in the parking lot would probably not be grinning and winking at prospective customers if it knew that its poultry friends and relations were on the menu.

The first stop for each of them was a trip to the restrooms to wash up. Bernie, in particular, always gave himself a good scrub after handling deceased victims, whether his own, or in this case, Bertie's. He guessed she probably felt the same, and even now would be up to her elbows in lather.

When he emerged from the restroom, she waved to him from a corner table where menus had already been delivered. "Hope you like fried chicken," she said.

He nodded with more enthusiasm than he felt. Their waitress, whose speed afoot would barely win her first place in a race with a snail, an older snail, at that, looked from Bertie to Bernie and from Bernie to Bertie, then completed the cycle all over again.

"First cousins," Bertie offered by way of explanation, although the woman deserved no such clarification. What she deserved was a firecracker up her ass to move her along more quickly.

After she plodded away, still in first gear, came the awkward silence, since neither of them possessed any skill at small talk. But Bernie was determined to give it a try. "You come here often?" he asked, such a banal question surprising even him.

"Not so often," she said. "Just sometimes when I have to do the river thing, you know. It's convenient."

It made perfect sense to Bernie, labor followed by lunch, especially when the results of that labor now floated somewhere downstream, destined for the open sea. Even without all the preliminary chitchat, he felt he knew a lot about Bertie, because he knew these things about himself, and, by simple extrapolation, he transferred that information onto his new friend. That she should share his feelings and probably some of his methodology about righting some of the wrongs of the world, by extreme measures, if necessary, made this a unique event, a one-in-a-million chance. He didn't have to guard his secret life because she already knew about it, just as he knew about hers.

Still, he thought he'd toss in a few details of his own, extra stuff that might not usually be on the agenda with a new acquaintance. "I'm in therapy," he said. "ECT treatments for depression."

She grasped both of his hands, squeezing tightly. "Oh, my gosh, so am I."

Of course, they would share ailments and treatment, how could it be otherwise?

"Where do you go for your treatments?" She seemed so excited to discover yet another shared aspect of their lives.

"The state hospital." He could have hedged a bit, said he was still having treatments at Dr. Bowman's office, even though she was no longer there, but lies had a way of catching up, and he didn't want to risk jeopardizing what seemed to be a unique and intriguing relationship.

"Why do you drive all the way out to the state

hospital? That must be thirty miles or so. There are closer places. I can even set you up with my own therapist, she's very nice."

"My old therapist died," he said.

"Oh, that's too bad. What happened?"

"I strangled her, but you have to understand, it was an accident. She provoked me. I couldn't help it."

"So, it wasn't your fault." From the rather mellow tone of her voice and sympathetic look on her face, Bertie appeared to understand that, even when killing was involved, sometimes you've got to do what you've got to do. Enough said.

"No, afterward there was a hearing, and the committee decided the whole thing was her fault, not mine, but I'd have to continue therapy in a supervised setting. So, I'm stuck with the state hospital for two years, by court order."

"Oh, my poor Bernie, I'm so sorry you had to go through all of that. Your therapist must have done something awful to set you off like that."

"She did. She threatened to cut off my ECT program. You see, it's not so much the depression; without the ECT I get night terrors, these horrible visions of other people I've had to kill. ECT keeps them away. It's the only thing that works. Pills don't help at all. Without ECT, I don't think I could make it. That would be the end for me."

"Have you had to do lots of other people?" Bertie asked.

"Not so many, things just happen, you know, and I have no choice." So, there, now she knew. He'd just confessed to criminal acts, more than one of them. Maybe it was over for Bernie and his new friend before they really got started, although he hoped not.

She moved alongside and embraced him in a fierce hug, drawing looks from the other few diners who weren't completely immersed in their dinners.

"Oh, Bernie, I should have known. It's the same with me, those awful, awful things in the night, swooping around my bedroom. Before ECT, it got so bad I almost stopped, you know, my work with my icepick. I didn't know anybody else had the same problem, but I should have guessed you'd have it too. We were made for each other, don't you think?" This last pronouncement came topped off with a big smile.

"Have to be," he said, so relieved he felt faint. He hadn't even told her about the verbal cues that set him off, forcing him to strangle Dr. Bowman, bludgeon others, but that would wait for another day. He'd found his soul mate, and nothing else mattered. Instead of what might have required some long, extended discussion, which he hated, all that unnecessary blabbering, they'd reached an understanding quickly, and nothing more needed saying. This girl was a keeper for sure.

With all that preliminary stuff out of the way, he could focus on lunch which he found quite up to his liking. "Good chicken," he said about halfway through the meal. They were both eating wolfishly now having worked up an appetite with their earlier strenuous endeavor; moving bodies was hard work, not to mention the personal revelation Bernie had just put forth, successfully it seemed.

Bernie particularly liked the way the sections of the serving plates were set off by raised ridges that prevented the mashed potatoes and gravy from mixing with the creamed corn and kept both from invading the space around the chicken. His dishes at home were designed in the same fashion. Food portions that ran together making for an inedible mess really set him off.

Lunch, or any other meal, for Bernie rarely lasted longer than fifteen minutes, twenty minutes tops. That's because mealtimes were for the consumption of food, so there was never the distraction of watching TV or poring over a newspaper, or, worst of all, talking. Those were separate activities, each to be done in its own time. Bernie didn't like combining activities any more than he liked combining food groups.

But this meal, his first with Bertie, had somehow run over the half hour mark, a new record for him. Then it was over, and they both stood at the same time, as if some non-verbal signal had passed between them. Bernie smiled. Bertie smiled, and that was it. Making plans for a repeat visit never occurred to him. This was unknown territory. If there was some standard protocol to cover such a situation, he didn't know about it. So, as casually as they'd met—the dead body notwithstanding—they parted.

Bernie had no recollection of the drive from the Chicken Shack to his own driveway. There was a new disturbance in his world dominating his thought processes. He didn't even notice his neighbor, Mrs. Grosbeak, peeking through her blinds at him, although he knew she was always there. For a man who craved routine, who hated surprises, Bernie wasn't sure which way to turn.

He tried reading, but the story line kept switching from present action to backstory and back again, and he was in no mood for such silly games. He took his volume of *New York Times* crossword puzzles from the shelf, picked a page at random and started to work, at least, he tried to. But concentration on the printed word was not in the cards, not today.

But there was always his work room, the space where he could lose himself for hours amidst tubes of glue, paint, tiny brushes and assorted carving knives, all arranged neatly in convenient rows in a tabletop rack he'd built himself from an aromatic block of cedar. In the center of the workspace sat his current project, a model of a Lancaster bomber, WWII vintage, almost ready for painting. He had only to attach the plastic turret for the tail gunner, and he would be ready to apply the finishing touches, a prospect that usually brought him a great deal of satisfaction, but not today. Today there were ripples on the usually still waters of Bernie's mind.

The severity of the situation demanded action, and Bernie, who seldom ventured out of doors except to go to work or buy groceries, decided to go for a walk. In the grand scale of events, this wouldn't merit even a footnote, but in Bernie's world, it was seismic. He stepped across the threshold three times before he could finally take that step that carried him out onto the porch. His trips out to his truck, all ten steps of them, provoked no such reaction, because that sort of activity had a discreet start and finish. It was the idea of beginning something with no specific destination in mind that gave him fits. Bernie did not like open-ended situations.

Mrs. Grosbeak followed his progress up the street; he knew this because he saw the gaps appearing in the blinds covering her windows as she crept room to room, probably seeing something she never expected to see. Next to Mrs. Grosbeak's abode with its peeling paint, sagging roof, and unmown lawn, there was a vacant lot overgrown with tall grass and a few scrub pines. Her yard, unkempt as it was, seemed to blend in with the disorder next door.

Once or twice, maybe more, Bernie had been forced to use that vacant space, which backed onto a rather dense growth of forest, as a temporary holding facility for some of his victims. Detective Molinaro had, in fact, spent a night there before Bernie could make arrangements for a more permanent placement. It was, of course, a stopgap maneuver, forced upon him by the inconvenience of lugging around an often heavy and uncooperative body, particularly one that had, like the detective, stiffened up so quickly he had to wedge her into his truck at an angle.

Although he only made these emergency visits in the darkest hours of the night, Mrs. Grosbeak sometimes must have spotted him. But she'd called the local police so often, mostly about outlandish things she suspected Bernie of doing—some of which he'd actually done—that her credibility was shot, so they didn't bother to investigate until the following day, and by then, the incriminating evidence was elsewhere. Bernie wasn't stupid.

For this unscheduled and unusual hike, he might not be sure of where he was going or why, but for certain he would get there and back in an orderly, consistent fashion, neither deterred nor distracted by the early clutches of daffodils that had sprung up alongside the road. Likewise, the sound of bees buzzing about, doing whatever bees did—he neither knew nor cared—

got only a brief notice.

Each step he took was purposeful and identical to the step before, and the step before that, and so on. Consistency of stride and cadence ranked high on his list of priorities. In effect, Bernie was marching to his own tune, no one else's.

But why was he out there in the first place, outdoors where random events beyond his control could and sometimes did occur? That was the question, wasn't it? And he needed an answer because the disturbance that had begun as a ripple was reaching tsunami-force. Then, almost from out of the blue came the answer…Bertie. He said the name aloud, hardly believing that another human, a female one, at that, could cause his entire world to tilt.

So, now he knew. The purpose of his trek achieved, he stopped, turned, and retraced his path home, each step landing in the footprint he'd made earlier. It was all about Bertie.

Chapter Four

The source of his discontent, the same that drove him out of doors, rang his doorbell not ten minutes later. Bertie, wearing the same white work outfit he'd seen her in before, or one exactly like it, was waiting outside his front door. "Hi, Bernie, do you want to go bowling?"

It was too much too soon. Bernie opened his mouth, but no sound came out. How did she know where he lived? How did she know he'd be at home? Had she followed him? Where had this bowling idea come from?

"Well?" she asked. "Yes? No? Maybe? Come on, help me out here."

He stepped aside and waved her in. There probably would have come a time, if the relationship progressed, when Bernie would have issued an invitation to visit, maybe with snacks and something to drink. But it would have been at a time of his own choosing. Now he faced the uncertain prospect of having a stranger, even one who was his own mirror image, inside his own personal space.

"So, this is where you live." She made a short circuit of the room. Bernie got the feeling in that brief moment she had evaluated and memorized every item in the room, something he did himself whenever he entered a new place.

She walked into the corner and stood facing Alvin's plexiglass case. "Oh, Bernie, what's this? What a gorgeous snake, a copperhead, my very most favorite." Her smile extended ear to ear. "What's its name?"

"This is Alvin," Bernie said, ever so pleased at Bertie's response.

"I've always wanted one of my own," she said. "I just love the way it blends in with the rocks and branches in the case. You did a good job decorating for him."

"Yeah, unless he's moving around, you wouldn't even know he's in there."

"What do you feed him?"

"Mice, mostly. I can give him one now if you want to watch."

"Oh, could I? I'd love to see that." She clapped her hands like a child about to receive an eagerly awaited birthday present.

Bernie went into the garage where he kept the cage that contained Alvin's meals. The cage was reinforced with an extra layer of wire mesh, because Bitsy, the cat, shared Alvin's fondness for white mice, or any mice. He selected a victim and took it back inside where Bertie waited beside the cage. Alvin, perhaps sensing that something good was about to happen began to move about, his languid motion still barely detectable.

"Do you want to feed him?" Bernie extended his hand, the white mouse enclosed with only its nose visible.

"Oh, yes," Bertie said. "Please."

Bernie opened his hand so she could grab the mouse's tail. Then he slid back the small movable section of plexiglass through which Alvin's mice meals made a one-way trip.

Bertie dangled the doomed mouse above the opening then dropped it into the case. "He sees it," she whispered.

Indeed, Alvin must have detected something new, yet familiar in his habitat as his tongue flicked back and forth locating his prey.

"Do they always sit still like that?" Bertie seemed disappointed that the mouse didn't dash about trying to escape.

"Sometimes they run, but Alvin always wins."

The show was over quickly enough, the mouse disappeared, and Alvin became immobile once again, so Bertie continued her tour of the room, over to where Bitsy lay curled up on the sofa. "Oh, you have a cat."

"Careful, don't…." Bernie was only halfway through his warning before she began scratching the cat's ears. Had he completed his statement, he would have told her that Bitsy didn't like strangers and sometimes mauled them, but that was unnecessary now because the cat's happy purr was audible across the room. Bitsy must have thought Bertie was Bernie, an understandable mistake. That was the only possible explanation.

"Now, how about some bowling?" she asked. "It'll be fun, I promise."

But bowling? She might just as well have invited him to a cocktail party, a couple of hours of drinks and small talk, easily enough to cause his head to burst into flames, because Bernie had bowled before…once. On that humiliating and painful occasion, he'd gotten his thumb stuck in the ball and, instead of releasing and rolling down the lane, the heavy orb, still attached, came down striking his left knee, leaving him with a limp that lasted almost three months. Why couldn't she have suggested something less hazardous, cliff-jumping or alligator-wrestling, for instance?

Yet there was more at stake here than just the risk of physical discomfort, right? He'd scored some major points with Alvin and Bitsy, but there was another side to making a good impression. He didn't want her to think of him as a total klutz, somebody who couldn't walk and chew gum at the same time. So, he put up a token resistance. "I don't have anything to wear."

She laughed like he'd delivered a great joke. "There's no uniform for bowling, Bernie. It's strictly come-as-you-are. Besides, we're sort of a matched pair already, aren't we?" She took up a position alongside him, hands on her hips.

True enough, her work outfit and his looked as though they'd come from the same rack and were worn on very similar bodies. And the mirror effect extended beyond apparel. When he scratched behind his right ear—a nervous gesture—she scratched behind hers. When he hitched up his belt, she hitched up hers. So much like watching himself.

So, off they went, Bernie venturing out into the unknown for the second time that day.

"I'll drive," she said. "I keep my gear inside my vehicle…always ready." She climbed into a white van, no windows in the back.

The problem with sitting in the passenger seat was that the steering wheel, brake pedal, and accelerator were all on the other side and out of his control, a situation that made Bernie acutely anxious. He tried to allay some of that angst with deep breathing exercises Dr. Bowman had taught him.

"What are you doing?" Bertie asked.

"Just a breathing thing," he said.

"That's what I thought you were up to. I have to do the same thing sometimes," she said. "Honestly, Bernie, you're the only person I've ever met who might be as weird as I am." She laughed for the second time, and Bernie laughed along with her.

The bowling alley was set back off the road behind a long, narrow parking lot, full, at the moment with pigeons. Bernie had probably driven past it a number of times without noticing it.

"Here we are." She pulled into a spot well away from any other vehicles, just as Bernie would have done. "My stuff is in the back. All you'll need are shoes."

Shoes…shoes that had been on someone else's feet, probably any number of strange feet. He doubled up on his breathing exercises.

Bertie came completely equipped with her own ball in a dark green carrying case. Somewhere in that bag would be, he guessed, shoes to match.

Of the ten bowling lanes inside, the first two were taken by two groups apparently involved in league play. They looked to be quite skilled in their delivery and, Bernie guessed, never ever got their thumbs stuck in the ball.

Bertie led him all the way down to the end lane, far away from the experts. Then it was off to the shoe counter where the clerk slid a worn pair of size twelves across to Bernie.

"Don't you have anything newer?" Bernie asked.

The clerk looked over his shoulder, then selected another pair, only slightly less worn than the first. "Best we got," he said.

When he got back to their seating area, Bertie had her ball in the rack, her shoes on, and a big smile on her face. "Get ready for some fun." She rubbed her hands together, the very picture of happy anticipation. "I'll start us off."

Fun? Bernie? The two terms seemed at odds as if they couldn't occupy the same space. Wonder what his therapist would say about that?

While Bertie was busily knocking over pins, Bernie applied a liberal glob of Vaseline to his thumb from a tube he'd slipped into his pocket before they left the house. His trick worked only too well. Not only did his thumb not get stuck, he lost his grip on the ball altogether, so that his first ball skipped over two lanes before coming to rest in the gutter by the center lane. The league boys gave him a big cheer and a round of applause.

"Pay no attention to those jerks," Bertie said.

Bernie wondered whether he and Bertie, with their utensils of choice, of course—his axe and her icepick—might take out the whole lot of them. The piercing look in her eyes, unless he misinterpreted badly, said she was up for it if he was. But the convenience factor won out. Even if they were successful, there would be a hell of a mess to clean up, and, since the shoe clerk would see everything, they'd have to do him too.

Bowling, in spite of his inauspicious start, seemed to be the lesser of two evils, so, he selected another ball. Of his next five attempts, three ended up in the gutter, but it was his own gutter and his thumb didn't get stuck on any subsequent attempts.

"You're getting better," Bertie said after he'd converted his first spare. "A little practice and you'll do just fine."

All things considered, Bernie felt damned proud of himself and of his effort. He felt even better when he was able to change back into his own shoes and leave the public footwear with the clerk.

Bertie took his hand as they walked back to her van. "Well done," she said.

What he'd expected would be a fleeting grasp turned into a walking-hand-in-hand episode, all the way. "You really have big hands," she said. "Of course, so do I."

The day was getting better and better.

*＊＊＊

Oh, no, no, no, Bernie broke into a cold sweat two days later when he drove past the sign on the vacant lot beside Mrs. Grosbeak's place: FOR SALE BY OWNER. Somebody owned that lot? He'd never seen another soul there, except for those he kept there on a short-term basis, and soul was no longer a consideration for them. The thought of what might be found by someone clearing that lot, digging beneath the surface, made his palms so wet he could hardly hold the steering wheel. The very reasons for all the detective visits lay buried in there including one of the detectives. Bernie hit his brakes, backed up and fumbled in his glove compartment for a piece of paper. He scribbled down the owner's number.

Early in the afternoon, at a moment when he had the small break room at the Post Office all to himself, he phoned the number. He provided a fake name, then identified himself as being from out of town, looking for a place to build a small single-family dwelling, keeping in mind that this whole sales routine might just be a scam. He made an appointment with a Mr. Beeson to look at the lot the following day. In the meantime, he went by City Hall to check the property records. Sure enough, lot number twelve in the Clearfield district, Mulberry Street, which of course, included his own dwelling, was owned by Mr. Beeson. No other names were mentioned.

Bernie prepared carefully, mindful of the importance of this meeting. He must appear interested but not eager. He was, after all, looking at other properties in the area, right? There must be nothing to connect him to the location, nothing that might indicate his place of employment. If the sale went through, and he was determined it would, it would be a cash transaction, no credit checks or other financial agencies prying into his personal life. He considered using a rental car just to complete the disguise but decided against what was probably a needless expense.

****

Mr. Beeson, if that really was his name, climbed out of a huge Dodge Ram pickup truck. Tall and lanky, he seemed way overconfident considering that what he had to offer was a modest, overgrown lot that Bernie knew, because of some of the digging he'd done at that very site, drained poorly and would probably be deemed unfit for building by the city inspectors. Yeah, there was a reason that lot was still vacant, and a reason Bernie wanted it to stay that way.

"Tom Beeson," a gravelly voice, he extended a boney hand.

Bernie had dressed in what he thought of as his bumpkin outfit, baggy khaki trousers, a bright floral print shirt, and sandals with dark socks. In his own opinion, he looked like a chicken ready for plucking. So, let the games begin.

"Looking to build here, are you?" Beeson asked.

"Yeah," Bernie said, "something small, just me and the wife, no kids. Pretty quiet back here, is it?"

"Quietest street you'll find anywhere," Beeson said, although Bernie felt sure the man had never set foot in the neighborhood before.

Bernie walked along the edge of the lot, staying on the street, avoiding the interior. "What are you asking?"

"Fifteen hundred," Beeson said.

Bernie walked a bit farther, shaking his head ever so slightly.

"I could go as low as twelve-fifty," Beeson said.

Bernie stuck out his hand. "We have a deal. I'll pay cash." Twelve-fifty? He would almost pay that much to see the expression on Mrs. Grosbeak's face when she learned that he had her surrounded.

The only downside he could foresee would be the real estate listing in the newspaper showing him as the buyer. If she saw it, the old bat would complain to the city about the overgrown appearance of the lot, and he might be forced to tidy it up. Of course, he could get a step ahead of the old snoop, clean it up on his own without being asked, Bernie Mitchell, model citizen. The idea made him cringe.

****

On the second and fourth Tuesdays each month, Bernie drove to the state hospital west of Bandon for his ECT sessions. The drive of thirty-five to forty minutes took him through forested countryside that many would call lovely. Bernie couldn't care less. He had no great affection for trees, but if forced to choose between a landscape of trees and one filled with people, he'd take trees any day.

This arrangement had been in effect for almost six months now, following his discharge from that establishment. The facilities were not nearly as nice as those provided by his previous therapist, but they were his only option since Doctor Bowman had forced him to commit a heinous offense, the memories of which entitled him to a new diagnosis of Post Traumatic Stress Disorder in addition to his established diagnosis of severe depression. He could probably apply for disability payments based on this new insult to his fragile psyche, but he was comfortable with his current routine.

Bernie didn't mind that the facilities were a bit rustic or that the staff was a bit brusque compared to those in private offices. The critical thing was keeping up with his ECT regimen, and for this he had to convince Dr. Peele that the treatments were the only thing that kept him going.

"I'm afraid that, if I couldn't come here for my treatments, I just couldn't make it," Bernie, slouched in his chair, head down, gazing at the floor, had told the good doctor.

"I hope you're not thinking of harming yourself," Dr. Peele said, his face a mask of deep concern.

Bernie responded with a long sigh, one that he practiced on a regular basis, a sigh that said neither yes nor no, but both together, a cry for help from a tormented soul. When he looked up at Dr. Peele, the man was almost in tears. Time for Bernie to switch gears, to toss out a lifeline that Dr. Peele could tug on to draw his patient back to safety. "I can't tell you how grateful I am for all you've done for me, Dr. Peele. You've saved my life. I pray every night for you and your family."

The doctor, for all his professional gravitas, could hold back no longer, convinced once again that he alone was the link that kept poor Bernie in the land of the living. The tears came. He reached across and embraced Bernie, an embrace that Bernie returned warmly because, beneath the subterfuge, by now he felt genuine affection for Dr. Peele.

But that was enough chitchat. Time for Bernie to get his head microwaved, kill off those unpleasant recollections before they could cause him any undeserved distress. He lay back on the gurney while the nurse inserted an IV needle in his forearm. Then the game, "Count backward from one hundred, Mr. Mitchell," as the medication took effect. He never got past ninety-four.

The staff always wanted Bernie to hang around for an hour after his ECT session, waiting for the sedative to wear off and to assure that no complications arose. He was, after all, their only regular ECT outpatient. To Bernie—he was a veteran now and could write a monolog on ECT—this was no great inconvenience. He strolled around the grounds, taking in the sweet aroma of newly mown grass, the clusters of daffodils swaying in the light breeze. It was as if the ECT session made him more aware of things around him.

He checked in with the head nurse before he left, big smiles all around. He wanted to stay on the good side of the people who actually ran the place, and that would be the nurses and aides who kept the wheels turning while the higher-ups stayed hidden away in their offices. Next time he would bring a big box of candy, not on every visit, of course. He didn't want it to become routine; routine meant the gesture would go unappreciated.

When he got back to his house, he found a familiar van sitting out front in the street. Bertie jumped out as soon as he drove up. She carried packages.

"Hi Bernie, I was afraid I'd missed you."

"I went to the state hospital for my ECT treatment." He'd already told Bertie about the unfortunate circumstances that required him to continue treatment in a supervised setting. If only Dr. Bowman had been more considerate none of these trips would have been necessary. When he told Bertie the story, she seemed to understand his actions perfectly. He was both surprised and relieved, because he worried that when she knew the real story of his therapist's departure, on a permanent basis, with Bernie's help, she might think less of him. Then again, given the close match in their life experiences, perhaps she'd bumped off a therapist or two of her own. He wouldn't be a bit surprised.

"Such a long trip. How often do you go?"

"Twice a month, but I don't mind the drive." The state hospital arrangement, nobody's first choice for a treatment site, but the court order left him no choice.

"Depression?" she asked.

"Yeah." He wasn't sure why she asked these questions since he'd told her about his routine that first day they'd met. Maybe she forgot. She received ECT too, so maybe her own short-term memory had taken a hit.

"Me too," she said. "Medications just didn't cut it." She extended two packages to him, one bulky and heavy, one less so. "Look what I brought you."

"Oh, wow." He took both packages, one of them quite heavy. "Come inside," he said. There on his kitchen table, he unwrapped a glistening new bowling ball, complete with carrying case. "Oh, wow," he said again. "This is so great. Thanks."

"I had them drill out the finger holes extra large, because I know you have big hands."

Next came the bowling shoes, the same color as Bertie's own. "Try them on, make sure they fit," she said.

He did, and they did, a perfect fit, as comfortable as his well-worn bedroom slippers, and they smelled much better too. He made a couple of trips around the kitchen table, even bounced up and down a couple of times, aware of a big smile, growing bigger by the minute, spreading across his face.

"Well, what do you think?" she asked.

"Let's go bowling."

Chapter Five

Bernie didn't see his parents very often—not surprising, since they were dead—but on those rare occasions when it happened, such as one afternoon when he was driving home from work, he wound up trembling so badly he had no choice but to pull off the road and wait for the shakes to subside. Daytime spectral visits were rare now, thanks to the effects of ECT; only those from his parents persisted, apparently rooted too deeply to ever be expunged from his memory.

Northern California commune life in the '60s had formed Bernie's early world view, a view that seemed to lack any real purpose aside from the avoidance of anything that resembled establishment living, and a view where Bernie's innate preference for order and routine and structure had no place and was ignored. At any one time, some twenty to thirty adults and a variable number of children wandered about aimlessly, starting projects, leaving them half-done, then moving onto something else.

The three semi-permanent structures on the campus, erected by members of the clan, stood as porous reminders of this casual approach. There was no point in going into any of them to get out of the rain because the roofs let in almost as much water as fell outside. Yet, they stayed, most of them, because that's where the food and facilities were, and, more importantly, the drugs.

At the time, nothing about Bernie's nuclear family struck him as particularly odd or different, not even the multi-colored bus that he and his family called home, until shortly after he turned six, and his mom got bitten by the home-schooling bug.

He sat by the communal campfire as she delivered her impassioned plea for an organized approach to teaching the kids. Watched as her entreaty was met with either relief—someone was foolish enough to take on the job, or, resistance—any kind of organized effort was sure to instill the values of the hated system, whatever that was.

She passed the hat—an empty one-quart juice can—for donations for school supplies and received four dollars and twelve cents. She bought three notebooks and a twelve-pack of pencils for twelve kids. By week's end, the twelve kids had dwindled to one.

Bernie's attendance was not optional. "I will not have you growing up illiterate," his mom said, the grim lines of determination across her forehead saying she meant just that. "You won't be living in a commune forever, and, when you're out in the real world, you'll have to be able to read."

So, Bernie's early academic efforts were supervised by Mom and Dad with material gleaned from whatever communal textbooks happened to be available. Of the parental pair, his mom was by far the most demanding, insisting that Bernie develop reading skills along with some rudimentary knowledge of mathematics.

Each morning, Bernie struggled through the pages

of a worn first-grade textbook, his mother at his side, while the other kids ran and played.

"Pay attention, Bernie." Any time his gaze drifted away from the page, she pinched his ear.

Bernie much preferred those sessions conducted by his father, because no sooner had Bernie opened a book, than dear old dad lit up one of his fat hand-rolled cigarettes, and soon enough, both participants were enveloped in a cloud of cannabis smoke. From that moment on, his father's constructive comments went no further than "right on," to "far out," and the like. Bernie only had to wait for his father to drift away to that special place where he smiled and closed his eyes, then Bernie could toss the book aside and go back to whatever he was doing in the first place, such as torturing one of the feral cats that lurked just outside the commune grounds.

This little quasi-educational charade continued for a few years or so, until, on a very warm morning in mid-August, Bernie's morning instructional period was interrupted by the arrival of a white van with Plaice County Board of Education on both front doors. Two rather squat men in shirtsleeves and wearing ties emerged, along with a tall, rail-thin woman wearing a dark gray suit that hung on her gaunt frame more like a bathrobe than public apparel.

A deputy sheriff came along, too. He parked his patrol car behind the van, got out slowly, and moved around like he was on high alert, never turning his back to the crowd, keeping his hand close to the butt of his firearm.

"Who's in charge here?" The woman's strong, loud voice belied her spare physique.

Visitors to the commune were usually gawkers hoping to see *naked people having sex out in the open*, or kids hoping to buy drugs. Both types usually left disappointed. This new entourage, apparently official in nature, drew a crowd quickly enough. Bernie's dad, always ready to welcome newcomers, stepped to the front, arms open wide.

"Why, hello and welcome, folks. Horace Mitchell at your service. How can I help you?"

"We're here about the children," one squat man said, taking a step forward.

"They're around here somewhere and just as happy and healthy as can be," said Bernie's dad. "Will you be joining us for lunch? Love to have you eat with us."

By then, most of the adults in the commune had formed a semicircle around the intruders, with the children in question lurking close behind them.

Bernie got in close enough to the front row of adults to hear a heated exchange. His father, always the peacemaker, was trying to soothe ruffled feathers the best way he knew how. He rolled one of his special cigarettes and was about to light up when Bernie's mom jerked it out of his hand.

"You idiot," she said between clenched teeth. "Don't you know that's the law over there?"

"Nothing to worry about, I was going to offer him a toke too."

"Idiot," she said again.

The county officials had come up with the novel idea that, since the commune residents were using county resources, the children's education was now the responsibility of the county.

"But they're all home schooled," came the cry

from the commune adults.

"We'll see about that," said team county.

So, a day was set up when the commune kids would be brought to Public Schoolhouse Number Eight for testing appropriate to their ages and grade levels. Bernie had never been inside a public schoolhouse before, and he was impressed. Just as disorder was the rule at the commune, everything he saw now from what had to be the playgrounds to the raised seating around an athletic field to the imposing red brick building all spoke of order and purpose. Then he saw the kids, and they saw him.

They must have emptied out the entire school to watch the commune kids arrive. The regular students were jumping up and down, that is, those who weren't bent double laughing. It was like the circus had come to town, and Bernie and his group were the main attraction. All they lacked was elephants and a marching band.

Bernie's dad insisted on driving him along with several other kids, in the highly decorated VW bus. This would be Bernie's first experience with the manner in which the world outside the commune might perceive that bus and its occupants. "Freaks! Freaks! Freaks!" The kids yelled in unison; they must have practiced. The taunt quickly removed any doubts he might have had about being different.

At first, Bernie feared he and the other occupants might come under physical attack, but no, only derision. He would have preferred physical assault to being mocked. When he looked about the schoolyard at the assortment of sedans and station wagons, all of a single color, he saw nothing resembling his dad's bus, which, by comparison, was both unique and ludicrous. He hadn't noticed until they got off the bus that, in addition to the swirls, balloons and flowers already in place, someone had painted a family of rabbits, mom and daddy rabbit along with six little bunnies along the side. No wonder the kids laughed.

But his humiliation was not to end there in the parking lot. He and the other commune types were herded into a large room where they were to be divided according to age. Some of the kids weren't quite sure about their age category, so they were assigned on a best-guess basis. Bernie, now aged nine, fit into the next-to-oldest group, fourth grade.

Then the professional educator types got down to business. "The first part of your evaluation will test your reading comprehension skills. After you've read each of the three short paragraphs on your page, write out the answers to the questions listed. You have twenty minutes to complete your answers." The matronly type running the show wore a smirk that said she didn't have very high expectations for the group.

Bernie struggled, but eventually had appropriate answers for the questions. As he looked around him, he saw several blank pages. This would not be a red-letter day for the commune kids.

"Next you will write one half page on how you spent your summer. You will have twenty minutes to complete this task." The lady in charge still wore her smirk. As Bernie wrote about a fictional trip to the lake with his parents—neither the trip nor the lake existed—he heard the smirk lady say "pathetic, just pathetic," several times.

Only his mother's persistence with his reading

skills saved him from being labelled as either untaught or downright retarded. His math skills must have been humorous because the teacher administering the test laughed outright.

After the testing period, Bernie and the others were herded back into the large room where they were watched over by four of the biggest, meanest-looking women he'd ever seen. He wanted to ask for a bathroom break, but the sour looks on those four large faces made him wonder whether he'd even get out of the room alive. They looked like people who would clamp off pre-teen penises with clothespins...and laugh about it.

However bad Bernie's experience might have been, his parents and the other commune adults who had followed along must have been getting it even worse. He would learn later there were accusations of child abuse along with threats of taking the entire group of children into protective custody until a more suitable arrangement for their care could be found. His mother, when he finally saw her again, was in tears. She looked as if she'd aged several years over the course of the morning.

Home schooling days were over. Henceforth, the commune youth would attend the regular school. Of course, none of them would be placed with kids their own age, because they were years behind academically, years that had to be made up.

Bernie, because he could read reasonably well, albeit with little comprehension, was only dropped back to the third grade, where he towered over his classmates. He made no friends. He didn't like little kids to begin with.

Because the commune itself lay well outside the usual school bus routes, the commune adults would be responsible for delivering the commune youth to the front door of the school building no later than eight a.m. each day. Bernie's ever generous father volunteered to drive, apparently not understanding that he would have to begin that drive some forty minutes earlier to get to school on time, and that the trip would have to take place regardless of the weather, Monday through Friday.

So, Bernie's dad, probably the most mellow man Bernie would ever meet, not that it mattered at the time, routinely failed to make the connection between time of departure and time of arrival when he pulled the bus up to the school building anywhere from ten minutes to an hour or more after the designated time. The school principal's rants passed over him like so much hot air.

"Far out, man." How could the principal respond to that? Once, after another tirade when the frustrated principal jumped up and down, Bernie's dad hugged him right there on the front steps, because, he said, he felt the man needed one. The pained expression on the principal's face suggested Bernie's dad was right; the man needed a hug, maybe more than one.

And whether they were on time, late, or later still, Bernie and his group had to face the gleeful taunts of the regular kids. Some of the kids in Bernie's group laughed it off; it wasn't their VW bus, and wasn't their father driving, but not Bernie. For him, it was deeply personal. Every jibe hit home. He would remember every one of them, and he had plenty to remember.

Pizza-face they called him. Yes, he had a skin condition that in times of stress caused him to break out in a rash of pimples. Soon enough, the other kids caught on and passed up no opportunity to provide Bernie with all the stress needed to bring on an outbreak. They laughed as he fumbled over words in class, causing him to fumble even more and produce even more pimples.

He would always carry within himself this highly volatile mix of memories, waiting to be reignited, lurking deep in his psyche like hand grenades ready for detonation, and when that happened, woe unto the unfortunate who provided the spark.

The spark arrived when Bernie was struggling at the blackboard writing out a complex sentence. One of his tormentors, one who seemed to have made Bernie's misery a special project, whispered "Pizza-face," loud enough for everyone in the room to hear. Bernie's own response was beyond his control, and, therefore not his fault, or so he thought.

In a flash, he was on the kid. He dragged him to the floor, knelt on the kid's chest, and pummeled him with his fists. When the teacher tried to drag him off, Bernie pummeled her too. Very soon every teacher and administrator in the building formed a semi-circle around a tearful but defiant Bernie. They had him surrounded.

The other kids in the class formed a cheering section. "Get him. Get the freak."

They got him. Then Bernie got a free ride back to the commune in the back seat of the deputy sheriff's cruiser. The deputy seemed pretty put out about the whole affair. "If I hear one peep out of you, I'll put on the cuffs, so help me God."

Now, since the other commune kids were in school during the day, Bernie's expulsion left him as the only kid in camp, a situation that he actually preferred, but one which caused his mom no end of embarrassment. Dear old Dad was less troubled, though. "Far out," he said.

Bernie soon reverted to his former behavioral pattern, alone, secretive, and now harboring enough anger to make him truly dangerous. In a short time, he recognized a focal point for that anger…the hated bus. The bus had ruined his life, exposing him to ridicule. So, the bus had to go.

He siphoned some gasoline into a small wash tub, soaked some rags that he placed at the four corners of the bus, lit a match and stood back to watch the fire, a fitting end for the bus that destroyed his life. How could he have known that his parents would be inside, semi-conscious, in the thrall of a new shipment of unusually potent cannabis that had just arrived the night before? By the time he realized what he had done, it was too late to undo it.

"Maybe being so stoned as they were, they didn't suffer so much," one of the commune elders said. There seemed to be general agreement that, when it came time to make the big exit, whatever the means might be, stoned was the best way to go.

Under other circumstances, the commune might have opened its arms to a child who'd lost his parents in such a dreadful manner, but there were many in the group who had cause to fear this strange boy who always stayed outside the circle of love offered up by the commune. They questioned whether the fire was truly an accident, since Bernie smelled so strongly of gasoline. So, when social services arrived, Bernie was given over to them. The commune community breathed a communal sigh of relief, and Bernie began a new chapter in his life…as an orphan.

Bernie's downward trajectory from the free and easy commune days to more rigid foster homes, and finally, the orphanage, reinforced the idea that his path through life would mostly be him against the world, and there were many more of them than of him.

****

"Bernie, you're getting better than me," Bertie said.

Bernie had just rolled three strikes in a row, and no one was more surprised than he was. In the span of three weeks of weekly bowling trips with Bertie, in addition to several surreptitious trips he'd made on his own, he really seemed to be getting the hang of the game. For Bernie, whose athletic endeavors had never extended beyond those wretched high school gym classes where he was passed along by mutual consent—the instructors didn't want him around, and he didn't want to be there—this was new territory.

Bertie looked both elated and surprised at his success. At their last session, she had presented him with a bright yellow bowling shirt with vertical black stripes down the front. She had one to match. Their names were stenciled over the pockets on the right side. Bernie thought it the most horrible shirt he'd ever seen, but he wore it anyway, for Bertie.

"Hey, I thought maybe we could have lunch at my place today. What do you think?" she asked.

Bernie, had he not had a firm grip on his bowling ball would have dropped it on his foot. He knew where she lived—he'd checked that out—but had never been inside.

"That sounds great to me," he said. He finished his last frame, left four pins standing and didn't care a bit, because another big step awaited, lunch at Bertie's.

She gave his hand a little squeeze as they walked out of the building, and he squeezed right back. Yeah, he knew they probably looked like a pair of overweight canaries in their yellow shirts, but he didn't care. And if anybody wanted to make something of it, he'd invite them out to the parking lot where his climbing axe lay in the back of his truck.

Bertie's house was about a mile north of Bernie's, and, aside from its brick exterior, her house resembled his, smallish, single-story, unattached two-car garage. The front yard was neatly trimmed, and rose bushes bloomed beside the front entrance. Neatness and simplicity of design, two features that scored points with Bernie.

He liked the way she'd arranged the living room, large pieces, sofa and chairs on opposite sides of the space; proper balance, that was the key. Same with the few wall decorations she had, some paintings, a decorative hanging; the pieces themselves mattered less to Bernie than the simple matter of placement, of balance. Balance made him comfortable. Imbalance left him on edge, as if fearing the room might tilt.

Of course, balance was impossible in almost any kitchen. So many large appliances, refrigerators and such, crammed into a small space meant that expediency ruled the day. Not much to do but grin and bear it. Besides, his own kitchen was much the same, which was why he spent as little time there as possible.

"I should wash up," Bernie said.

"Bathroom's first door on your left."

Ah, yes, the bathroom, the *sine qua non* of orderliness. You could learn more from a few minutes in someone's bathroom than you could after hours of observation and conversation. Most places he'd visited had flunked on first glance, bits of clothing, damp washcloths lying about, used bars of soap with—God forbid—embedded hairs. But not Bertie. Hers was as tidy as tidy could be. So far so good, but there was one final test, wasn't there? The check that would tell him once and for all whether Bertie was a winner or a pretender—the medicine cabinet.

He turned on the water in the sink to cover any noise he might make, then carefully opened the door that would tell all. Bernie almost jumped for joy. All of the items were lined up like toy soldiers on parade. The cap was in place on the toothpaste tube, while the tube itself had been squeezed at the far end, forcing the goodies toward the opening. Little things counted, too.

He glanced over her medication labels and found they were taking many of the same antidepressant drugs. There were a few he'd never heard of before; the instructions said for diarrhea or constipation, and he wondered why she would be taking both, but no big deal there. He had leftover medications in his own cabinet. Most people did, he guessed. Before he left, Bernie checked himself in the mirror and tried to smooth out the wall-to-wall smile that had spread across his face. If he came out of the bathroom grinning like an idiot, she would know in a second what he'd been up to.

She had the table set when he returned, two large salad bowls filled almost to overflowing. "I'm trying to eat a little healthier," she said, patting her own generous abdomen.

"Looks great to me," he said. "What are the green things?"

"Avocado slices. You haven't had them before?"

"Don't believe I have." Then he did something he almost never did; he tried a completely unfamiliar food group, not just a nibble, but the entire slice all at once. "Not bad," he said, "not bad at all."

He'd never have dreamed that in the space of a few weeks he'd taken up bowling, worn a garish yellow shirt—twice—and eaten an avocado. Would wonders never cease? This woman had turned his life inside out. He must have smiled during most of the lunch because his jaw muscles actually ached. And several times he caught himself laughing. He would have to rehearse extra hard to convince Dr. Peele that his depression was just as bad as ever, if not worse, so he could continue his ECT program. Mustn't let happiness interfere with his treatment schedule.

If Bernie had to choose a descriptive word for his luncheon with Bertie, it would be idyllic, except he wasn't sure he had ever used the word before, and wasn't sure of the spelling, either. Even so, it sounded good and seemed appropriate for such a pleasant outing.

****

His bubble of well-being burst just before he got home when he spied a shirtless young man digging in the empty lot he'd recently purchased beside Ms. Grosbeak's house. Bernie hit his brakes and skidded to a halt. In an instant he was running across the lot waving his arms at the man whose small dog, on seeing Bernie flying at him, the tails of his yellow shirt flapping wildly, ran to hide behind Ms. Grosbeak's house.

"What are you doing?" Bernie yelled, hoping he kept the panic out of his voice.

"I was just going to turn over the sod here. Looks like it might be a good place to put in some tomato plants," the young man said.

"You can't do that here," Bernie said. "No digging."

"But it's just a vacant lot. What's the big deal?"

"It's my lot, and I'm telling you, no digging."

"Aunt Ginny said you were a weird duck."

"Who's Aunt Ginny?" Bernie asked.

"My aunt, Virginia Grosbeak, lives right here. I'm staying with her through the summer, if it's okay with you, of course." The rather lame attempt at sarcasm was dead-on-arrival.

Bernie paused, a trick he'd learned from his therapists, just stare and say nothing while you counted to ten was usually enough to make the other party start to squirm, wondering what would happen next. And it appeared to work on this man who claimed to be Aunt Ginny Grosbeak's nephew. He propped his shovel over his shoulder and stomped away, mumbling something that Bernie couldn't catch, except for the mention of weird several times.

A potential disaster nipped in the bud, so Bernie thought. But that didn't solve the problem of the dog. Dogs loved to dig, particularly when that digging produced bones, bones that could cause lots of trouble for Bernie.

He had to act fast. Early afternoon the following day, a truck parked in the street by the lot, and three brawny guys set about installing a six-foot high chain-link fence around the lot, plenty to keep out any bone-digging dogs or tomato-planting nephews. This would probably cause Ms. Grosbeak to gnash her teeth and tear her hair, all of which was fine with Bernie. Maybe she'd decide to move away altogether, one less set of prying eyes to worry about.

There remained one small chore, although a much more pleasant one he'd just thought of…a gift for Bertie, a tangible reminder of their developing relationship. He thought through the usual list of suspects…flowers, a possibility, but not his first choice, chocolates, no because they were now both committed to losing a few pounds, clothing wouldn't be very original since she'd already done the bowling shirt bit, and jewelry, he wouldn't know where to start.

But it didn't take him long to come up with an idea. The next day he drove across town to an upscale hardware store, the type that sold tools intended more for decorative effect than for actual work. The hammers had high gloss finishes that probably would never be marred by striking a nail. The wrench sets were displayed in leather carrying cases nicer than many purses Bernie had seen. They even had a small area set aside for gift-wrapping, truly unusual for a store that supposedly specialized in nuts and bolts.

By now, Bernie and Bertie had settled into a routine of late morning bowling followed by a lunch each Friday. When they'd rolled their last frame at the bowling alley—Bernie's game continued to improve—he presented her gift, a slim box about ten inches in length, wrapped in shimmering gold paper.

"Oh, Bernie, what's that for?"

"It's for you."

She returned to her seat, then slowly unwrapped the box, careful not to tear the lovely paper. When she opened the box and took out the shiny new stainless-steel icepick, her face lit up like a child's at Christmas. "Bernie, this is the most thoughtful thing anyone's ever given me."

Bernie got a hug and a big wet kiss on the cheek, as best he could recall, his first adult kiss from someone who wasn't family. He'd nailed it!

Chapter Six

Sunday mornings, particularly rainy Sunday mornings, were for sleeping late, then later still, coffee and the Sunday newspapers, enjoyed while he was still in his pajamas. Everybody knew that, everybody but the idiot who kept ringing Bernie's doorbell. Bernie pulled his pillow tight over his ears, but still couldn't block out the incessant ding-dong-ding.

Soon enough, Bitsy got in on the act. Usually the cat needed no excuse to sleep in at any time of day, but this morning she kept jumping back and forth across the bed, hurdling over Bernie like he was some obstacle at a track meet.

His Sunday morning wrecked beyond repair, Bernie crawled out of bed and headed for the door. He didn't bother with his robe and slippers. His sole purpose was to chase the doorbell offender back under whatever rock he or she had crawled from.

And the soggy, bedraggled man standing on his doorstep might very well have crawled from beneath a rock or wherever homeless people took up temporary residence. Tall and thin—emaciated, actually—he wore a jacket that just retained enough of its former characteristics to still resemble corduroy. Likewise, his trousers had probably been khaki at some time in the past, but now bore so many stains and deposits as to be of questionable origin. His dirty toes, complete with long curving toenails the color of mustard, protruded from holes in his shoes.

"Good morning, Bernie, I'm your Uncle Bob." He stuck out a hand that Bernie had no intention of touching, and it didn't matter because the screen door was still closed and latched.

"I don't know you," Bernie said.

"Well, it's been a long time," the dirty man said. "You were just a kid the last time I saw you. Look at you now, a full-grown man." He smiled, revealing teeth the same color as his toenails.

"I don't remember any Uncle Bob." Family ties in Bernie's commune recollections had been tenuous and often as not, imaginary. They—the adults—all considered themselves family, and so, their kids were all related too. "The family of the world," his father often said, his head partially hidden in the cloud of smoke that seemed to be his constant companion.

"Your dad's brother, Bob Mitchell. We've both changed a lot since then."

"What do you want?"

"Just let me come inside, will you? You can't leave me standing out here in the rain. We're family."

"Stop saying that. I don't know who you are, and if you don't go away, I'll call the police."

Bernie, being a bit of a hustler himself, got the clear impression that he was being hustled. And the mark of a good hustler was they always had a Plan B. Uncle Bob's Plan B was tears, not just silent tears, but tears with wailing, probably audible up and down the street. This could not go on. Of course, Bernie had a Plan B all his own, and Bob or whoever had just made a huge mistake by dredging up memories of a past Bernie hated.

He unlatched the screen door and let Uncle Bob inside. The tears disappeared in an instant. Bob rubbed his hands together. "That's more like it."

Mission accomplished, Bob must have thought. "Long time since those days in the commune, huh? You was just a little kid then, always running around starting fires. That's what I remember most. Too bad about your folks, though. Accidents will happen, I guess."

Now he had Bernie's full attention. The thing about pushing someone's buttons is that sometimes you pushed the wrong one, as Bob had just done. If he'd played his cards right, Uncle Bob might have walked away clean with a ten, fifteen-buck handout, enough for cigarettes and a cheap bottle of wine, but he obviously had bigger plans.

He walked into the hallway. "Looks like you got a lot of room here, Bernie. Maybe room enough for your old uncle to bed down for a while, you think?"

"Maybe."

"You know, I haven't eaten since yesterday. How about some breakfast?"

"Kitchen is right through there." Bernie pointed the way. As Uncle Bob shuffled on ahead, his footsteps marked by grimy deposits on the floor, Bernie made a quick stop by the fireplace to grab the heavy poker.

The deed itself was over and done with in a flash. Bernie was left to wonder whether he and the dead man lying on his kitchen floor were actually related and how much he might have known about Bernie's past, but it didn't matter now, did it? "Sorry, Uncle Bob, you had a chance to leave. You should have took it."

Uncle Bob had stumbled into a pattern that was

established early in Bernie's life, one that he would later share with his pet copperhead, Alvin. Left alone, Alvin posed no threat, but provoke the snake, or Bernie, and bad things happened.

****

Clean-up and disposal were particular problems when the event took place in his own home, and this time the difficulty was acute; he was low on supplies. He had none of the heavy-duty plastic wrap he needed to wrap up Uncle Bob, and he couldn't very well run out to the nearest hardware store, not with Uncle Bob lying there. He needed help, so he called Bertie.

"What should I bring?" she asked.

"Plastic wrap, for sure. I have plenty of duct tape and latex gloves." He was so lucky to have a friend like Bertie who asked just the right questions and nothing more.

When she got there, she backed her van right up to his garage door, facilitating transfer of Uncle Bob once they had him securely wrapped. It would also help conceal the transfer when they were ready to go. This simple, considerate act made Bernie go all warm. She thought of everything. What a perfectly marvelous woman.

Inside, Bertie surveyed the death scene. "Kind of messy," she said. "Bernie, you really ought to try the icepick method. There's so much less to clean up."

"I don't know; they seem kind of flimsy. Do they ever break off?"

"Oh, no, remember, a block of ice is a lot harder than someone's chest. Besides, I sharpen them up before I use them."

He had, in fact, considered a switch to the smaller

tool. It would be much easier to conceal, but he had some reservations about the effectiveness of what seemed to be a rather flimsy weapon compared to his axe or his fireplace poker. Those items had some heft. With the icepick, who knew? A larger victim might not die quickly enough, and a rowdy scene could ensue in which Bernie himself might sustain some damage.

"The trick is, you have to practice," she said, as if anticipating his reluctance.

"You practice, on people?"

"No, silly, I keep a heavy burlap bag filled with sand hung in the garage. It's not an exact match, but you can still practice your moves. See, I think of them like tennis strokes." She stepped away from him and swung her arm toward him at shoulder height, and he was so thankful she wasn't holding a weapon. "This is the forehand stroke, here's the backhand, and my favorite, the overhead smash. There's also the straight jab, sort of like a volley. I use both hands for that one, and you have to get your weight behind it. I practice a couple of times a week. If you practice some, you should pick it up in no time. Remember how fast you caught on to bowling? You should come over, try it sometime."

"Maybe I will." But he thought the icepick a bit too methodical. His own events were acts of passion, and bludgeoning seemed to be the best way to get the job done. Perhaps, if he hung around long enough with Bertie, he could watch her in action and learn more about her technique.

Today, with Uncle Bob, he had a special request. His usual holding ground for items awaiting disposal was now fenced off and inaccessible. "Do you suppose we could use your spot on the river?" he asked. "Just this one time."

"No problem," she said with a smile. The woman was a marvel. She helped wrap Uncle Bob, then mopped the kitchen floor. "Who was he?" she asked.

"A bum that wandered up, claimed to be my uncle. Never saw him before."

"I just hate those," she said.

Once they had the newly deceased securely stashed behind a stack of cardboard boxes in the garage—they wouldn't move him until after dark—Bernie suggested breakfast, his specialty.

"Oh, Belgian waffles," she said as Bernie whipped up the batter and warmed up the waffle maker. "I do love them." She fried up a side dish of sausages, and soon they set down to a late morning feast. Later, they settled back with the Sunday papers. This was a routine Bernie could become fond of very quickly, minus the part with Uncle Bob, of course.

The rest of the Sunday was close to perfect. Tummies loaded with carbohydrates, they snuggled on the sofa and shared the crossword puzzle. Later, a nice long nap. Could life possibly get any better?

Of course, there was still Uncle Bob waiting behind the boxes in the garage. Shortly past sundown, they loaded him into Bertie's van for the drive to the river.

"Bastard seems to have put on weight," Bernie said.

"They seem to do that, don't they?"

****

"This is such a romantic place," Bernie said. They stood close together, arms linked while the darkness became complete. Only the sound of the stream gurgling close by and an owl deep in the forest intruded on the quiet.

Moments earlier they had unwrapped Uncle Bob, now stiff and cold, and rolled him over the embankment where he dropped into the stream with a soft splash. Bernie's last sight of him was just before he floated into the more rapid current that would, if all went according to plan, sweep him out to sea where he would never again ruin anyone's Sunday morning.

"I love it here," she said. "It's so peaceful."

"Are you sure he's gone?" Bernie asked. "I can't see him in the dark."

"They all go away," she said, snuggling closer to him. "I've seen it lots of times. Don't worry."

How many times? Bernie wondered.

****

Bernie didn't need to fake remorse when Dr. Peele told him he was leaving the state hospital for a new job in Phoenix, AZ; his anxiety was real and acute. Having carefully trained the therapist over several months, Peele had developed into a man Bernie could depend on, a man he could control.

"Dr. Carruthers will take over your care. She's an excellent therapist, and I'm sure you'll like her."

"What about my treatments?" Bernie asked, beginning to tear up. Yeah, that was the critical item, wasn't it? Without ECT, Uncle Bob would be back ringing Bernie's doorbell in his dreams, an intolerable situation. Just as quick as that, Bernie's emotional climate shifted from despair to anger toward Dr. Peele. How dare he desert Bernie, leaving him to the mercy of some second-string therapist? Rage, which was always just beneath the surface with Bernie, began to build, and he knew that he'd better get it under control, or he would blow the whole deal. Bumping off a second therapist in the same year would buy him a permanent living space in the locked ward of a building that smelled like Bitsy's litter box.

"Bernie?" Dr. Peele looked concerned. "You seem to have drifted off there."

"I'm sorry," Bernie said. "I just get so scared when I think how bad my depression can get. You've helped me so much, Dr. Peele. I don't know how I'll get along without you." He forced a smile that he hoped would convey his trepidation about a future that would now depend on a new therapist.

"I've spoken with Dr. Carruthers about your ECT. I'm sure she'll work out a plan for you."

She? Bernie must have missed that earlier. Another curve ball. Female therapists, in Bernie's experience, could be tricky. He'd learned that during his time with Dr. Bowman. He could never be sure he had the situation under control as tightly as he'd like. There was always the possibility she'd want to try something new, and that wouldn't do, not at all.

He told Bertie about his new dilemma during their luncheon of tuna salad over leaves of Romaine lettuce the following Friday. He described Dr. Peele as receptive and cooperative, which, in Bernie-lingo, meant malleable. He expressed his great concern over Dr. Carruthers. Would the same techniques he'd used on Dr. Peele work on her as well?

"I don't know what I'd do if I lost my doctor," Bertie said. She had a piece of lettuce stuck to her front teeth giving her a comical gap-toothed appearance, until

Bernie pointed it out to her.

"Thanks," she said. "That probably looked kind of funny."

Bernie shrugged.

"I've been on ECT for almost over a year now, and I'd be a wreck without it," she said.

"I'm just afraid she'll want to start me back on pills, and I'll be staggering around like a zombie. She has to understand that sorting in the mailroom requires quick decisions and precision. A lot of people wouldn't get their mail if I was all doped up, not to mention what it would do to my bowling."

She took his hand. "Don't you worry about it. If she needs convincing, we can handle it."

****

For two people so used to working alone, asking for help was a big step, but the advantages of this united approach became apparent quickly enough.

"You know, this could work out, you and me together, like our own little Justice League, fixing what needs to be fixed. Just something to think about. I like being with you. We make a good team."

She made this suggestion right after they'd dropped a body into the deep ravine behind Bernie's house. The ravine was blocked from Mrs. Grosbeak's view—he still couldn't think of her as Aunt Ginny—by Bernie's house.

As they worked, Bertie gave him some of the history of this, her latest victim, a drunken driver who had crashed into a vehicle at an intersection killing a mother and her twelve-year-old daughter. Even though the driver had several DUI charges on his record, he apparently had friends in high places and got off with a fine and probation.

"That's how this all got started," she said.

As Bertie told the story, she became more and more agitated, pacing back and forth, her arm swinging in an arc that Bernie could easily imagine ending up in a fatal blow from an ice pick.

"I had a younger sister," she said. "Mom was driving her to her piano lesson when they were struck from behind by a drunk driver in a pickup truck. My sister died in the crash, and Mom never recovered. She went into a deep depression and never came out again.

"That driver got off too. A year later, he crashed into a bike rider and killed him. He got a six-month sentence, suspended, but he was out and at it again. Something had to be done. The courts let those bastards off, and they were right back on the streets. The very thought of it gets my bowels in an uproar."

Her fists were clenched so tightly that her knuckles shone white through the darkness.

This was familiar territory for Bernie, when the internal temperature approached boiling, the point of no return, the point where someone died, and he didn't want it to be him. Partly out of compassion, partly as a measure of self-defense, he embraced her and held her firmly until he felt her relax. "I understand," he said, and he did, and she would have known he did.

This was a huge step forward in their growing relationship, this sharing of internal motivation, linking cause and effect. He held her long past the time the tension had left her body, just because he liked doing it, and she seemed to like it too.

Eventually she began to squirm ever so slightly. "Let's go back to your house," she said. "It smells back here."

Which was, of course, why it made such a good drop-off point. The foul sulfur smell, emitted from somewhere down below, kept away any sightseers or hikers who might make a startling discovery were they to investigate the depths of the ravine. He drove the short distance back to his house with the lights off. Bertie's van was still parked in the street, and he pulled into his driveway. When they got inside, Bertie had no sooner sat down than Bitsy jumped into her lap.

"I still can't get over how much my cat likes you," Bernie said. "She's never taken to strangers before."

"Well, I'm not exactly a stranger, am I?" She winked at Bernie.

"I'll make coffee," he said. He brought out chocolate chip cookies he'd bought earlier in the day. "Not exactly on our diet plan, but we deserve a treat, don't you think?"

He thought Bertie was the perfect picture of domestic bliss, chocolate chip cookie in one hand while she stroked Bitsy with the other. And now he understood her activities with the icepick. It had seemed all along that, while his own homicidal acts were spontaneous, hers were more calculating. She planned ahead. Now he knew why. She had to select her targets carefully, and he respected her for that. Bernie's targets selected themselves by their own actions which forced him to act. Not that it made a lot of difference, because whatever her motives might be, they were fine by him.

"There's something else I should tell you." She looked almost shy, as if about to reveal her darkest secrets, even darker than those they already shared.

"It's medical, I have irritable bowel syndrome."

He had no idea how to respond to this announcement or whether he should respond at all. So, he sat, waiting for her to continue.

"It's kind of connected to the icepick thing. I've had it for years. I've tried everything imaginable, high fiber diet, low fiber diet, gluten free diet, non-dairy diets, none of them helped. And pills, my medicine cabinet was full of pills for diarrhea, constipation, depression, all for naught. I even tried meditation, relaxation therapy, but it didn't help. Then my doctor tried me on a short course of ECT for depression, and my symptoms disappeared. I threw out most of the pills in my medicine cabinet, and now I can eat pretty much anything I want. I only have to go for treatment once a month, so it's not much of an inconvenience at all.

"About the only thing that gets me stirred up is stress, like when I read about that drunk driver getting off with just a slap on the wrist. I had to do something."

"Oh, I get it," Bernie said. "The ice pick, it's like a type of stress management." He leaned back, smiling, partly because he'd caught on so quickly, and partly because the entire sequence made such perfect sense. And now, too, he understood the rather odd assortment of medications in her bathroom cabinet.

"Yeah, you could say that. Every time I do it, I feel such a relief."

Bernie felt relief too, like the final pieces in a puzzle had slipped into place and a very clear and pleasing picture had emerged.

****

Dr. Carruthers, the new therapist who would take over Bernie's care, didn't fit his expectations. Over the nine months or so that Bernie had been making trips for treatment at the state hospital, he recognized two categories of therapists: a younger group like Dr. Peele, for whom the state hospital was a stepping stone to bigger and better things, and an older group for whom that same hospital appeared to be the final stone in their career sequence. This latter group, into which he assumed Dr. Carruthers would pool her clinical skills, were typically older, and, on more than one occasion, Bernie had mistaken one of them for one of the inpatients. Dr. Peele seemed to find this amusing. The older therapists did not.

When Bernie arrived at the interview room, Dr. Carruthers was already there, her back to him, looking out the window. "You're late," she said without turning around.

When she finally turned to face him and fixed him in place with her blue eyes, Bernie, had he been able to move, would probably have run out of the room. This new therapist towered over him. Her blonde-mixed-with-gray hair was shoulder-length, and those same blue eyes, framed by wire-rimmed glasses, looked like blue pieces of ice embedded in silver strips.

Something was dreadfully wrong here. This doctor looked more like the tyrannical CEO of some major corporation than an end-stage therapist at a state hospital. And she gave him nothing. Aside from the chill radiating from her eyes, Bernie was staring into a void, a therapeutic black hole where feelings were drawn, never to emerge.

He began the day with a serious miscalculation. Assuming that he would be matching wits with one of the state hospital standards, he had dressed down for the occasion, hoping to blend in with the current clientele. He'd let his hair go uncut and unwashed. Bernie, whose beard grew in heavily and quickly, hadn't shaved for two days. He'd worn the same shirt for the past three days. Now, standing across from the most perfectly coiffed woman he'd ever seen, Bernie, looking foul and smelling worse, felt like a bum.

He kept his gaze directed at his feet, the proper angle for the depressed patient. He also tried to work in an attitude that he hoped would be interpreted as penitent. She would know that he was here because he had done a dreadful thing, even though it was all Dr. Bowman's fault for pushing him over the edge.

Dr. Carruthers took her seat behind the small desk by the door and opened the folder that, from its thickness, must have contained every event in Bernie's entire life. He didn't know whether to sit, remain standing, or jump out of the window. He sat. What he had hoped would be a rubber stamp meeting, continuing Dr. Peele's innocuous regimen, was not to be.

"I knew Dr. Bowman, your former therapist. We were classmates in Chicago. We became close friends." Her voice was low, like a murmur and full of threat.

Then came the flash of recognition, the photos in Dr. Bowman's office of her and another woman; that other woman was right in front of him. Bernie was dead-on-arrival, being treated by the friend of a therapist he'd had to do away with.

"Maybe you shouldn't be my therapist." It was a Hail Mary attempt, but what else could he do? This woman had a score to settle, with him. How could Dr. Peele whom he'd considered a friend, have left him at the mercy of this harridan?

"That's up to me to decide, not you. I'll remind you that regular attendance of your treatment sessions is mandated by the court. If you don't appear, you will be confined here in the locked ward until I say you can be released. Is that clear?"

Horror of horrors. Sweat turned his armpits into swampy bogs. He was melting and could do nothing to save himself. Then the questions started, rapid fire, giving him barely enough time to respond before she was at him again.

"Why did you murder Dr. Bowman?"

"What? I didn't murder anybody."

"You took her life in a very brutal act. What would you call it?"

"I was provoked. Everybody agreed."

"Provoked? That's a good one. I doubt Dr. Bowman ever provoked anyone, not in her whole life. She was a sweet, gentle soul, and now she's dead, because of you."

No escape in sight. Why-oh-why couldn't she be more like Dr. Peele? Ah, Dr. Peele, those casual, easy-going interviews. Dr. Peele understood him, cared for him. Dr. Peele's interviews lasted thirty minutes at most. Carruthers' inquisition might go on forever.

But he had to stay the course. This blue-eyed monster could, with a phone call, yank away his life as a free man, confining him to a nightmarish back ward in the hospital where, in time, he would probably become like one of those lost ones who sat strapped in wheelchairs, drooling, fed with a spoon, soiling himself. Or, she could simply discontinue his ECT, leaving him to the tender mercies of the dreaded dream people.

Neither option looked good at all. Bernie hung his head like the doomed man he was.

And the day had started out so well. Bertie had brought over a chocolate cake with three candles to commemorate their three months together. She had commented on his unkempt appearance. "New therapist today," he'd said. "Just part of the game." They'd both laughed then, but now he wondered whether it might be a long time before he laughed again.

Carruthers' voice sounded like a growl. "Since you don't want to talk about that incident—and I can see why you wouldn't—let's go back to your childhood. Dr. Bowman wasn't your first victim, was she?" Carruthers ran a boney finger down a page in a thick file open on her desk. His life story? How could she have known that? He'd always been so careful with the information, most of it fictitious, that he'd doled out to his earlier therapists.

Through no fault of his own, things began to shift inside Bernie. His internal thermostat climbed into the red zone. Soon his rage would boil over and out of his control.

Carruthers must have been well aware of what she was doing to him and given some sort of signal, because two hefty attendants entered the room and took up positions on either side of her desk. "Now, Mr. Mitchell, are you going to cooperate, or not?"

Cooperate? As if he had a choice. Lost, he was totally lost. "What do you want from me?"

It became clear soon enough, the adversarial tone of it all, attack, attack, attack—she wanted him split open, his guts spilled out onto the floor. Meanwhile, sweat and more sweat, his shirt plastered to his body, the smell of his own fear rising up in a stench she couldn't have missed. Did this woman have not even an ounce of compassion? He was a sick man. In addition to depression, he suffered from Post-Traumatic Stress as a result of the Dr. Bowman episode. She should know that. She had all of Dr. Peele's records right there in front of her.

"Did you hate your parents, Mr. Mitchell?"

"Huh? No, of course not."

"Why, then, did you kill them?"

"I didn't kill anybody. There was a horrible accident."

"You seem to be involved in a lot of accidental deaths, Mr. Mitchell. Are you an angry man, the kind who kills people for no reason?"

"No, not at all." Accidental deaths? If she only knew how close she was to becoming one, accidental death, that is. He gripped the sides of his chair, anchoring himself. He had to cooperate, as she put it, to have any chance of getting out of the room.

She turned a couple of pages of the hospital record. "Your first foster home, destroyed by a house fire, right, Mr. Mitchell?"

So unfair, how she was splicing together a string of unrelated incidents, trying to make him out as a villain. Dr. Peele would never do this. It was downright unethical. If he got out of this room alive, Bernie was never coming back, ever. God, how he wished he had his axe or his fireplace poker.

"You didn't answer my question, Mr. Mitchell."

"I didn't know you asked one."

"Fires and accidents, as you call them, Mr.

Mitchell; they seem to follow you around. Do you have anything to say about that?"

"I don't know what you mean." Desperation crept in, quietly at first, then roaring in on all eight cylinders. He considered pulling his complete breakdown routine, tears, loud wailing, rolling on the floor, much the same as he had done many months before in Dr. Bowman's office. It had worked back then, but he doubted it would be effective with Dr. Carruthers. She'd probably laugh at him. No, he needed something more drastic.

She bored into him with those iceberg eyes, but before she could continue her assault, a stroke of pure genius, a bolt from the blue born of the deepest desperation, saved him.

"A rat, a big one," Bernie yelled as he pointed. "Right over there, it ran behind the bookcase."

Her pale complexion turned even paler, her features twisted into an expression of horror. She grabbed the file and bolted for the door. "Let me out of here."

A direct hit, one of his best ever, one he'd have to remember for future use.

The two hulks stepped aside, and, as they turned, one of them winked at Bernie. Round one to Bernie, although it had been close. He released his grip on the chair, settled back and waited for his tormentor to come back and dismiss him, and when she failed to return (the imaginary rat was a gift from heaven), Bernie dragged himself out to his car for the drive home.

But he still had a serious problem on hand. His therapist's morbid fear of rodents was certainly good news, something to be kept for future use, but her adversarial temperament would not do. If she continued to use him as a punching bag, he would be forced to take countermeasures. He was sure he could count on Bertie's help.

Chapter Seven

Dr. Carruthers had, without question, scored a number of direct hits, albeit on an innocent victim, because to Bernie, his conscience was clear. The rather slapdash association she had drawn between him and fires would never hold up under close scrutiny, he was sure. Accidents happen, everybody knows that. Yes, he had been in the same vicinity as both fires, and several others she hadn't mentioned, no denying that, but being present did not prove he had actually set them, and if he was innocent in the eyes of the law, Dr. Carruthers didn't have a leg to stand on.

Cheap shots, that's all she had to offer up, kicking a poor guy who'd already been kicked around way too much. If she'd had to survive a series of foster homes as he had done, she probably wouldn't be sitting so pretty herself.

And they'd acted like they were doing him such a huge favor back then, taking him out of the commune, the social work lady and her assistant, who, as far as Bernie could tell just got in the way, placing him with the Winkle family. "Just what he needs," she'd said, "more structure in his life. Heaven knows, he didn't have any at that commune." She said commune like it was a garbage pit.

"Don't you worry, we'll set him straight." Mr. Winkle, large, loud, and abrasive—all the things his father was not—Bernie would learn, clapped a heavy hand that reeked of vinegar on Bernie's shoulder, establishing ownership in no uncertain terms. Mrs. Winkle, half her husband's size but twice as malevolent, stood there radiating all the warmth of a stone that had been immersed in ice water. Their son, William, four years older than Bernie, completed the loving family. Bernie never had a chance.

Yeah, structure, and lots of it, that must have been what he needed, because that's what he got. Meals at the commune had always been free-flowing events. Since no one had to be anywhere at any specific time, folks drifted in and out on their own schedules. There was lots of talking, singing sometimes, and always plenty to eat. But those days were history.

"Bernie, why is it taking you so long to get the leaves raked?" Mr. Winkle stood at the edge of the yard shaking his head and frowning like he'd just bitten into an unripe persimmon. "And you haven't even started washing the windows yet. Honestly, you're the laziest kid I've ever seen. Maybe you'll just have to work right through lunch. That should teach you to keep up with your chores."

Bernie said nothing. He certainly didn't say that every time he raked the leaves into a pile, William ran right through them, kicking them every direction so that Bernie had to do it all over again. At the Winkle house, every minute of Bernie's day was scheduled. He frequently got behind in his chores, because William, large, malignant and stupid, was always there lurking in the background, tripping him up, breaking down whatever Bernie had set up.

Always smiles and kind words when the parents

were around, when they were alone, William showed Bernie his true colors. "Touch any of my stuff and I'll kill you." His favorite pastime became administering painful pinches to Bernie, always where the marks wouldn't show.

The time it took Bernie to repair whatever damage William had done was subtracted from his mealtime, so he was always late and always hungry. Only when he said his evening prayers, on his knees beside his bed watched closely by Mrs. Winkle, Bible in her hand, did he extract some revenge. Instead of silently blessing all the Winkles, as he'd been instructed, he wished them all to burn in hell and wondered how he might speed up the process.

"Why can't you be more like William?" Mrs. Winkle asked him almost daily, as if becoming like William was a good thing. Bernie would have to lop about fifty points off his IQ to drop to William's level, besides having to learn to drool on command. No, there were no role models in the Winkle household, no hope for young Bernie, either.

"We caught him for you, Mrs. Winkle. He didn't get far. We kept him overnight down at the juvenile detention center. Didn't see any need to wake you up so late." The officer who had a very firm grip on Bernie's upper arm—he left a bruise—pushed him through the front door into the waiting arms of Mrs. Winkle.

"I just don't understand it," she said as she grabbed Bernie by the ear. "We try so hard to make a good home for him, then he ups and runs away like a common hoodlum. We'll see how you like going a few days without supper, young man. I guess we've just been too lenient with you. Young boys need discipline, that's for sure."

Bernie's first attempt at escape from the Winkles had ended abruptly when he was caught within the hour by the local authorities. After a terrifying night in the local juvenile detention center that he was sure he would not survive, he was almost glad to return to the loving arms of the Winkles, almost, but not quite.

Eight months was all he could take. Bernie lost weight—not good for a growing boy—and he'd begun to stutter, so, he did what he had to do. The fire started on a Wednesday evening when Mrs. Winkle was at her Bible study group, William was at band practice—tuba, a perfect match, Bernie thought—and Mr. Winkle was stretched out in his recliner working his way through a second six-pack. Bernie swiped a pack of the master's cigarettes and hid them in William's nightstand, all except for the one he lit and tossed into a pile of rags in the basement.

The fire smoldered for a while, and Bernie wondered whether he'd really done the job, but when the flames reached upstairs, and smoke poured from the windows, things improved quickly. He got to watch a drunken Mr. Winkle stagger out the front door to collapse on his lawn and watch the blaze consume his recliner along with everything else he owned. Soon enough everybody was homeless, the Winkles and Bernie too. The only loss was Mrs. Winkle's parakeet, but that was enough to keep her in hysterics for several days. Bernie felt bad about the bird, about Mrs. Winkle, not so much.

Oddly enough, the pack of cigarettes Bernie had stashed in William's nightstand survived the blaze, scorched but still recognizable. The fire marshal displayed them for the Winkles. "It wasn't me, it was Bernie," William said. "I caught him smoking just yesterday."

Denying it would get him nowhere, so Bernie remained silent. He should have guessed that William, though remarkably stupid, would try to blame him for the blaze. Still, it was a lovely fire that left the Winkles homeless and William without a place to sleep. Not a bad night's work, Bernie thought.

The Winkles went to stay with her sister in a neighboring town. Bernie was not invited.

The next two stays in foster homes were of even shorter duration, one ending when, on a surprise visit, the social worker found Bernie nursing bruises over his face and most of the rest of his body, courtesy of the man of the house and his ever present bottle of gin. After that, only the orphanage remained for Bernie. Along the way he decided people were no damned good and were to be avoided whenever possible. For the foreseeable future, it would be him against the world, or more specifically, the world against him, and there were many more of them than of him.

On his first day at the orphanage, just after he'd received his bed assignment, one of the big kids grabbed Bernie by the shirt and said, "When the lights go out tonight, I'm going to kick your ass." And he did just that, on that first night and on many nights to follow, until Bernie, using the club he'd fashioned in woodworking class, put the big kid into the local hospital for an extended stay.

Yeah, run the great Dr. Carruthers through a childhood like that and see how she'd turn out.

****

His first clue when he arrived home after his initial Carruthers inquisition that he'd best do something about his physical state came from Bitsy. Usually very tolerant of odors, the cat would have nothing to do with him. "Sorry, Bitsy, guess I don't smell so good." And if his cat found him repulsive, his appearance, which he'd hoped would elicit a sympathetic response from Bertie, was more likely to bring forth revulsion.

Later, showered and shaved, his rancid interview clothes stuffed into the bottom of the laundry hamper, he called Bertie.

"How'd it go with your new therapist?" Her voice had the effect a drowning man might feel when a rescue vessel sailed into sight.

"Not so good, in fact, not good at all."

"Shall I come over?"

"Yes, please."

He was not alone. For the first time in recent memory—since his parents, at least—he had someone in his corner. The feeling was new and a bit overwhelming. Bernie teared up.

By the time she arrived, he'd recovered and was well into preparation of an early dinner.

"What's this?" he asked as he opened the door for her.

"Flowers, you sounded a little down over the phone."

Bernie's world tilted in much the same way as on that first time he met Bertie. He felt he should grab onto something lest he slide off. He grabbed onto Bertie.

"Wow," she said. "If I'd known you liked daffodils so much, I'd have brought some before. Do you have a vase? I'll put them in water."

"Vase?"

"Yeah, you know, a tall, cylindrical kind of thing. "I guess you don't have one. Let's look in your kitchen. Maybe we can find something."

She did indeed find a dark green vase in the back of one of his cupboards. Bernie couldn't remember seeing it before. Had she simply conjured it up? Anything seemed possible with Bertie.

"Perfect," she said. "It's just right for the daffodils, don't you think?"

"Yeah." The dark pool of despair in which he had been flailing had somehow receded. The light he saw was not just that fabled glow at the end of the tunnel; it filled the entire room. Salvation!

She took a quick look at the edibles Bernie had begun preparing, zooming in on one particular item. "Avocados? Bernie, you're amazing."

"Yeah, I remembered you liked them." He wasn't sure, and there was no way to check, but he might have blushed.

Over a light dinner at which Bernie served a chilled chardonnay—it was another day of firsts, it seemed— he went over his near-disastrous encounter with Dr. Carruthers. Bertie listened intently without interrupting, but her facial expression alternated between alarm and anger.

Only when he finished did she speak up. "What the hell? I thought she was supposed to help you. That's what therapists do, right?"

"It was awful," Bernie said. "She was so fixated on this therapist I had before, said they were classmates in college, and there were photos of them together in Dr. Bowman's office. She blames me for her death. I know she does."

Bertie cocked an eyebrow but said nothing.

"But it wasn't my fault," Bernie said. "I was in severe distress, temporary insanity, they call it. Instead of helping me, Dr. Bowman provoked me. Dr. Carruthers has all the records. I don't see how she can hold me responsible for something I couldn't control."

"So, this new therapist is pushing you, on purpose, it seems." She helped him load the dishwasher, then they took their wine glasses into the living room, chased Bitsy off the sofa, and sat side by side, pondering Bernie's new dilemma.

"What if she just disappeared?" Bertie asked.

"Only as a last resort. They're watching me for sure." Yeah, he might get away with one dead therapist, but he'd have a hard time explaining another one.

"You said there were two attendants in the room while she was grilling you. Do you remember their names?"

"Wrote them down, Lassiter and Perkins. From the way they both looked at her, I don't think she was at the top of their list of favorites."

"So, if you explained to her boss how she'd mistreated you, they would probably back you up," Bertie said. "Sounds like she's a real bitch."

"I think so, yeah. All of the attendants seemed to like Dr. Peele, and she's completely opposite from him."

"Good, now we just have to find out whether her thing with Dr. Bowman was professional or personal. I know somebody who might be able to help." She took a long drink of wine, then pointed at Bernie's glass. "You're not drinking fast enough. How am I going to get you drunk if you won't drink?"

"Why would you want to get me drunk?" he asked. He found out soon enough.

As make-out sessions went, this one, their first, was rather low-key and chaste. Buttons remained buttoned, buckles stayed buckled, and zippers stayed zipped. Teenagers, even pre-teens, would have laughed at the slow, deliberate pace of their explorations.

Not that Bernie was unfamiliar with the process. In his days of wandering about the commune, he had come upon all manner of couplings, twosomes, threesomes and more, as well as solitary figures making love to themselves. Even his parents invited others over for occasional love fests. Bernie peeked but never could quite catch on as to what they were doing and why.

But those first halting moments with Bertie were unlike any of those he'd seen or known before. This was not what might be called a quickie. He had feeling things now he hadn't felt before, and he wanted to bask in the pleasant glow as long as possible. He could only hope Bertie felt the same, but they were reaching the point of no return, that moment when the consummation of all their cuddling would result in a furious clash of bodies. Bernie was not completely enthusiastic about this prospect, so, he was somewhat relieved when Bertie pushed him away and held him at arm's length.

"I should have told you before," Bertie said, becoming tearful for the first time since he'd known her. "I can't do anything. My stuff is all messed up down there. I was born that way. They said it would take surgery and hormone injections to fix me, but even then it might not work out."

Silent tears were the worst. They were the ones, Bernie figured, that came from real pain.

"I didn't say anything before...." She turned and took several steps away. "It never seemed to matter. Nobody ever gave me a second look anyway. It was always like I wasn't even there...until you. It's the first time I ever wanted to, and I can't, I just can't."

He knew all he needed to know. The medical specifics might have been interesting but would in no way change the way he felt about Bertie. He crossed the short distance between them and wrapped his arms around her. "It doesn't matter," he said. "We're together, and that's what counts, nothing else." And since his words came straight from the heart, he didn't need to say anything more.

The malevolent Dr. Carruthers was forgotten, a problem pushed off until a later date. More important issues took precedence. Even without committing that final act, he felt the bonding between them was now complete.

****

It was late. They had cuddled on the sofa for more than an hour. "You could stay over," Bernie said.

"But I didn't bring anything," she said. "And I look a perfect fright in the morning."

"I have some things you can wear tonight, and I'm sure you'll look just lovely in the morning. We'll have Belgian waffles for breakfast."

"You've found my weakness. You've got yourself a roommate, for tonight, anyway. You don't happen to have a spare toothbrush, do you?"

"As a matter of fact, I do."

"Why do you have twin beds?" Bertie asked as

they walked into the bedroom.

"They were here when I moved in. It wasn't much more trouble to take care of two, so I kept both of them."

"Or maybe you were just waiting for me to come along," Bertie said, smiling broadly.

"Maybe so."

Same bedroom, separate twin beds. Other couples would have found the arrangement untenable, but Bernie and Bertie were not like other couples. They were new at the game and proceeding cautiously, but proceeding, all the same.

"Good night, Bertie."

"Good night, Bernie."

"Bertie?"

"Yes."

"You make me want to be a better person."

The soft sound coming from Bertie's side of the room sounded like Bitsy purring.

****

"This is the third one this month." Bertie had three newspapers spread out across the kitchen table leaving Bernie no place to put his beer." I can hardly keep up," she said.

Bernie leaned in to get a closer look, although he could make a good guess of what she was studying. Each paper was opened to an article about a drunken driver and an auto accident involving fatalities. She'd used a yellow highlighting pen to mark certain specifics in each case, specifics that she then copied into her notebook. Bernie could also make a good guess of what happened to people whose names were written in Bertie's notebook and hoped his own never came to be among them.

This was her passion, this put fire in her eyes. When drunken drivers caused death and destruction on the highways, then were allowed to skip through the legal system with little or no consequences, Bertie, who was very conscientious about her work, went into action, taking over where the legal system failed. "I don't have time to fix dinner tonight," she said. "Can you find something to eat?"

"No problem." So long as there were microwave dinners in the freezer, he would not go hungry. "Anything I can do to help?" This woman who had brought bowling, avocadoes and daffodils into his life was bringing complications as well...more bodies. Bernie felt obligated to assist her in her quest, even though the idea of bludgeoning somebody who posed no threat to him left him queasy, too much like real murder, but, when the time came, as he knew it would, he'd help however she wanted. It was the least he could do.

"Maybe later, I might need some help moving things around." She glanced up at him, smiled, then went right back to her notebook, making her battle plans. When she was on the hunt, gathering intel about her quarry's habits, she was relentless. The process consumed her. So, when three miscreants were passed along by a lenient judge within the same one-month period, Bertie embraced a formidable task, but one that she would not let go by unpunished. She compiled files on each of the culprits—home addresses, jobs, vehicles, family information.

"Why do you bother with all that information, especially the family details?" Bernie asked.

"Even habitual drunks have families, and I have to take that into consideration when I'm making my plans. You know, all actions have consequences, mine more than most."

Bernie found this very thoughtful of her.

It looked and sounded like a military campaign, the cool calculating way she set out her objectives, then went after them. Her methods contrasted so sharply with his own, which weren't really methods at all.

The wild card in Bernie's life had always been the unfortunate remark or act that flipped the switch and forced the action that complicated his day and usually ended someone else's. He had no control over such incidents, so there was no way to plan or set aside a time, much less collect background data.

He thought once of keeping a written record of his deposits and where he'd made them, but that might just serve to reinforce the tendency of the dreaded dream people—the nocturnal manifestations of those deposits—to make their unwelcome visits. Why tempt fate when fate had treated him so unkindly in the first place?

Bertie's activities, being more deliberate, could be planned, in fact, required planning. Bernie was not entirely surprised when she showed him a list in her notebook of victims dating back five years. "So many," he said as he ran his finger down a second page.

"You don't count yours?" she asked.

He shook his head. He wanted no reminders, most of all he didn't want to do anything that might stir up those dreaded specters.

During Bertie's frantic data-gathering period, while she scoured newspapers and other sources about her intended victims, Bernie saw her at their Friday bowling-lunch, but that was about all. Even then she insisted on discussing the information she'd gotten with him.

"Well, two down, one to go," she said as they settled into a lunch of tuna salad sandwiches.

"You mean you've already done the other two?" Bernie never expected she would move so fast, and she hadn't requested his assistance with either of them.

"Didn't have to," she said. "One had two previous DUI arrests, and the judge gave him two years. I'll keep my eye on him. I doubt he'll serve the whole time, and I'll be waiting for him when he gets out. Number two is off the list permanently. The fool, probably drunk as usual, crashed his car into a bridge abutment, killing him instantly. At least he didn't hurt anyone else, and he saved me a lot of work," she said.

Bernie wondered why she didn't stand back and let nature take its course with the others, since the inebriates seemed to self-destruct so frequently, but he did not mention this to her.

"The third one is still a work in progress, and the sooner I get him off the road, the better. He hits the same bar several times a week and staggers out at closing time. I followed him one night. You should have seen him weave all over the road. The judge should never have let him go. It's just a matter of time before he hits another vehicle."

So, the following week, late Wednesday evening, Bernie and Bertie sat in her van outside her target's bar while a misty rain covered the windshield, giving everything a ghostly haze. Bertie had parked a couple of car lengths from a battered pickup truck with dents in both front fenders.

"Are you sure that's his truck?" Bernie asked.

"Absolutely, just look at the front end. I wonder how many collisions he's had. Besides, I checked the license number, no mistake."

It wasn't long before drunk number three emerged, and Bertie put an end to the public health menace. He staggered out of the bar toward his truck, but never completed his trip. As he fumbled for his keys, Bertie crept out of the van, and, moving with the grace of a very large cat, slipped alongside him with her icepick poised at shoulder level. She grabbed her victim by the shoulder, spun him around, and with a single thrust, dispatched the inebriate with a degree of strength and skill that left Bernie slack-jawed. He was watching an artist at work, no doubt.

The man's arms and legs continued to quiver as Bernie went over to help with the lifting. Bertie knelt down, her knee on the man's chest just beside her ice pick, and seizing his head, gave it a vicious twist producing an audible cracking noise. Then he moved no more.

"Sometimes I have to do that," Bertie said, "when they keep wiggling about. We don't have time to wait around for him to stop."

The advantages of working with a fresh subject were obvious; the parts were warm and pliable, and, since Bertie's icepick made only a small hole, not gory at all.

"This is really great, having you to help out with this. I've thrown my back out a couple of times," Bertie said. They wedged the body into the passenger's seat, then Bertie drove the truck a few miles up the road with

Bernie following along behind in her van. When they reached their destination, a sheer drop-off, they switched the body to the driver's side beneath the steering wheel. The flight of the truck after they pushed it off the road and over the edge was spectacular, and the fiery crash at the end left only a ring of scorched earth at the bottom of the gully.

They watched for a moment, then drove to an all-night diner for a heavy dose of comfort food to recharge their internal batteries. They tackled mounds of pancakes in silence but without enthusiasm. Eventually each of them pushed aside a plate only half-consumed. Bertie, in particular, looked morose. "The thrill is gone," she said.

"Thrill? What thrill?" Bernie asked. This was hardly a thrill sport. What had he missed?

"I didn't mean it like that. Before, I always felt like I'd done a good thing, a sort of public service, you know. This time didn't feel like that. I almost wish I hadn't done it."

Bernie, perhaps not the most perceptive guy on the block, still knew something momentous was afoot, something more than the aftermath of the sugar load from the imitation maple syrup they'd poured over their pancakes. Without thinking, he made what was probably his best move; he took her hand and kept his mouth shut. Later, he would look back on this as yet another act of instinctive genius. From the way she squeezed his hand, he guessed she must agree.

"Maybe I'm just tired, I need a break," she said. "I think we both do. You get most weekends off, right?"

"Yeah, sure." A weekend with Bertie, he was certainly up for that.

"You like fishing?" she asked.

Fishing, ugh, a waste of time if ever there was one. Many months before, during his therapy with Dr. Bowman, he'd created an imaginary fishing expedition with imaginary friends and imaginary fish, finally feeding the whole line to the doctor to convince her that he really was trying to get out there in the world and connect with other people. But now, coming from Bertie, the whole idea took on a new light. If she wanted him to fish, he'd fish, even though he couldn't recall ever having done it before.

"Sure," he said with enthusiasm that surprised him. "But I'll have to buy some gear."

"I have plenty," she said.

What must this woman's storage closet look like…bowling balls, fishing tackle, icepicks to spare, what else?

"I hope you're okay with camping out," she said.

"Sure, no problem."

She looked a bit surprised at his quick answer but probably would not have been had she been more familiar with his childhood in the communes where his parents took up temporary residences. When he was old enough to explore on his own, he was left to wander about as he pleased, sometimes with the other kids, more often by himself. Play dates and sleepovers were not events to be arranged; they just happened, or not.

In the warmer months, he slept outdoors almost as frequently as he slept inside the bus with his parents. Having Bernie elsewhere seemed fine with both of them and gave him the opportunity to spy on the nocturnal habits of the other commune dwellers. So, in effect, he was camping out for much of his childhood and learning about many behavioral oddities that went on after dark, some of which would be forced upon him during his later orphanage years.

****

Friday afternoon, the second week in May, both Bertie and Bernie managed to get off work early, so the ninety-minute drive north to the campground still left them with plenty of daylight to get set up. Bernie brought only a change of clothes and a few toiletries, since Bertie insisted she'd packed everything they would need, and, from the stuffed appearance of her van, she'd done just that.

The drive took them through rolling hills of forest. "It's so beautiful through here," Bertie said. "Don't you just love it?"

"Absolutely." He rode with his arm out the window, breathing in the scent of evergreens, enjoying things he'd seldom even noticed before. Travelling with Bertie made it all special.

The campground lay in a narrow valley with a stream gurgling down the middle. Bernie paid the attendant, a gaunt man wearing a straw hat with a hole in the crown, twenty dollars for a two-night stay. Bertie parked the van beside a site just a short walk from where the stream formed a pool some twenty feet across.

"Perfect, just perfect," Bernie said as he did a three-hundred-and-sixty-degree turn, taking in the entire vista. "How did you ever find this place?"

"One of the girls from the store told me about it. She comes up with her family several times a year. Are you thinking about going for a swim?"

"I'll pass," he said.

"Good move. That water comes right down from the mountains, and it's really cold. There's some firewood by the showers over there. If you'll bring some over we can start a fire. It's starting to get chilly already."

Bertie's tent was one of those easy-to-assemble models with the frame extensions on the outside, and they had it erected and standing in only a few minutes. She'd brought along a propane gas stove for cooking and set it up on the picnic table next to her van.

"Tonight's dinner will be beef stew from a can," she said. "Tomorrow I'm expecting fresh trout. That will be your job."

Bernie's gut went into a mild spasm as he considered fishing for trout. If their dinner depended on what he was able to catch, it might be a meager meal.

After the surprisingly tasty beef stew, she served up hot coffee and sticky buns she'd wrapped in foil and warmed over the campfire. She hummed as she bustled about the campsite. Time in the great outdoors seemed to be the perfect antidote for the temporary gloom she'd expressed after their last adventure.

"I'm in shock," Bernie said, "the way you've planned all this out." He'd seldom seen her so light-hearted, so carefree. Soon enough, he found himself caught up in her good humor.

"Just trying to impress you," she said.

"You've done that for sure. I feel like I'm not holding up my end here. You're doing all the work."

"You can start by washing out the pots in the sink by the showers. Your big test will come tomorrow…two nice fat trout for dinner."

The pressure was building. She clearly expected

him to perform the manly duty of going out into the wild and securing food for them. Maybe he could fake an illness.

After he had completed his clean-up duties and everything was packed away—can't leave any food lying about, Bertie cautioned, attracts bears—they took a stroll around the campground, hand-in-hand, their usual arrangement now. The gurgling from the stream reminded Bernie of the place where Bertie launched her icepick victims, but when he mentioned it to her, he didn't get the response he expected.

"Let's talk about something else," she said, a bit sharply.

He didn't mention it again.

Farther along, after they'd passed the last empty campsite and the road doubled back toward the entrance, she said, "Sorry about snapping at you back there. I'm just not feeling too good about all the river things right now."

Bernie could think of nothing to say. What in the wide world was happening to them? In some ways they were almost becoming different people…together. He could make do with the different part, enjoyed it, actually, so long as the togetherness persisted. He didn't want to lose her.

An evening chill had set in by the time they got back to the tent. Bernie stirred the embers of the campfire and added a few more pieces of pine that caught quickly. Moments later, a happy fire—if a campfire could be called happy, and Bernie saw no reason why not—burned within the ring of stones.

All the aromas blended, smoke from the campfire, the spicy smell of millions of pine needles, the musty loam of the earth underfoot, and coffee grounds from their meal earlier. Just to sit and inhale was enough, but to share the experience with Bertie made him want to stop the world, freeze the moment in time. He was almost giddy…almost.

Sometime later—how long? Who knew? Who cared? They stretched a sheet of plastic cut from the same roll they sometimes used to wrap up their victims across the floor of the tent and spread out their sleeping bags.

"Probably going to be a chilly night," Bertie said. "If you get cold, you know where to find me."

Bertie's little tease—she was teasing, wasn't she?—was Bernie's last sound before the twilight in his mind became total darkness. Perhaps there had been an owl, maybe two, perhaps some small creature snuffling in the underbrush, but those memories were vague, encased in the soundest night's sleep he'd had in a long time. And even in the depths of his darkness, no specters, no dream people. Bernie slept the sleep of the innocent.

Chapter Eight

Then someone was tugging at his foot. Someone was saying, "Wake up, sleepyhead, the sun is up, and the coffee's hot." Someone was laughing. Soon enough, Bernie was laughing too.

Bacon, scrambled eggs, hot coffee, and Bertie, if there were better ways to start off a day outdoors, he didn't care to know about them. She kept on surprising him, pulling rabbits out of hats he couldn't even see.

Another day in paradise, that was his thought as he stood gazing up into a cloudless blue sky spread out above the ragged rim of the dark pine forest. "I can't believe I've been missing all this," he said, as much to himself as to Bertie, and he had no doubt that much of the wonder of this pleasant experience came from the presence of his companion, that she could turn an ordinary day into something extraordinary.

But Bertie had heard him. "We're going to have to get you out more," she said, linking her arm through his. It was a rather possessive gesture, and he didn't mind a bit.

They had just finished cleaning up after a breakfast that had Bernie rethinking his routine every-day-the-same-thing meals. Maybe it was time for a little variety. Once again, a thought that would have caused him considerable anxiety before, now seemed altogether reasonable.

"Let's walk off that breakfast." She took his hand and tugged him along behind her. "There's supposed to be a lovely trail on the other side of the road."

Yep, paradise, had to be. The path was too narrow for them to walk side-by-side, and even with Bertie leading single file, they were still caressed by outcropping branches. Bernie, who usually objected to anything alive and green, had no trouble at all, this new man of adventure.

About one hundred yards into the forest, with most of the sunlight blocked by the overhanging foliage, the otherwise friendly path turned cold and forbidding, and steep. Before long, Bernie was panting like a long-haired dog on a hot day.

"How about a break?" Bertie said.

"You read my mind."

"Drink?" She passed him a canteen.

Bernie, who had given no thought to provisions, water, least of all, gulped it greedily.

"Careful, not too much all at once," Bertie said. "Make you sick."

"Thanks," he said and passed the canteen back to her.

"We should have brought jackets," she said. "Sorry, I forgot how chilly it gets under the trees. It levels off a little farther along. You up for another short climb?"

"Lead on," Bernie said. The decision of whether to bring jackets was no more her choice than his own, but she had accepted responsibility. With every flip of the coin, she ascended several more rungs on the ladder of Bernie's esteem. Soon enough, she would reach the top…then what?

The level spot she'd mentioned was also open, yielding up an unbroken green expanse in three directions, changing only off in the distant west where a great rolling sea dominated all. Bernie was breathless once again but not from exertion. Now something completely different welled up within him, so strong that it compressed his tear ducts, bringing little rivulets halfway down his cheeks.

He turned away in shame and confusion, but too late, Bertie had seen. She grabbed his shoulders and turned him back around. She kissed away the tears. "Bernie, whatever am I gonna do with you?"

Someone who might have come upon the two of them embracing there on that rocky point would have taken them for a pair of lovers, totally lost in each other, and someone would have guessed right.

The trail formed a loop, coming down on the other side of the ridge and leaving the two lovebirds with a substantial downhill hike to reach the campsite. By the time they got back, the sun was well past its zenith, but Bernie had other concerns.

"I think my blisters have blisters," he said. He took off his shoes and found a bloody spot on his right heel.

"Oh, damn," Bertie said. "I should have seen this coming." She propped both his feet up on a camp stool and applied a soothing white creamy lotion to the blistered areas. "No more mountain climbing for you, not for a while, anyway."

"But what about dinner," he asked, "the fish?"

"I'll catch some later for us." And, after they sat back soaking up the scenery for a while, that's exactly what she did.

Bernie had never seen a fly rod handled with such

dexterity. The trout never had a chance as Bertie laid beautiful loops of line across the pool. Bernie imagined the fish jostling one another to see which would have the honor of taking a fly presented so skillfully.

After she'd caught several, most of which she returned to the pool until she had exactly the two she wanted, she held them up for Bernie's approval. He hardly had time to get the fire rekindled before she brought over four perfectly prepared filets.

"Where did you learn to handle a knife like that?" he asked as the filets sizzled in a cast iron frying pan.

"It's what I do. I'm a butcher, been doing it for years. I'm head of the meat department at the market. Sometimes I do fish. I thought I mentioned that."

"I don't think so." He would have remembered for sure. "But even if you had, I've never seen anybody slice and dice the way you do. You're like a Rembrandt with a filet knife."

"Years of practice. How do your blisters feel?"

"Much better. That ointment you put on was like magic." The blisters seemed like a blessing in disguise, having spared him the embarrassment of fishing for their trout dinner, an endeavor doomed to failure for sure.

Once again, Bertie had saved the day. In addition to succulent trout filets, from the depths of her cooler she dug out plastic cartons of coleslaw and potato salad, along with chocolate pudding for dessert. Who could ask for more?

They were far enough into the evening hour that the sparks from the campfire flickered like so many fireflies, glowing for an instant, then gone.

"That trout was delicious," he said. "Best I've ever

eaten."

Bertie's smile was barely visible in the twilight. She came over and sat beside him, and they both stared into the hypnotic embers. He thought how different this evening was compared to how he usually spent them, some time working on his airplane models, sometimes reading, but mostly the same night after night. Routine was comfortable, and he liked it. Now, evenings with Bertie had taken on a more madcap *anything goes* aspect, and he liked that even more.

"Penny for your thoughts," she said.

"This is just so nice, no, it's perfect." He pulled her close and they blended, forming one rather ponderous body. "Just a few weeks ago, I would never have dreamed we would be here like this together."

She moved even closer until there was no space at all between them. This, in Bernie's mind, was just as it should be. Life was good, very good…until he began to detect a slight tension in the air. Was there trouble in paradise? Something he hadn't picked up on yet?

"Bernie, I need to tell you why I snapped at you back there."

"Hey, you don't need to explain anything to me, ever. I'll be happy to hear whatever you want to tell me, but don't ever think you have to."

"There are some things I've wanted to tell somebody for a long time, but until you came along, there was nobody I could trust. I mean stuff I don't even tell my therapist."

He wrapped an arm around her waist and pulled her even closer. Other times, other places, other people, he'd have done almost anything to avoid exchanging confidences with someone. Intimate knowledge entailed commitment, but this was different, this was Bertie.

"That guy, the one you helped me drag down to the river, the first time we met, I knew him." A deep breath. "He was my uncle. I lived with him and my aunt in New Hampshire for a couple of years." She halted to take another deep breath.

Bernie had no doubts about the pain that came up along with this revelation. "You don't have to go on, if you don't want to," he said.

"No, I have to finish what I started. It's been buried too long. There was some sexual abuse, a very painful attempt at rape. I sliced his arm open with a kitchen knife, and that pretty much ended that. I left New Hampshire as soon as I was able and never expected to see him again, but now several years later, he turns up at the market where I work. He didn't see me, and I don't even know whether he was looking for me or not, but I couldn't take that chance. So, I did what I had to do, and fortunately you came along to help with the heavy lifting."

"Oh, my God, that's a terrible story. I'm so sorry," he said.

"That was probably more than you wanted to hear." She hung her head as tears coursed down her cheeks.

"I know it must have been hard to do, but I'm glad you shared it." But that wasn't the important thing, was it? It wasn't so much what he did or did not want to hear, it was what she wanted to say that was important. So, he borrowed a trick from his old therapist…silence…trying to convey something by doing and saying nothing, *if you want to talk, I'm always ready to listen*. It must have worked.

"You want to hear more?" Her grin was rueful at best. Even considering their rather advanced state of communication, advanced because they were so similar in so many ways, rooting around in the psychological basement, digging up some of the really unpleasant stuff would always be tough sledding.

He nodded, no words, not when the merest of gestures would get his point across.

"It doesn't get any better," she said.

Couldn't be much worse than mine. He thought it but didn't say it.

"When I was growing up, my sister, Sherry, and I couldn't have been more different. I mean, I loved her to pieces, but she was talented, pretty, the perfect daughter, as my parents said many times. And I was much the way you see me now, on a smaller scale, of course. It was hard to believe we were sisters. Everybody seemed to say that, my parents included. So, the boys always chased after Sherry. If they looked my way at all it was to throw something at me or punch me. So the best thing for me was to try to be invisible, and that's what I did."

This was familiar territory for Bernie who had so many times wished for an invisibility cloak for himself. If they don't see you, they can't hurt you, not on purpose, at least.

"That worked out okay until the auto accident when Sherry was killed. Of course, it wasn't an accident. When a drunk driver rams into your car and kills your sister, that's homicide in my book. Always has been, always will be.

"Sherry's death destroyed our family, such as it was. I had nothing to do with it, but my mom seemed to blame me anyway. 'It should have been Bertha.' She always called me Bertha. I heard her say that to Dad several times, how the wrong daughter got killed. He agreed with her. I heard him say it. As time dragged on, and Mom slipped deeper and deeper into depression, and Dad got more and more distant, they made me feel like nothing, like I didn't matter at all. I guess I never got over that feeling, until I met you. Now you see how important you are to me. Without you I feel like I would sink, and nobody would save me."

"Same here." He knew a bit about feeling like the world would be better off without him, like nobody would notice if he was gone. He could relate directly to Bertie's one-to-one testimonial. "That's just one of the reasons we have to stay together." It must have looked more like they were wrestling than hugging, so fierce was their embrace.

****

Late in the night Bernie woke up to what sounded like someone or something slapping the side of the tent.

"Wind came up about an hour ago," Bertie said. "Seems to be getting worse. I wonder if we shouldn't move into the van in case any limbs blow down."

They rolled up their sleeping bags, grabbed a few items of clothing, and made a dash for the van. The wind was fierce and cold and drops of icy rain had begun to fall as they threw their gear into the van.

"My poor tent," Bertie said. "I hope it's still standing in the morning."

The wind buffeted the van for another hour during which neither of them slept. When daylight finally crept in through the front windshield—still intact—they emerged from the vehicle to find their orderly campsite now filled with rubble. The tent remained standing, bowed but not beaten.

"Would you look at that." Bernie pointed to where a large falling limb had crashed through the toilets reducing them to firewood. "Must have been that big crash we heard about an hour ago. Good thing nobody was inside." Although anybody inside the toilet in the middle of a stormy night probably had problems enough of their own.

It was almost nine o'clock before they'd retrieved their personal items and began dismantling the tent. The caretaker pulled up in an ancient Ford pickup, rolling along on tires so slick they could not have provided much traction, if any. "Just wanted to check, see how you folks made out last night."

"We're okay," Bertie said. "We'll just get our stuff together and be on our way. Is there a pancake house nearby?"

"Yeah, just drive back out the same road you came in on, then make the first right turn. Restaurant's about a mile down that road." The attendant looked around the littered campsite as if hoping Bernie would tidy it up, but storms came under the act-of-God heading, not Bernie's problem.

The pancake house had survived the storm with only the loss of their roadside sign.

"You really have a new thing for blueberry pancakes," Bertie said as Bernie mounted a vigorous attack on the stack in front of him. "Since you liked Belgian waffles so much I wasn't sure you'd go for pancakes."

"Yeah, the waffles will always be my first love, but this is like a special treat." For Bernie, this was just another new item he'd been introduced to by Bertie. Oh, he knew about pancakes, of course, everybody did, but this break from his rigid routine that allowed him to have them any time he wished; this was another major change.

Bertie must have seen how much he was enjoying himself, because she didn't even mention their diet and that blueberry pancakes were nowhere on the list. Oh well, what was the fun of a diet if you couldn't break it once in a while?

When the stack of pancakes along with bacon strips and honeydew melon slices were reduced to moist streaks on his plate, a very content Bernie leaned back. "You know, this has been a great trip, even with the storm and my stupid blisters. I've had a great time."

"We'll have to get you some real hiking boots and heavy socks. Blisters are no fun."

"You might give me a few lessons with that fly rod, too," he said.

"Easy enough, we can do it right in your back yard. Turn you into an expert in no time."

Their drive back was an extension of the happiness ongoing. Bernie rummaged through Bertie's stack of tapes and came up with one of Christmas carols, and, notwithstanding the fact that it was still the very merry month of May, they went through about a dozen choruses of Jingle Bells before they tired of it. Yeah, life was good.

They both spotted the dark blue sedan parked in front of Bernie's house about the same time. The driver of the sedan must have seen them as well, because, when Bertie partially blocked the street with her van, the sedan cleared out the ditch on the other side then sped away.

"What the hell?" Bernie said.

"Have you seen that car before?" Bertie asked.

"Not around here."

"I've seen it parked in front of my house twice," Bertie said. "I got part of the plate number this time, so maybe I can find out who it was."

"Are we in trouble?" Bernie asked, assuming that, if one of them was in a jam, they both were.

"Let me see what I can find out about this car first," she said.

They unloaded Bernie's few items from her van. "Can you come in for coffee?" he asked.

"Thanks, but I'd better get home and make some phone calls." She kissed him on the cheek, then she was gone, and with her, the joy of their first camping trip. Gone too was Bernie's newly found placidity. In its place, his usual rage reaction reappeared. If the driver of that car, or anyone else for that matter, wanted trouble, he was just the guy to dish it out.

He didn't have to wait long for a target; there, among the bills and ads he'd received in the mail was a letter from Dr. Carruthers. The return address at her office in the state hospital was Denise Carruthers, Ph.D., not M.D. This difference gave Bernie's innards, already in a twist because of the mystery car, another jerk. By now he had a good idea of what M.D. therapists were all about, but what if Denise Carruthers, Ph.D. was a different animal altogether? What if she didn't really have Bernie's best interests at heart in the first place? After all, she'd accused him of murder during their first interview.

What if she came with new ideas about his

treatment? What if she planned to change things around, make him suffer as much as possible? His fears were confirmed as soon as he read the letter; she wanted to increase his visits to weekly. What was she up to? This did not sound like a friendly gesture to Bernie. This Carruthers person could become a real problem, and it might take more than imaginary rats to get rid of her, although it was nice to know that strategically placed rodents really got her panties in a bunch.

If he needed any further proof of Dr. Carruthers's evil intent—and he did not—Bernie was called into his supervisor's office Monday afternoon. The supervisor, Molly McCoy, had been in place as long as anyone could remember, and, while as rigid and demanding as any military NCO, she also protected her employees in a fierce and maternal way.

She waved Bernie into her office about one hour before closing time. "I got a call from a Dr. Carruthers at the state hospital, said she wanted to interview me, had some questions about you. Anything you need to tell me about, Mitchell?" she asked.

McCoy, a fireplug with arms and legs, looked every bit the battle-scarred veteran she was. The winds of political change had blown in all directions, sometimes several at the same time, but she still had her job and would do so until the final bell rang, and she was ushered off into retirement, her inflated pension at the ready.

"Oh, no, Ms. McCoy, I only met Dr. Carruthers once." Bernie could express surprise and dismay with the best of them. All it took was practice and a mirror. "I'm sure my former therapist can provide you with a lot more information than Dr. Carruthers can." He slid Dr. Peele's card across the desk to McCoy. He had no worries about getting it back. When Dr. Peele had left his card with Bernie at their last meeting, Bernie had had a stack of duplicates made, in case he needed one at some future date. One could never be too careful, not with malignant types like Denise Carruthers lurking about.

"I don't plan to meet with this doctor, then. I don't appreciate her going behind your back in the first place," McCoy said.

"Thank you," Bernie said.

In her letter, Carruthers informed Bernie that his subsequent appointments would fall on each Friday at noon. She added that, failure to appear would constitute a violation of a court order, and she could have him placed in a locked ward until she deemed him fit to return to society, which, Bernie guessed, would probably be never.

"That bitch," Bertie said when he told her about his new schedule. "She knows that's our day for lunch and bowling. I'm sure of it."

The scowl on Bertie's face made Bernie fear she might do something rash, so he put his hands on her shoulders. "She'll get hers," he said.

"Damned right she will. She'll regret she ever made that threat about a locked ward."

****

The morning of his second session with Dr. Carruthers, Bernie got up an hour earlier than usual, showered, and shaved carefully, then put on his best uniform shirt, the one with the bright new shoulder-patch identifying its wearer as a proud member of the

U.S. Postal Service. Bernie figured he'd made a serious miscalculation when he showed up at her office before, looking and probably smelling only slightly better than your average homeless guy. He wouldn't make that same mistake again.

He fed Bitsy, then dropped a white mouse into Alvin's glass case. For himself, he made coffee, then selected a packet of instant oatmeal from one of three identical boxes lined up in the cabinet above his kitchen sink. Breakfast was no time to get adventurous.

His truck coughed twice before starting up properly, not surprising for a vehicle that had traveled just under two hundred thousand miles. Bernie had considered getting a new one, but such a transition would involve changes, something that always made him cringe. Change might produce the desired outcome but just as easily might deal out a disaster, so, why tempt fate? He patted the dash lovingly, "Just take your time, old girl, we'll get there eventually."

When he arrived at the Post Office, a red brick building with a flat snapping in the breeze out front and U.S. Post Office spelled out in large white letters above the door, he met his supervisor, Molly McCoy just inside the door.

She looked him up and down. "Looking sharp today, Mitchell. Got a hot date later?" She grinned, and his two co-workers standing beside the counter laughed. Bernie's status as a confirmed loner was well known around his workplace.

"Got to see my therapist this afternoon, the one that contacted you about me," he said for Molly's ears alone. He ducked his head and walked quickly toward the mailroom, the one place aside from a bathroom stall where no one was likely to try to engage him in conversation, small talk, not exactly a fate worse than death but close enough…more in line with dental work without anesthesia.

He left work shortly after noon for his drive to the state hospital. The sky was clear when he left, but the situation changed abruptly bringing dark gray clouds and heavy rain. Bernie made the drive without incident, but the parking lot at the hospital was some fifty yards from the door he had to reach, and he was soaked by the time he got inside.

The wing where the staff physicians met with outpatients jutted out from the main building like an afterthought. Because the elevator always gave off a fishy odor, Bernie took the stairs to the third floor where Dr. Carruthers' office was located, his soaked shoes squishing with every step.

The receptionist looked up as he sloshed to the desk. "Oh, my, looks like someone got caught in the rain. Let me see if I can find a towel."

She returned a few moments later with only a hand towel. "Sorry, it's all I could find."

At least he could dry his hands and face.

"Go right in. Dr. Carruthers is expecting you."

Bernie checked his watch. He still had almost ten minutes before his scheduled time, but probably Dr. Carruthers would blame him for being late, no matter how early he showed up.

"You kept me waiting again." If Dr. Carruthers noticed or cared that he was dripping all over the floor, she gave no sign.

The room temperature was chilly, and within moments Bernie was shivering in his wet clothes. If he expected any kind of greeting or civility from his interrogator—he didn't—he would be sorely disappointed. She wasted no time on such frills. She opened up his file and began firing questions at him.

Her game plan of full frontal assault seemed much the same as before; maybe it was the only one she knew. No matter, Bernie knew the game and its variations better than she did, and this time there would be no element of surprise, a good thing, too, because she launched right into him.

"Why did you hate your parents?"

"I didn't hate my parents."

"Why did you kill them?"

"There was an accident. Check the court records."

"Why did you hate Dr. Bowman?"

"I didn't hate Dr. Bowman."

"Why did you kill her?"

"I didn't mean to."

"Another accident?"

"Yes."

Her silent treatment was even less effective. Bernie could play this one all day long. She fixed him with what she must have thought was a steely gaze, but it had no more effect on him than the rain he'd dashed through in the parking lot.

The balance of power had shifted; they both knew it. She still held the high card, her threat to have him locked up in what was marginally better than a dungeon being the nuclear weapon. It would take no more than her signature to have him put away and medicated to the point where he couldn't wipe his own ass, or even find it. But Bernie's arsenal was far from empty. Carruthers' morbid fear of rodents that he had discovered during their first meeting gave him a very big cudgel to hold in reserve in case the doctor required further disciplinary measures. Once during the interview, he took a quick look into the corner of the room where he'd claimed to have seen a rat before, nothing dramatic, just a quick glance. But it was enough. She blanched. Even across the room he could feel her chest tighten, her airways constrict. *Yeah, fuck with me, lady, and you'll find rats in your desk, rats in your closet, rats in your bed, and rats in your cornflakes.*

So, at the moment, it was a standoff, this interaction that was adversarial and anything but therapeutic. But would it stay that way? He didn't look forward to driving to these court-ordered sessions where he would be kicked around like a deflated soccer ball. Something would have to be done about Dr. Carruthers, and soon.

****

Bernie pushed his dinner plate to the side, having barely touched his fried chicken.

"Are you okay?" Bertie took his hand.

"No appetite tonight."

"It's that Carruthers bitch, right?" Bertie's eyes narrowed to mere slits, the way they did when somebody was about to be introduced to her icepick.

"You should see the way she comes at me. She's more like a prosecutor than a therapist, calling me a murderer."

"She still harping on that bit with Dr. Bowman?" Bertie asked.

"Yeah, that's most of it, but from the way she makes it sound, I've killed more people than Hitler. She

135

must think I'm some sort of mass murderer."

"Okay, I have some people looking into her, and they're supposed to get back to me soon. Then we'll know what makes her tick and how to stop it."

"Who checks things out for you? You have some sort of team?" Bernie was ever so slightly alarmed. He'd always assumed that the team consisted of himself and Bertie, no one else.

"Just a couple of people I trust," she said. "Let me put it this way, they know better than to cross me."

Bernie breathed a deep sigh of relief. His secret weapon, Bertie, was about to take the field, or had done so already, along with her co-conspirators. Everybody had a past, and soon enough they would know Dr. Carruthers' better than she did herself.

"One good thing that's come out of all this, she might have done us a small favor by moving your treatment schedule around. I kind of enjoy our new Wednesday evening bowling and dinner schedule," Bertie said. "It's like a real date."

With that, conversation halted, and they sat gazing into each other's eyes. Just two thirty-somethings at the Chicken Shack, two streets over from the bowling alley, on a date night, an event that would go unnoticed by anyone and everyone, save these two, because for Bernie, it was a first, and he guessed it might be the same for Bertie.

All of those landmark events, proms, holiday dances and such that would involve co-mingling with members of the opposite sex had passed right by Bernie, a shy, reclusive youth who preferred his own company to that of anyone else, without leaving a mark. Had Bertie had similar experiences? Maybe so, he could only guess.

So, he sat, starstruck, caught up in feelings he never knew existed.

"Anyway, you're getting too good for me," Bertie said.

"Huh? What?" He'd drifted into a warm, comforting place and didn't want to leave just yet, but whenever Bertie talked, he listened.

"Our bowling, you've gotten so good you're trouncing me every time now. Would you consider joining a league? I'm sure there are league groups that would love to have you."

"You're my league," he said in an inspired moment, and he must have come up with just the right response, because he got a big kiss in return.

****

When he arrived for his Friday session with Dr. Carruthers, a nurse who seemed quite young, although he could only see her face from the side because she never looked directly at him, met him at the reception desk. "Dr. Carruthers will see you in the treatment room."

"Are you sure about that? I'm not supposed to have a treatment today," Bernie said. Abrupt changes always upset him, and such changes in his medical regimen were particularly bothersome.

"You'll have to discuss that with her." The nurse still looked away as if hiding her expression. What was she trying to conceal?

Bernie followed the nurse down the hallway past the ECT lab and into a small, windowless room that reeked of disinfectant. There was barely room for a gurney that had restraining straps draped across its upper and lower halves and a couple of chairs, one of which was occupied by Dr. Carruthers who sat alongside the gurney, her face expressionless. "Get on the gurney, Mr. Mitchell."

"Why? I'm not due for a treatment today."

"I'm going to ask you a few questions, but first I'm going to give you an injection."

"I don't understand." Bernie was getting messages from his feet telling him to run like hell. This was all so very, very wrong.

"The injection will help your memory. Now, get on the gurney like I told you, and remember, failure to comply with treatment means I can admit you to this hospital and keep you as long as I see fit, and you won't have any choice about your therapy. Now, are you going to cooperate, or not?"

Like a condemned man mounting the steps to the gallows, Bernie climbed onto the gurney with no idea what lay before him, or why this doctor was behaving in this bizarre and hostile fashion. The only thing he felt sure of was that being confined to the hospital under the control of Dr. Carruthers was a fate he wouldn't wish on his worst enemy.

The anonymous, apparently faceless nurse fastened restraints across his legs and chest.

"Why are you tying me up?" Bernie asked.

"It's for you own safety, Mr. Mitchell, so you won't roll off the gurney and injure yourself." Dr. Carruthers' voice was almost taunting, as if the possibility of Bernie tumbling to the floor and cracking his head wouldn't bother her in the least.

The nurse tightened a tourniquet around his upper arm and began swabbing a section of Bernie's right forearm with alcohol. "A little pinch now," she said. In other words, here comes the needle.

But there was more than a single pinch as she continued jabbing the needle around under his skin. "I'm sorry, Mr. Mitchell, I seem to have missed the vein."

"What's going on over there?" Dr. Carruthers' harsh voice.

"I'm so sorry, Doctor, the vein rolled. I'll have to try again." She sounded close to tears.

"Just get it done and hurry, will you?" Carruthers again even harsher than before.

More swabbing, another pinch, and a sigh from the nurse so prolonged that she must have been holding her breath the whole time. She opened the valve on his intravenous line and began infusing a clear liquid. He couldn't see the label on the bag of fluid. "What's in the bag? What are you giving me?" he asked.

"Just something to help you relax, Mr. Mitchell," Carruthers said.

Relax? Why did he need to relax?

He heard a click followed by a whirring noise. Was she recording this?

He was close to outright panic, but the medication took effect quickly, and after a few moments the overhead lights became indistinct, blending together into a yellow haze. Dr. Carruthers must have moved her chair because he could no longer see her.

"I can stay if you need me," the nurse said, her voice almost a plea.

"No, I want you to leave. I'll call you if there's a problem. Otherwise, stay out. Then Carruthers began, some of the same questions from before, some new, and he responded, but he wasn't sure whether the answers were coming from him or somewhere else in the room. This had to end. He tried to struggle against the restraints, but his arms and legs wouldn't cooperate.

"Why did you murder Dr. Bowman?"

"You've committed other murders, right? Tell me about them."

"Tell me about the fires. You've killed people with fire, haven't you?"

And there were more, many more, and he answered because he couldn't help himself.

Eventually the grating sound of Dr. Carruthers's voice ceased. The overhead light receded merging into a single orb. She must have summoned the nurse because he felt her removing the intravenous line from his arm, but she left the restraints in place. When he tried to sit, the nurse pushed him back down. "Don't try to get up, Mr. Mitchell."

He could no longer see or hear Dr. Carruthers who apparently had left the room.

"What happened?"

"I'm so sorry, Mr. Mitchell, for all of this," the nurse said.

"Sorry for what? What did you do to me?"

"Dr. Carruthers will explain everything to you."

Yeah, right.

He was able to bend far enough around to see the wall clock: three o'clock. He'd been there for two hours, two lost hours. Dr. Carruthers had had her way with him for two hours.

Both the nurse and his tormentor-in-chief returned. The nurse removed the restraints and tugged him into an upright sitting position. "Stay where you are," she said, when he tried to stand.

"The nurse will stay with you until you have recovered from the medication," Carruthers said. "I'll expect you back for another session next week. Remember, if you don't return voluntarily, I'll send someone after you."

When he was able to get a look at her face he saw that look of triumph, that look that said, "I can have you trussed up whenever I want to, and there's not a damned thing you can do about it."

Bernie wondered for a brief moment whether he might be able to leap far enough to get his hands around her throat, that way she couldn't scream and all this nonsense would end once and for all. Could he make it look like another accident? Probably not. More likely the residual effects of the medication would leave him sprawled on the floor. His so-called therapist would probably find that highly amusing.

Chapter Nine

"Are you sure you feel well enough to drive?" The nurse who had walked him up and down the hallway several times still clung to his arm as if, should he try to run off, he'd have to drag her along.

"I'm okay," he said. He bounced up and down a few times to convince her. He wanted to get away from that place as soon as possible.

Even though he felt steady enough on his feet, Bernie discovered soon enough that the residual effects of the medication Dr. Carruthers had pumped into him were still floating around. Several times during the drive home he found he'd wandered across the dividing line into oncoming traffic, and only the sound of horns blaring furiously jerked him back into a more alert state just in time to avoid a collision.

He spotted a cleared area alongside the road and pulled off. He'd stepped only a few paces away from his car when he vomited. A passing motorist stopped across the road from Bernie's car. The elderly driver walked over to Bernie. "Hey, fellow, are you okay?"

Bernie, halfway annoyed at the intrusion and halfway grateful that someone cared enough to stop, said, "I'm all right, just something I ate for lunch."

"Anything I can do to help?" the man asked.

"No, thanks for stopping," Bernie said. He watched the man drive away. His session with Dr. Carruthers had brought him lower than he'd been in a long time, and he had no idea what kind of information she'd extracted from him while he was drugged. What if she decided to do it again? Clearly, this could not continue. It was only a matter of time until she pushed him past that point of no return, and he would be forced to take action, and Dr. Carruthers would be no more.

Still, there had to be another way, some way that would let him escape the likely consequences—imprisonment or long-term confinement in a locked ward—of her death, justifiable as it might be. Perhaps he could request another therapist, but Carruthers, now that she had him in her clutches, would probably not consent to a switch. Unless he could come up with an alternate plan, he was doomed, for sure, as was his therapist.

So, late Friday afternoon, a confused and exhausted Bernie pulled into his street to find a car parked out in front of his house, but not the mystery sedan this time…Bertie's van. He was barely out of his car before she walked over carrying a cardboard box with the top taped shut.

"What's all this?" Bernie asked.

"Oh, my gosh, sweetheart, you look terrible. What happened to you?"

"Bad day at the office," he said. "What's in the boxes?"

"Lots of stuff," she said, "and I hope you haven't eaten because I brought Chinese takeout for dinner."

"Great," Bernie said. The nausea he'd felt earlier was gone. "I'm starved. Eat first?" Bertie was the sole ray of light in an otherwise gloomy horizon. If there was a way out of his current predicament, she was it.

They settled in at Bernie's kitchen table, aromatic cartons spread all around, one of which certainly contained Bernie's new favorite, Kung Pao chicken. His own contribution was a chilled bottle of plum wine.

"How was your day with the wonderful Dr. Carruthers?" Bertie asked as she heaped fried rice and entrees onto the plates. "From the looks of you, not so great."

"Awful. She strapped me onto a gurney and injected me with some medication that knocked me out, then started asking me questions, at least, that's what I think happened. I don't remember much."

"What?" Bertie's eyes started out as great round orbs, then narrowed to slits. "Did she explain anything to you? Did she get your permission?"

"No." Bernie told her the sad story, ending with Dr. Carruthers's threat to forcibly hospitalize him if he didn't cooperate. "I don't know what she asked me. I don't know what I told her. Could be she has some really bad stuff on me."

"Was there anybody else in the room with you?"

"No, I don't think so. She told the nurse to leave, so it was just the two of us."

"Didn't want any witnesses. She can't do that, the bitch." The way Bertie gripped her knife suggested she'd like to perform that same filet action on Carruthers that she'd done on the trout she caught when they were camping out.

"Well, she did it. I can't go back in that hospital. That was an awful experience, and I can't do it again. I just wish I had a better idea of what she did to me."

"Narco-interrogation," Bertie said.

"Huh?"

"Interrogation under drugs, sodium pentothal, amytal, something like that, what they used to call the truth serum. It's not legal. She could never present that in a court of law. It's a clear violation of your Fifth Amendment rights. And she can't very well disclose it to anyone else either. She would lose her license for a stunt like that."

"What am I going to do?"

Bertie drummed her fingertips on the table and stared off into space the way she did when the wheels were really spinning. "She's really crossed the line this time, but don't worry about it. I've got some information I'll show you after supper. Now, eat your chicken."

Once again, he followed the orders of a woman, but this one he didn't mind following. This one had his best interests at heart. This one he trusted. This one brought him Kung Pao chicken. "This chicken is really good."

Later, they took Bertie's mystery box into the living room because she said she had to spread things out on his coffee table. She lined up several folders and opened the first one.

"What's this?" Bernie pulled a spray bottle from the box.

"Luminol, but it has to be dark for it to work, so, we'll have to wait a bit."

"I know about that," Bernie said. "That's the stuff they use to detect blood spatter on TV crime shows. Well, you won't find any in here. I'm a very thorough cleaner."

"We shall see," she said. "This first folder is some background information about your new best friend,

Denise Carruthers. She got her undergrad and doctoral degrees in psychology from Columbia, no less."

"I'm impressed." Even though Bernie's own academic background was less than stellar, he still respected those who had excelled where he had not.

"And guess what her thesis was about?" Bertie asked.

"Fear of rodents?"

"Not even close…serial killers. I haven't checked out her thesis in detail, but she's written a number of really interesting papers. Mostly she's interested in creating psychological profiles, so you can catch the bad guys before they cause too much damage. I've read all of these. You should too."

She placed the folder in front of him, and Bernie looked at it as if expecting it to leap up and grab him by the throat. "I don't think I want to." He pushed it away.

"I can see her game now. It all starts to make sense, the way she's been going after you. She thinks you fit her profile, and for the time being, you're her guinea pig."

"It's all wrong," Bernie said. "I'm no serial killer, and she can take her profile and shove it up her ass. Anyway, that's no excuse for the way she's tormenting me now. Why does she hate me so much? I told her that thing with Dr. Bowman was an accident."

Now Bernie was on the boil again, or very close. The spiral in which he found himself caught up had begun, of course, earlier in the day when he was being abused by Dr. Carruthers. The drugs she shot into him probably kept the lid on his rage for a while, but never put out the fire completely. Now he was back in the red zone, fists clenching, teeth grinding, sweating profusely. If Denise Carruthers had walked into his living room at that moment, nothing, not even her attendants, could have saved her.

Bertie slid away from him, probably recognizing the warning signs. She didn't touch him, but there was her soft voice just the same. "Bernie, it's just you and me. We're all that matters now. Bernie, can you hear me?"

It took several minutes and a lot of soft crooning from Bertie before his internal pressure gauge dropped into a safer zone that would read, if labelled, *Agitated but in Control.* Usually, when he spun into the red zone, control was lost, and, through no fault of his own, someone or something suffered. This time, though, a little voice that began softly and grew louder and louder reminded him that Bertie was his friend, and he was not to smash his friends.

When it was over, he found himself still sweating profusely and needing a physical outlet. "Want to go for a walk?" he asked.

The cool evening air and his special friend at his side, this was all he needed. Mulberry Street, his home for the past twelve years or so, was a narrow two-lane road of just over two hundred yards, intended for light traffic. On Bernie's side of the street there were only two houses, his and Ms. Grosbeak's. On the other side there were six houses of the same size and design as his, as if the homes had all been built from the same set of blueprints.

They'd just begun their walk when a car full of kids roared by, yelling insults. His fight or flight mechanism flipped on once again, but before it climbed into the danger zone, there was Bertie, patting his forearm. "It's okay, it's okay. They're just some stupid kids. We probably did worse when we were that age, don't you think?"

He took both her hands. "I'm never letting you go, just so you know."

A new crescent moon had climbed well above the horizon by the time they got back to his front door. "Makes me think we should plan another camping trip," Bernie said. They waited together on his porch enjoying a cool spring breeze which, blowing away from the ravine behind his house, smelled better than usual.

"Should I make coffee?" he asked when they were back inside.

"Why don't we check out the Luminol first?" Bertie asked. "I want to see what happens."

"You're not going to find anything." Bernie said again. He'd always done a good and proper cleaning job, and he was sure Bertie's CSI technique would turn up nothing at all.

Bertie had her spray bottle in hand. "Turn off the kitchen light," she said. The reaction was rapid and extensive. Almost everywhere she sprayed she scored a hit. In no time at all, much if not most of the living room carpet showed fluorescence. Same when she sprayed the walls. "Oh, my gosh, Bernie, what happened in here?"

"It was an accident." He'd scrubbed the entire area after each incident. How could there be blood stains everywhere?

"Just one? Looks like several. I had no idea you've been so…active," she said.

"It's been over a long time. I've lived here almost twelve years, and you said yourself, some methods are messier than others." It wasn't his fault that head wounds bled like crazy.

"Yeah, this is one of the reasons I suggested the ice pick. It doesn't leave nearly so much to clean up."

She continued into the hallway where several sets of bloody footprints stood out starkly in the Luminol. "What's this door?" she asked.

"Closet." Bernie didn't understand, he'd cleaned so carefully, every time.

"Can we look inside?"

Bernie opened the door, and the fluorescent footprints followed right up to a pair of his shoes. Bertie picked one up and sprayed the sole—bingo, blood all over. "Is there anywhere else we should look?" she asked.

"Maybe the kitchen."

More of the same. Bernie wasn't feeling well, not at all. It was like in his truck when he had to pull over and throw up. Bertie was going to think he was a complete slob, somebody who didn't know how to clean up after himself.

"How about your truck?" she asked.

"Yeah, we'd better check there too."

That same breeze that brought spicy floral scents earlier had shifted and now turned offensive with the sulfuric aroma that welled up from the depths behind his house. He opened the gate on the rear of his truck, and Bertie sprayed the incriminating agent inside. Fluorescence on the floor, the walls, the ceiling…everywhere. He couldn't possibly have been so careless. Perhaps there was something wrong with the Luminol reagent. "Have you tested this stuff?" he asked. "Do you know for sure it works like it's supposed to?"

She looked at him over the tops of her glasses, the way she did when he'd said or done something impossibly stupid. "Yes, it works just fine."

Bernie closed and locked the truck gate. They went back inside, leaning on one another but mostly Bernie leaning on Bertie, not feeling too sure of himself at the moment.

"Coffee now?"

"Do you have anything stronger?" she asked.

He mixed gin and tonic for each of them.

"I thought I had everything cleaned up." He stared into the depths of his glass, hoping to find a way out of his dilemma.

"We have a big problem. I'm not sure you can ever get it completely clean. Luminol is always going to pick up something."

"Oh, shit," he said. "I completely forgot the garage and the basement."

"This calls for something drastic. You know that, right? If Dr. Carruthers or any cops ever saw any of this…." She stopped there, stared at him, a deeply pained expression on her face.

"But there's no reason they ever would, do you think?" He thought back to nosy Detective Molinaro. What if she'd brought along a bottle of Luminol on one of her visits? Wouldn't she have had fun, before Bernie bashed her, that is?

"Do you want to take that chance?" she asked. "You know what would happen."

"I'd be locked up forever, I know."

They turned on all the lights, having seen all either of them wanted to see of what, given the amount of fluorescence that appeared, looked like the inside of a slaughterhouse.

Bernie mixed two more drinks, then sat beside Bertie on the sofa, as low as he'd ever felt in his life, lower than those days when he was shuttled between foster homes, lower than the day the door closed behind him at the orphanage. He saw no way out. It was all so unfair. First, Dr. Carruthers, now the unmistakable evidence of Luminol. "What can I do?" he asked, not really expecting an answer.

"Burn it down," she said. "There's no way to clean it up, and so long as it's here, you're in danger. You said the cops have been here before, right? What if they come back? All it takes is one little bottle of this stuff, and it's all over for us." She held up the bottle of Luminol that lighted the way to hell for Bernie Mitchell, and probably Bertie too.

"You can come and live with me," she said. "I have plenty of room, and there's a place where you can work on your models, so you wouldn't lose any of them. And you can bring Bitsy and Alvin too, and Alvin's mice. It will be just like home. Of course, you'll have to leave some stuff behind so it won't look like you've moved out completely. That would be suspicious."

For a man who disliked change, even small changes, the thought of moving into another space set his head spinning. He wished he could have another ECT treatment right that very moment.

Bertie put her arm around his shoulders. "I know this is very upsetting for you, I really do. Just think about it for a while. I can help. You can always count on me."

Bernie turned to look at her, difficult because she was sitting so close her lips were touching his ear.

"I set off a gas explosion once," she said. "The house was a bit larger than yours, and afterwards there was nothing left but the foundation. That would take care of your Luminol problem forever." She gave him a good strong squeeze like she'd solved all his problems at once.

There were probably things he could say, should say, but whatever they were, they remained hidden from him at the moment.

"I should go," she said. "I have to get to work early in the morning. I hate to leave you like this. Why don't you go for another walk after I leave? Some fresh air might do you good."

"Okay."

But he didn't go for another walk that evening. In fact, he remained sitting in the same spot until the rosy fingers of dawn crept across his carpet, prying him off his sofa. When he got up, his movements, mind and body, were stiff, robotic. Now, he decided, might be a good time for the walk he should have taken last night.

His joints ached as he crept outside. For a man like Bernie Mitchell, to whom Mother Nature was as much an adversary as an ally, all that exuberant spring growth emerging just outside his front door wouldn't usually put a smile on his face or a zip in his step. Today there was something special about the dawn of the new day, particularly when that day fell, as this one did, in early May, bringing swaths of bright yellow where clutches of daffodils smiled up at Bernie, as if trying to make up for the unwelcome tidings that had fallen on him the night before.

Burn down his house, as Bertie had suggested? A terrible thought. Sure, it wasn't such a great house, a bungalow, three small bedrooms, and yes, there were more attractive neighborhoods out there for the taking.

But Bernie had grown attached to this small place. He knew which doors creaked, which windows were stuck and remained shut, and now he knew what appeared to be clean floors and walls were covered with invisible bloodstains. Every time Bertie had pressed the lever of the spray bottle of Luminol, the fine spray highlighted more damning evidence against Bernie. After a while, it turned into a new game, trying to find a spot that didn't show fluorescence. Only his bedroom and workshop area where he built his airplane models had escaped the carnage.

"Bernie, Bernie," she'd said. "You've been such a busy boy."

ECT might remove some of the memories in Bernie's brain of those who had forced him to take violent action, but the electric shocks did not erase the evidence on his floors and walls. Bertie, for reasons known only to her, had even directed the spray onto the ceiling of his living room, and there, like stars glowing on a clear night, were tiny fluorescent spots all around.

"Bernie," she'd said again, as if disbelieving. She seemed to want to say more but couldn't bring herself to do it. Bernie himself could not explain the fury that had sprayed blood to such remote areas.

Such were the thoughts of an unquiet mind—Bernie's own—as he plodded along the street, now almost oblivious to all the spring finery spread around him. It was almost a relief when the pesky little dog he'd seen with Ms. Grosbeak's nephew came running out of her house, making a bee-line for Bernie's ankles. Bernie raised one foot, preparing to flatten the yapper, when Ms. Grosbeak herself, ratty dressing gown flapping around her knees, ran out and scooped up the dog.

With the obnoxious little beast secured in the crook of her arm, she waved a bony finger at Bernie. "She's gonna get you now," she said. "I told her plenty about you and your weird ways."

Her laugh came out as a coarse cackle, and all that was lacking was for her to mount a broomstick and fly away over the rooftops. "Told who?" he asked.

"That Dr. Carruthers, she stayed all afternoon."

"She came out here to talk to you about me?" Bernie's knees quaked, and the back of his neck turned clammy.

"Oh, yeah. You're done for now, Mitchell." She headed back toward her house, cackling all the way, probably not knowing that, had she been standing a few feet closer to Bernie, no power on earth could have saved her…from him.

If he'd needed a final straw—he did not—the uninvited interview with Ms. Grosbeak was just that. For all the harm she'd done him and for all the harm she was likely to do in the future, Dr. Carruthers had just bought herself a one-way ticket to oblivion. Now all that mattered was the details.

As best he could recall—and there were gaps in his memory, thanks to ECT—most of his earlier activities had been impulsive, spur-of-the-moment affairs that required no advance planning. Actually working out the steps in someone's demise as Bertie did was new territory for Bernie. The neatest solution would be if he could lure Carruthers into his own house, since the dwelling was slated for a fiery end anyway, both jobs could be done at once, but he could see no way to pull that off. But whatever method he chose, the bottom line remained the same: Dr. Denise Carruthers had to go, and she'd brought the whole thing down on herself.

He still didn't know how much incriminating evidence she'd gathered so far, potentially quite a lot. Who knew what she might have learned as she grilled him while he was drugged up? If she already had enough to put him away, she probably would have sprung the trap by now.

On the other hand, maybe the bitch enjoyed watching him squirm, agonizing over what she would do next. She would have known that Ms. Grosbeak would have wasted no time in flinging the news of the interview in his face. Now she was probably sitting in her office feeling pleased with herself guessing she'd really put one over on poor old Bernie Mitchell. But poor old Bernie, had a few tricks up his own sleeve, and one of them was named Bertie.

****

Bertie usually worked late on Monday evenings, so he waited until shortly past eight before he called Bertie. "Dr. Carruthers has to go," he said.

"I know. I'll stop on the way over and pick up some Chinese. And never say anything like that over the telephone," Bertie said. "Besides, first we have to go through some of the information she has on you."

"You know already?" he asked. "Tell me now."

"I have some information, yes, but there's probably more in her office that we might have to get. We should eat first. I'll bring something over."

It was a real council of war, convened around Bernie's kitchen table. First, they ate—armies always fought better with full stomachs—even though Bernie was writhing in anticipation. He'd waited a long time to learn what Bertie knew, but it was her show at the moment, so he'd have to be patient, easier because she'd brought Kung Pao chicken.

Then they cleared the deck. The first item on their agenda was intel. The background Bertie had collected earlier went into one stack, and to that she added another smaller folder. "Motive," she said, tapping the new folder with a stiff forefinger. "Dr. Carruthers and Dr. Bowman were an item, had been for several years. That's why she has you in her sights; you killed her lover."

Her lover? The thought shocked Bernie, not quite so vigorously as his ECT treatments, but enough to give him pause. He couldn't think of anyone less lovable than Dr. Carruthers, so, the idea that she had a lover caused his worldview to tilt slightly. Even so, it would easily be enough to bring her wrath down upon his poor depressed head. "So, that's why she hates me."

"Right, it's personal now, has been all along."

"But it wasn't my fault."

"I doubt that Dr. Carruthers sees it that way or that she cares. Now, could you make coffee? It might be a long night."

Bernie, glad for the opportunity to contribute something, even coffee, practically jumped out of his chair.

By the time he returned, Bertie had spread a map across the center of the table. "Here's where she went during the past two weeks." She traced out a red line across the map, most of which ran back and forth between the state hospital and her apartment. There was also a red line running from her apartment to Bernie's street, not once, but twice.

"What the hell?" Bernie said. "She made another trip out here? How'd you find out?"

"I put a tracking device on her car." Bertie's grin spread across her entire face.

"You're a genius," Bernie said.

"It's a start, but we have a lot of work to do. We have to find out what she knows, so we must get her files. I'm thinking she used Pentothal on you to get extra information. So long as those extra files are out there, you'll be in jeopardy, even after Carruthers is gone."

"I think she might have taped that last session," he said.

"Then we have to get the tape, too."

"How do we get them?" His usual method would involve a quick bash on the head with his axe, then he could take whatever he needed. But his partner-in-crime, Bertie, was way ahead of him in the planning department, so he simply sat back and listened.

"My guess is that she takes them back and forth with her on the days when she sees you. She wouldn't leave them in her office at the hospital, because if anybody discovered the kind of data she's been collecting on you and how she interrogated you under anesthesia, she would be in big trouble."

"Coffee's ready." Bernie jumped up to get cups for them.

"Now, get this, every Tuesday night, she drives out to a private residence at the beach, a really nice one, waterfront and all that, just north of here. She always stays overnight. She has a new friend. Apparently she's gotten over the loss of Dr. Bowman."

Now Bernie's smile made an appearance. "I don't know how you do it, but this is amazing stuff."

"Here's the really neat part. There's just a husband and wife in that big old house. On the night that Dr. Carruthers stays over, the wife stays home, but the husband leaves and spends the night with his own friend. They're both gay. It took me forever to figure that one out."

"But they're married," Bernie said.

"Yeah, I don't know if they even knew about the gay thing before or after, but they have the perfect arrangement. At least, they did until I found out about it."

"But Dr. Carruthers could still say you made the whole thing up."

"Not when she sees the videos."

"Godalmighty, Bertie, you are incredible. So, how do we get her files?"

"We pick a Tuesday night when we know she'll be out at the beach house, break into her apartment, and steal them," Bertie said. "I can't think of a better way to get them, can you? We can look them over if we have time and just take what seems most incriminating."

****

Bernie's next Friday session with Dr. Carruthers was even more adversarial than his last. She'd placed his chair so the afternoon sun struck him full in the face, blinding him, then she fired questions at him like she was throwing darts, the same questions she'd asked him several times before, and probably when he was drugged, as well. There seemed to be no answers that would satisfy her, so his only thought was that she was doing this out of pure malignancy, something for which she would pay and pay dearly.

"Okay, Mitchell, I'm through with you for the day, but I'm going to keep after you. Just so you know, I'm going to break you, however long it takes. Then your sorry ass belongs to me." Dr. Carruthers grabbed her notes and stalked out of the room.

Bernie's reprieve came when he was carted off to the ECT lab for treatment. Even there, he wondered if she might play some nasty trick, like sneak in and turn up the voltage, cooking his brain, reducing his functional level to that of some of the pathetic long-term residents of the hospital. Yep, it was time she got a message.

****

The night of the great break-in, they took Bertie's van, leaving Bernie's own truck parked in his driveway with the lights on inside his house. Bertie brought along a couple of bags, one empty, one filled with objects with a combined weight of around ten pounds.

"What is all this?" Bernie asked.

"Just stuff, always be prepared, you know."

Bernie's own contribution was a small cage containing six field mice he'd caught behind his house. He thought about taking along some of Alvin's white mice, but Alvin deserved nothing but the best. Dr. Carruthers, on the other hand, would get the wild variety. Maybe they carried some type of disease, or, at the very least, fleas. Bernie liked that idea.

"But she'll know it was you when she sees the mice," Bertie said.

"I want her to. I want her to know who she's messing with. Field mice today and next time rats the size of chihuahuas."

Bertie wore a white jacket with LARRY'S PEST CONTROL in black letters. She had baseball caps for each of them with the same logo. Bernie had stopped being amazed at her seemingly endless repertoire. He simply smiled and nodded.

The apartment complex was relatively large, three floors with a little courtyard in front, considering the remote location. Bertie went in first, taking only a moment to jimmy the front lock with tool from her bag. Then she waved Bernie over, and they proceeded up the stairs to the second floor to Dr. Carruthers' apartment.

"How do you know which one is hers?" he asked.

In return, he got a Bertie smile that told him she knew a lot more than he could ever guess. She jimmied the second lock with apparent ease.

"Wow, this is quite a place." Bernie dragged his feet through the plush carpet, checked out the high-end furnishings. Not what he would have expected for someone employed by the state hospital. "The doc must be doing well."

"Dr. Bowman left her some money in her will," Bertie said. "They had an arrangement where each was the other's beneficiary."

Bernie had no idea how Bertie might have acquired that information, but somehow it did not surprise him.

The room that apparently served as her office, complete with a walnut desk, floor-to-ceiling built in bookcases and a swivel desk chair, was right next to her bedroom. Bertie searched the desk while Bernie went through the adjacent file cabinet. In the top drawer, right front-and-center, he found it, a fat file with a tab that read B. Mitchell.

He and Bertie opened the folder on the desk and made a quick scan of its contents, which included a small tape cassette. "Good grief, Bernie, she must have your whole life story in here, like she's going to write a book about you."

"That or she's gathering evidence to put me away for a long, long time or maybe both. Either way, I don't like it."

"Check the other drawers," she said. "Make sure we're not missing anything."

Before they left, Bernie released his carton of mice in the bedroom. Most of them scampered under the bed, but a couple dashed through the open door into her office.

"She's going to be one pissed off lady," Bertie said.

"Had to be done. She started it."

"You leave first," Bertie said. "Walk back up to the corner and wait there. I'll drive by and pick you up, so it won't be so obvious we're together."

Chapter Ten

There, they'd pulled it off without a hitch. Even so, the mood in Bertie's van was not one of elation. They had crossed a line, a line that almost always existed between opposing parties. So long as that line was not crossed, either or both parties had the option to agree to disagree and walk away. But Dr. Carruthers had cut through the line by her unethical and unlawful gathering of personal data on Bernie. And now Bernie, with Bertie's help, had hopscotched across the line as well. If there was ever any doubt about his intent, leaving a half dozen rodents in her apartment made it perfectly clear: this was war.

Bertie pulled into his drive but stayed in her van.

"You're not coming in?" Bernie asked, thinking they should at least toast their success.

"Not tonight. I should keep this file," she said. "That way, if anyone asks, you can say truthfully that you don't have it."

"I wonder if she'll send the cops after me," Bernie said.

"She would have to be pretty stupid to do that. What she's done here, putting together this file on you without your knowledge or permission is not legal. Just be careful and keep your head down. Let her make the next move."

Bernie knew what this meant—role-playing,

something he was good at. All it required was discipline, a quiet place, and a mirror. He had all three. Becoming the complete and total picture of innocence and maintaining that façade in the face of the barrage he knew Dr. Carruthers would launch at him, all it took was practice.

So, the following Friday, when Dr. Carruthers stalked into the interview room, jaw tightly clenched, steam seething from her nostrils, Bernie didn't bat an eye. When she called him a miserable son of a bitch for leaving rats in her apartment, he looked straight ahead, eyes wide, apparently horrified that anyone would be so cruel as to do something like that to the good doctor…and the rats.

He was somewhat bothered by the fact that she had not brought her security detail into the room this time. Soon enough, he learned why.

"This isn't over, Mitchell," she said through clenched teeth. "You didn't get my office notes, and that's what I'm going to use to bury you."

"I don't understand," he said, still the picture of innocence. "Why would you want to bury me? And why are you always so angry with me?"

"I'm sure you know exactly why, you sneaky bastard. Laura Bowman was worth ten of you, and I'm not going to quit until I've nailed you for what you did to her."

Bernie knew better than to argue with her. He sat looking at his own feet. Making eye contact with her would be like provoking an angry dog just looking for an excuse to bite. "My advice to you, Mitchell, get your affairs in order, because as soon as I review my clinical notes on you with the rest of the staff, I'm sure I can convince them you're a threat to the community. Then we'll put you away, lock the door, and throw away the key. Have a nice day, Mitchell. You won't have many more of them."

The only reason Dr. Denise Carruthers passed through the door of the interview room that day as a living, breathing, intact person was the extensive mental preparation Bernie had done before the session, which allowed him to maintain strict self-control, even under severe duress. As it was, he was right on the brink, fists clenched, sweaty, and hyperventilating. Another moment or two in the room, and Carruthers would probably have become a member of the dearly departed. And things wouldn't have worked out so well for Bernie either. Killing one therapist, Dr. Bowman, in a moment of passion might be forgiven. Killing a second was a step too far.

His hands shook that evening as he told Bertie about the meeting, how Dr. Carruthers made him sound like a murderous monster, a threat to society.

"I guessed as much." She cocked her head to the right and nodded slightly, as if she'd known what Bernie was going to say before he said it. "We don't have a lot of time."

"What am I going to do?" His earlier confidence had melted away, and he was close to tears. The possibility of being locked away in the state hospital was worse than death, particularly since he'd done nothing to deserve such a fate.

"I'll take care of everything. I have it all planned out." She gave him a reassuring pat on the shoulder like one might give a child who had just asked for information that was well beyond his comprehension.

Why is the sky blue? Pat, pat. "It's better you don't know what I'm going to do. I'll let you know ahead of time so you can go somewhere you'll be seen, you know, for an alibi." She gave him another pat.

Wednesday morning, he got the call. "Make yourself scarce tonight," Bertie said.

"I think I'll go bowling." Not something he wanted to do alone, but this was all about making an appearance, establishing whereabouts while Bertie did what had to be done.

"Good idea. Make sure to chat up the shoe clerk guy so he'll remember you were there. No more questions now." She hung up.

So, his fate rested in her hands. Whether he would continue life as a free man or succumb to the ongoing assault of the evil doctor depended on Bertie. This was a leap of faith far greater than any Bernie had taken before or would likely ever take again.

Bernie went bowling alone, wearing his gaudy, unforgettable yellow shirt. Even though he now owned his own pair of bowling shoes, he stopped by the shoe rack to chat with the clerk who was chewing gum so furiously it seemed as if he was trying to kill it. "Your friend not coming tonight?" the clerk asked in between chews.

"She said she might be late, not feeling so good." Bernie rested his elbows on the counter and leaned across. This apparently made the clerk uneasy because he took a step back. But that was okay. Bernie wasn't there to make friends and influence people, only to create an impression.

He bowled a few games, taking his time. He went to the bathroom…twice. He visited the snack bar and purchased the vilest cup of coffee he'd ever tasted, killing time, although drinking the coffee might have killed him as well. He managed to dawdle away two hours, then tucked his bowling ball and shoes in his bag and prepared to leave. He waved to the shoe clerk. "Guess she's not coming after all." Bernie Mitchell spent the evening of May 11, at the bowling alley, and he could prove it with several eyewitnesses, should anyone ask.

Two evenings later, just after he'd rinsed off his dinner dishes, Bertie called. "I'll need your help. Meet me at the market. Park behind the white refrigeration truck. Wear old clothes, coveralls if you have them, and gloves. It might get messy."

He'd been to the market before and didn't like the large building with the glassed-in front through which could be seen an almost endless variety of products. Bernie wasn't into variety. He shopped at a smaller market where the same products sat on the same shelves at the same price week after week. Variety was just a lot of wasted motion.

Bertie's area of that market was in the back of the building, closed off from the rest of the store by a pair of swinging doors. That's where large chunks of meat were magically transformed into small packages neatly wrapped in cellophane that bore little resemblance to the original source.

She was waiting for him beside the truck, a big eighteen-wheel rig that emitted a low growling sound. She wore a large black apron that covered her from neck to knees.

"What's that noise?" Bernie asked as he hurriedly donned his coverall suit and gloves.

"That's the refrigeration unit, runs all the time. We have to hurry." Bertie bounced from one foot to the other, as if that might move him along more quickly. "It will take at least an hour to cut her up."

Bernie's knees went weak, and he had to brace himself against the truck. "Cut who up?"

"Dr. Carruthers, of course, who did you think?" Bertie increased the pace of her little foot-to-foot shuffle.

"Why do you have to cut her up at all? Can't we just put her in the river like the others?" He maintained contact with the side of the truck. If there had been handles, he would have clung to them like a drowning man.

"She's frozen, Bernie, she won't sink. She'll bob up and down like a cork, and somebody might see her. We can't take that risk."

"Oh, God, where is she?" He pushed himself away from the truck, knowing well enough the horror that waited inside.

"Right here in the freezer truck with all the rest of the meat."

"It's locked." He pointed at the padlock on the rear doors of the truck, hoping for a last minute reprieve from a task he'd do almost anything to avoid.

"I have keys." She dangled a large steel ring with what looked to be enough keys to unlock every door in the shopping plaza. "I have keys to everything."

He followed her inside past the hanging frozen carcasses, to the back of the truck, half expecting a bloodied, frigid Dr. Carruthers to leap out and grab him by the throat.

"Here we are," Bertie said. And there, between the

carcasses of two pigs hanging from hooks, was the former Dr. Carruthers, wrapped in heavy plastic and hanging upright from a hook.

"Bertie, she's naked." The nausea came roaring back.

"Of course, I couldn't very well leave her in a dress. Anybody who came into the truck would have spotted that right off."

"But you took off everything." Of course, Bertie was right about the dress. Leaving Dr. Carruthers fully clothed would be silly at best, dangerous at worst. But the harsh fluorescent light left nothing to the imagination.

"Look around, Bernie, do you see any meat hanging in here wearing a bra and panties?"

Bernie couldn't move. He was frozen like his former therapist, absolutely certain that this image, wrapped in plastic, hanging from a hook, would haunt him as long as he lived. It would take more than ECT to flush this horrific vision from his brain.

Bertie elbowed him rather sharply. "Come on, Bernie, get with the program. We don't have all night."

He closed his eyes as he wrapped his arms around the frigid figure and tried to hoist her off the hook. "It feels like she's stuck," he said when the body remained suspended despite his efforts.

"Yeah, the hook is still in," Bertie said. "Sometimes that happens. I'll have to get the ladder." She retrieved a small two-step ladder from the far corner of the truck, climbed up, and freed the hook, leaving Bernie with the full weight of his therapist.

"She's heavier than I thought," Bernie said.

They carried the stiff, frozen body out of the truck

like a board of lumber, Bernie at the feet, Bertie at the head. Then they propped her against the wall while Bertie unlocked the door.

Inside, Bertie flicked on the lights in a cavernous room with smooth concrete floors leading to a drain in the center. "Here we are," Bertie said, "my home away from home."

The walls were crisscrossed by black hoses ending in nozzles not unlike the one on Bernie's garden hose. He could only imagine how this room would look and sound when all of the workers were hacking and sawing. Suddenly his little mailroom workplace at the Post Office, so quiet and peaceful, looked rather good.

The acrid stench of disinfectant reminded Bernie of the small room at the state hospital where the woman whose carcass he'd just carried inside had persecuted him with drugs and an endless barrage of accusations. But thanks to Bertie's intervention, Dr. Carruthers' evil reign was now over and done with. *Any more questions for me now, Doctor?*

They laid her body out on a stainless-steel bench, and Bertie began stripping away the plastic. Without even the transparent plastic covering her, Bernie looked away. No one should have to see his therapist naked.

"You've never seen a naked woman before, have you?" Bertie asked.

Bernie shook his head. "Well, just at the commune, but that was a long time ago." And now he was sure he wouldn't want to see another one.

"I can see you won't be much help with the cutting part, so why don't you bring over some of those large Styrofoam boxes. About three should do it." She nodded toward the wall behind them where the boxes that would soon hold parts of Dr. Carruthers were stacked head high. "When I hand you the pieces, wrap them in plastic and put them in one of the boxes. When I'm all done cutting, we'll cover them with dry ice."

Bernie pulled a metal stool to what would become his temporary workstation, Styrofoam boxes on one side, a roll of heavy plastic on the other. He glanced over at Bertie who appeared not upset in the least over the gruesome task at hand. She had laid out a pair of carving knives, a large cleaver, and a saw, just to her right, all of the implements spotless and gleaming in the overhead lights. Dr. Carruthers' earthly remains lay stretched out on the bench in front of her.

"How did you kill her?" Bernie hadn't noticed an entry wound when he carried the carcass in from the truck.

"Ice pick, same place as usual. See, you didn't even notice the spot. If you'd been using the ice pick method all these years, you probably wouldn't have bloodstains all over your house and truck."

"I guess you're right. How many people work in here?" he asked, trying to postpone the inevitable.

"Eight, usually, I'm the only woman, not that anybody ever notices," she said. "Okay, Bernie, enough chit chat, time to get to work. Where should I start, head or feet? Your choice."

"Huh? I don't care." Now he wanted to be somewhere else in the worst way possible. For years, he had bashed in heads without hesitation, dumped bodies into ravines, over cliffs or simply buried them and never gave it a second thought. But the very thought of carving someone up, caused his stomach to revolt. When had he become so squeamish?

"You look like a leg man, Bernie, so I'll start there." Bertie sounded almost cheerful. Just another day at the office for her, was it?

A few moments later, "Here you go, one lower right leg, foot attached. Say, are you okay? You look a little green."

"I'm fine." No, he wasn't. And it wasn't just him that had turned green, everything was green, and things were moving that shouldn't be moving.

"Bernie, get to work." Her voice was sharp, and she had a cleaver in her hand.

Take the piece, wrap the piece, put the piece in the box. He could do that, maybe. How he wished he had something to stuff in his ears to block out the sounds of chopping and sawing and, most shocking of all, Bertie whistling.

"One right thigh coming next," she said.

Bernie never would have guessed one of Dr. Carruthers' thighs would be so heavy. It seemed he barely had the thigh wrapped and boxed before Bertie called out again. "You know what's coming next, don't you? One left leg, foot attached." She dropped the leg in front of him where it landed with a soggy thump.

"Bet you forgot to make sure I didn't switch feet on you, didn't you?"

"Huh? What?"

"Just joking, Bernie, just joking."

Take the piece, wrap the piece, put it in the box, don't think about it. Okay.

Then the left thigh, of course. Bernie marveled at how closely and expertly she had separated the thigh at the hip joint. Not just carving up a body, she was disarticulating it. Why, with a few screws and some wire they could probably reassemble the entire thing. A ghoulish thought if ever he had one.

"Right arm coming up, Bernie."

"It won't bend," he said. Indeed, the elbow joint was stiff as could be, and the arm extended would not fit in the box.

"That old rigor mortis," she said, "That and freezing. Here, I'll fix that for you." She took it back, gave the elbow joint two whacks with her cleaver, then handed him the upper and lower arms separately. "Two for the price of one."

Take the piece, wrap the piece, etc.

"Oh, look, Bernie, she's smiling at you." When he turned at the sound of Bertie's voice, he found himself face to face with his former therapist, a sight he never wanted to see again. Bertie had set Dr. Carruthers's detached head on the cutting surface facing him. Instantly his gut began doing backflips.

"No, please, don't get sick there," Bertie said. "Go over by the drain if you have to."

He barely made it before he disgorged everything he'd eaten for the past two weeks.

"I'm so sorry, Bernie…bad joke." Bertie now had the therapist's severed head covered in paper and rolled in plastic, but the damage was done. He had seen, and he would never forget. Bertie apologized a few more times, but otherwise, they worked in silence until the job was mostly complete.

"There, all done except for the torso. Usually I do the big pieces with the electric saw, but all of the insides have been removed by the time I get to them. It will make a huge mess if I cut her in half, all that stuff inside coming out, splattering around. Bernie, you're looking a little green again."

"Can't help it. Anyway, there's nothing left to throw up." If this wasn't the worst day of his life, it was close enough.

"Sorry about all that," she said. "I think I'll just have to leave what's left of her in one piece. Nobody's going to recognize her, no arms no legs, no head, you think?"

"Whatever." He shook his head slowly. Rapid movements made his world spin, and he'd had quite enough of that already.

"Oh, I forgot to check for tattoos. Wouldn't it be a hoot if she had Dr. Bowman's name tattooed on her butt, you know, with a little heart?" Bertie laughed as she rolled Dr. Carruthers' remains over. "Nope, nothing here. Seriously, though, can't leave any identifiable marks, you know. Should we spank her, Bernie?"

"Absolutely not."

"You're no fun. Okay, let's see if she'll fit in a box."

They were able to fit two boxes on each cart, and it took both of them to load the bulky boxes into Bertie's van. "So, we're finished here?" he asked, thinking he might never eat meat again.

"Oh, no, it's clean up time. This place has to be spotless before we leave. There will be workers in here tomorrow, and I'll be one of them."

Sometime later, after the cutting counter was spotless and the floor washed clean, all the instruments scrubbed and put away, Bertie stripped off her apron, and he shed his coveralls. Then he followed Bertie home and parked in her driveway behind her van.

"I don't have a cart here," she said, "so we'll have

to carry these boxes around to the back porch."

Since Dr. Carruthers was now in several separate parts, the boxes were not too burdensome, except for the one with the torso. "Maybe I should have cut her in half after all," Bertie said, struggling with the weight.

"What now?" Bernie asked, guessing he would hear an answer he didn't want to hear.

"We empty each box into one of these plastic bags and then store her in the freezer until we're ready to ship her off."

Ready to ship her off...it seemed to be a day for euphemisms. "You mean take her down to the river, right?" Bernie said.

"Of course, honestly, Bernie, you shouldn't take everything I say so literally. Lighten up a little."

They didn't talk much during the final stage of bagging up the disassembled therapist, partly because there was nothing much left to say and partly because Bernie was so tired that moving his hands was all he could manage.

On the other hand, his partner in crime didn't seem fatigued in the least. She gave him a vigorous pat on the shoulder that must have left a mark. "You did good in there, Bernie. I'm proud of you. It's not easy the first time, all that cutting and sawing."

"But it didn't seem to bother you at all," he said.

"It's what I do every day, and after a while, it's all just meat, whether it's Black Angus or psychotherapist, you know?"

"Yeah, I guess I get that." How absolutely marvelous the way she could cut right through a problem...*it's all just meat after all*, nothing to get worked up about.

"What about the box with the torso? I can come over and help you carry it when you move it."

"I can manage," Bertie said. "I'm a strong girl, and anyway, she's not as heavy as some of the guys I've had to lug around."

"Okay, but I don't think I'll make it to my next session with Dr. Carruthers," he said.

"No, you have to go." Bertie grabbed him by the arm and shook him. "Listen to me, you absolutely must go."

"What's the point? She won't be there. She'll be here in the freezer, most of her anyway."

"That's exactly the point. You know nothing about that. When she doesn't show up, you have to look surprised, disappointed, even. Bernie, look at me." She stretched her arms apart, eyes wide as if acting out the part. "You have to understand how important this is."

"Okay, I'll be there." There was a break in his fatigue, like sun shining through a cloudy day, and he saw things more clearly. "Thanks," he said. "I know you're doing all this for me, and I appreciate it. Don't worry; I'll be there on time."

****

And so, there he was, two days later, right on time, shuffling along toward the side door of the state hospital as if a great weight pressed down upon his poor shoulders. After all he'd been through with the remains of his former therapist, feigning depression was easy enough. He took a few deep breaths before he reached the reception desk, slipping further into character, leaving nothing to chance.

"Good afternoon, Mr. Mitchell. How are you feeling today?"

The receptionist had one of those ideal poker faces that remained perfectly neutral no matter what. He could imagine her announcing that the building was burning down with the same lack of expression.

"Not so good today," Bernie said. "I think my depression is getting worse. I'm looking forward to talking with Dr. Carruthers."

"I'm afraid I have some bad news. Dr. Carruthers won't be in today. She phoned us a short time ago and said she's not feeling well herself. Otherwise I would have called you and saved you a trip."

Why would the receptionist make up such a lie? He knew very well that Dr. Carruthers was in no condition to phone anyone. Yeah, he knew it, but they didn't, so maybe they were just trying to cover their butts until they found out more. Still, he had to play along...no problem.

"I'm sorry to hear that," he said. "Could I maybe make an earlier appointment to see her next week?"

"I'll call you as soon as she's available for appointments."

Bernie crept away, faking disappointment he did not feel. Of course, Dr. Carruthers would not be making any more appointments, ever, unless they needed therapists in hell. This time she'd tangled with the wrong twosome and paid the price.

Chapter Eleven

Bertie was waiting for him at the front door when Bernie arrived from his trip to the state hospital, his first visit there since they'd sent Dr. Carruthers down the river.

"Tell me everything," Bertie said. "What did they say about Dr. Carruthers?"

"Well, I acted real disappointed that my doctor was a no-show," he said. "All they said at the hospital was she called in sick." It was all practice now, even when he talked with Bertie, and they both knew perfectly well where Dr. Carruthers was, most of her, anyway.

"That's kind of weird," Bertie said. "I don't know why they'd lie like that. Are they going to set you up with another therapist?"

"I'm sure they will because I have to get my treatments there for at least another year, that court order thing."

The following week the receptionist from the hospital called saying Dr. Carruthers would be on extended leave for personal reasons, and they had scheduled an appointment for Bernie with a new therapist, Dr. Doolittle.

"Doolittle, really?" Bernie's interest level jumped several notches. "Any relation to General James Doolittle?" Doolittle, it seemed like such an odd name, one he'd never come across at the Post Office, that there might be a connection.

"Who?" The receptionist apparently had neither time nor interest in the subject that Bernie found so fascinating.

"He was a famous pilot, World War II." Bernie had a wooden model he'd carved of one of the old B-24s that General Jimmy Doolittle had flown in that legendary bombing raid over Japan, marking his place in history for some, but not for the history-challenged receptionist.

"Never heard of him. Your appointment is at nine o'clock on Thursday, May 14."

****

Dr. Doolittle's office was on a separate hallway from the room where Dr. Carruthers had tormented Bernie. The sparse furnishings looked the same in both places as if they'd been purchased in bulk from some cut-rate supplier, but, whereas the Carruthers domain had felt barren, uninhabited even, Doolittle's had more of a human touch. Small mementos lay scattered across his desk, a few stuffed animals, key rings, a snow globe from Niagara Falls, and other trivial items that probably had value only to the doctor and whoever might have given them to him. Photos of family and staff covered most of one wall. It even smelled nice, a pleasant floral aroma, although Bernie couldn't see any flowers.

Dr. Doolittle was tall, looked late fortyish, some gray streaks in a beard that made his face look long and horsey.

"Ah, the famous Mr. Mitchell," he said in a low, sonorous voice. "You seem to have bad luck with therapists, one dead and one gone missing."

"Dr. Carruthers has gone missing? They said she

was taking some personal time off."

"Well, okay, if that's what they said."

"Wait, I don't understand. How could she be missing? You really don't know where she is?" Bernie asked.

"I can't say any more about that," Doolittle said, his tone suggesting that misplacing Dr. Carruthers was no great loss.

But Bernie felt he had to show some reaction, and responding to this news, although it was hardly news to him, was as simple as reaching into a closet, choosing a mask, and putting it on. For this occasion, he chose dismay. He was lost, hopelessly lost, his lifeline, Dr. Carruthers having abandoned him without warning. He stared at his feet. "She should have let me know. I depended on her." He shook his head as he spoke.

"I'm sure we'll know something soon," Doolittle said. "People don't just disappear into thin air. In the meantime, why don't you tell me about yourself. You've been on ECT for a long time," Dr. Doolittle said. "I don't have Dr. Carruthers' notes, so I don't know why she continued it so long."

"The reason is, without the ECT, my depression takes over. I don't eat, I can't sleep, I turn into a zombie. ECT is the only thing that gets me out of it, keeps me going."

Of course, Dr. Carruthers hadn't disappeared into thin air, had she? She'd disappeared into the river. Bertie had taken care of that. And of course Doolittle didn't have Dr. Carruthers' notes because Bertie had them. Those incriminating pages were part of the midnight raid he and Bertie had pulled when they'd taken her files and left her mice in return.

179

Dr. Doolittle peered at him above the rims of his glasses as if trying to decide whether Bernie was the genuine article, just another depressed man who'd realized his life was going nowhere fast. He scratched his chin and made a few notes. "Before we continue, I'd like to do some cognitive tests, make sure we haven't damaged your functional capacity."

Some patients might have felt intimidated by the prospect of cognitive tests, but not Bernie. He'd been taking them since he was a teenager. By now he could not only ace any cognitive test, he could write them, if need be. No sweat, no sweat at all.

"I also want to do an MRI, make sure there are no structural changes in your brain."

Bernie had no objection to the brain scan either. They could scan to their hearts' content. Actually, he would like to know for himself whether his brain structure was normal. For some time now, he'd suspected it was not.

He went through the cognitive testing; a standard Wonderlic Test of fifty questions that he'd seen so many times he almost had them memorized, that same day in a room with no windows where he was the only test taker. Even though the process was totally familiar to him, he took pains to appear to struggle with the answers.

"I'll go through these test results, and we can discuss them at our next meeting," Dr. Doolittle said.

Bernie turned away and managed to turn a laugh into a sneeze. There was nothing in the entire series of tests he hadn't seen before several times, so there wouldn't be much to discuss, would there?

The MRI two days later was more of a chore,

because Bernie suffered from a touch of claustrophobia, and his large body was a close fit inside the scanner. "I'll give you a small injection of Versed," Dr. Doolittle said. "It's the same sedative you get before your ECT." Bernie liked Versed.

****

About a week after his appointment with Dr. Doolittle, the cops came to his house, two of them, a man and a woman wearing matching dark blue suits with blue and yellow striped ties. Was this some new uniform policy, he wondered?

"We're checking with people who know Dr. Carruthers," the lady cop said. "You've been seeing her for a couple of months, right?"

"My sessions with Dr. Carruthers are covered under doctor-patient privilege." Bernie had to let them know right off they weren't dealing with some brain-dead yokel they could push around.

"We know that." This time the man cop spoke. "We're mainly interested in any changes in her attitude lately. You probably know she's gone missing. Did she seem upset about anything?"

"Not that I noticed, maybe a little down sometimes, but everybody has good days and bad days. Do you have any idea where she went?" Bernie asked injecting a note of concern into his voice.

"We can't comment on that." The lady cop this time. "How would you describe your feelings about Dr. Carruthers? Did you like her?"

"Sure, I thought we got on well. She helped me a lot. I hope you find her soon."

"Some of her staff members felt she'd been angry lately. Did you notice that?" The male cop's voice was eerily similar to his companion's.

Same question with a subtle variation, just enough to trip him up if he wasn't careful. He was careful, always. Bernie shook his head.

The cops left after half an hour or so. Bernie doubted he'd seen the last of them. He was just glad they hadn't brought along a bottle of Luminol. That would certainly have added a new twist to the conversation. As he watched them drive away, there, silhouetted by the lights behind her, was Ms. Grosbeak's little pinhead, watching through her kitchen window.

He called Bertie to tell her about the police visit.

"I'm so glad we got her clinic notes," she said. "I've been looking over them, and some of what she wrote down could have been trouble."

"Should you be looking at that?" he asked. "It's kind of personal, you know, me and my therapist. I haven't even seen what she wrote about me."

"I'll stop if you want. I'm just trying to look out for you. I don't want anything to happen to you."

Hearing her say that made Bernie feel warm all over. She cared, and that meant the world to him. "I'm worried about Ms. Grosbeak," he said after a few moments. "Did you find anything in the notes about Dr. Carruthers visiting her?"

"Yeah, there's nothing specific, lights in your house going on and off at odd hours, things like that. Old lady Grosbeak is not your biggest fan. Dr. Carruthers asked her to keep an eye on you."

"I wonder whether we should be discussing this over the phone. Let's go bowling."

"I'm starved. How about we hit the fried chicken

place first?" she asked.

Bertie looked none the worse for wear after what must have been a gruesome task, sending Dr. Carruthers down the river, piece by piece. He gave her a vigorous kiss on the cheek, equivalent to what between other couples would have been a full-bore lip-locked embrace lasting long enough to leave both participants gasping. But Bernie and Bertie were not exactly like other couples.

"Wow," she said. "I guess you're glad to see me."

He grinned and nodded. "I just appreciate all you've been doing to help me."

They attacked their fried chicken with a fury pent up during several days of stressful and highly unusual labor, which, without Bertie's butchery skills, would have been far more taxing, messy too. Later, with plates of cleanly picked bones in front of them, a miniaturized version of what was probably left of Dr. Carruthers, they began cleaning off with the moist wipes provided by the eatery.

"You still up for bowling?" he asked.

"Hell, yes, I need some action."

****

The fury of their efforts drew stares from other bowlers. This was bowling with a vengeance. No finesse here, the pins were bludgeoned and bruised, some of them flying off into adjacent alleys. Bernie almost felt sorry for them, being smacked about as they were. Between frames, he went to the snack bar and brought back two cans of Budweiser.

"Bernie, you're really living on the edge tonight." Bertie laughed as she popped the top on her can.

Here at their usual lane on the end, their refuge,

they put their heads together. "So, I'm thinking about your situation," she said. "Your whole house glows with Luminol, and you have that old bat next door watching every move you make. And who knows what kind of information Dr. Carruthers gave her? Sooner or later she's going to find enough to get the cops interested."

"Maybe it's time to clean house, once and for all, get rid of everything." There was no middle ground here. He loved his little house, but it had to go and Ms. Grosbeak as well. If Dr. Carruthers hadn't drawn the old lady into the mix, things might have been different. But she'd done it, and now Ms. Grosbeak was a point of vulnerability, just like Bertie's Luminol spray can.

"You still think I might move in with you?" he asked.

"I'd love that," she said.

"What's the best way to do this, you think?"

"I'm pretty handy with gas lines. I've never tried a double explosion, but I'm sure I can manage it, yours and hers at the same time."

"Can't they tell if the gas lines have been altered?" he asked.

"No, the way I do it, everything is inside, and it all goes up at once. Don't you worry about a thing." She gave him a reassuring pat.

"It's gonna be really hard to get into Ms. Grosbeak's house. She never leaves," Bernie said.

"No problem. If I create a big enough blast at your place, it should take out her house as well."

"My gosh, you're talking about a real explosion."

"Sure, what did you think it would be? We can't leave anything intact; have to destroy all the evidence at once, including Ms. Grosbeak."

"When can I move in?" he asked.

****

Moving his household goods in small installments so as not to attract attention—although Ms. Grosbeak's snout poking through her kitchen curtains was a constant feature now—took a long time, spilling over into a second week. And he couldn't very well take everything. A fire in an empty house would look a bit too convenient, so he left behind everything he could do without, and therein lay the catch.

Bernie had relatively few possessions but was quite attached to what he had. In the end, he took over his own dresser and toiletries, leaving behind his beds and living room furniture. He needed little closet space because most of his clothes were the same ones he wore to work. But he could not part with his model-making equipment. Bertie had cleared out her third bedroom for his hobby, and there was room for the cedar worktable he'd made himself. And his axes, couldn't very well leave them behind.

He made a separate trip with Alvin's heavy plexiglass case, which he installed in the room alongside his model-making gear. Bernie loved his snake but was careful moving him about. He'd seen too often what happened to the mice when Alvin bit into them and didn't want to share the experience.

Bertie entered the room just as he was making the final adjustments on Alvin's case. "So, you're really settled in now."

"Yeah." He put his arms around her. "You're one in a million, you know? How many women would take in me, my snake, my cat, and a crate full of white mice?"

She laughed. "I'm glad we're all together now, like a weird little family."

"Luckiest day of my life when I met you," he said.

"Don't get carried away."

"Okay, back to business. I think I'll leave my truck in the garage, get rid of it along with everything else," he said.

"Good idea," Bertie said. "From the way the inside glowed with Luminol, we'd never be able to get out all of the bloodstains, no matter how hard we scrubbed."

****

"Take a look, Bernie, this is how we'll do it, really simple." Bertie was working with a couple of small gadgets on the kitchen table. "This little timer is battery-powered, and when it reaches whatever time you set it for, it causes a little spark in this gizmo. Watch."

She set the timer and they waited a few minutes until it clicked, setting off a small spark in the apparatus connected to the timer by a single wire. "And it's mostly plastic, so it will melt away in a fire, nothing left behind."

"That's not much of a spark." Bernie couldn't quite figure out how such a small flicker could set of the kind of conflagration she'd described.

"It doesn't take much when the room is full of gas. That's why we have to be far, far away when it goes off." She wound the wire around the timer and put both pieces into a small box. "What do you think, can we be ready by Friday?"

****

After several weeks of planning and preparation,

they were finally ready. The Friday morning of their great adventure featured an auspicious and cloudless sky, like a stamp of approval for their plans. Most of Bernie's essential household goods were now stowed in Bertie's house. Both his snake and cat had managed the move with minimal fuss. So long as they were fed on time, everything else was small potatoes. Bertie had already introduced him to the neighbors as her brother who had come to stay with her—not at all a hard sell, since they looked so much alike.

Their cover story would be a camping trip, similar to the one they'd taken earlier in the spring. When the big bang occurred, they would be far away, safe and sound, and crouched beside a campfire. As they packed the last of their camping gear into Bertie's van, Bernie was already planning a dinner of fresh trout, caught, expertly fileted and cooked to perfection by Bertie's own capable hands.

"Okay, then, let's go back inside and get to it. "Bertie walked over to Bernie's kitchen stove. "Your gas range is almost identical to mine," she said. "This will be a piece of cake."

"You make it sound so simple. How many times have you done this?" he asked.

"Just once, but it's not complicated. Gas explosions are pretty impressive. I almost wish we could stay behind to watch this one, but that's not going to happen." She lifted the cover off the burners on the stove, then turned off the gas. "Once I'm sure the pilot light is off, I'll turn the gas back on. Then I can hook up the timer, and we're all set. It's just about nine o'clock now, so I'll set the timer for ten. That will give us plenty of time to get away."

"While you're doing that, I want to take one last look around," Bernie said.

"Saying goodbye to your house?" she said.

"Yeah, something like that." He wandered from the living room into each of his bedrooms. They looked small and forlorn now emptied of most of their contents. Pangs of regret mixed with guilt washed over Bernie; not only was he going to abandon the house, he was going to burn it down as well. Not a nice thing to do to a place that had provided him with shelter and warmth for twelve years.

"You'd best wind up your farewell tour," Bertie called from the kitchen. "I've turned the gas back on, so it's just a matter of time now."

"Just a minute, I have to check the garage." He rummaged around in the glove box of his truck until he found it way in the back, still tucked away inside a red bandanna. He unfolded the bandanna and held the ring in his hand. He'd almost forgotten one of his most important treasures.

His mother had a beautiful ring with a large red stone. It was the kind of heirloom a mother would pass along to her daughter, but since there were no daughters in the Mitchell family, and Bernie would be the last of the line, it really should be his, so, he took it. His mother didn't discover the theft for a week or so—she never wore the ring in public—and when she confronted Bernie, he turned his empty pockets inside out. "Not me," he said.

Of course, it wasn't in his pocket because he kept it hidden away in the trunk of a large oak that grew at the edge of the commune. Somehow as he later got shuffled between foster homes, then to the orphanage, he'd managed to keep it away from prying eyes and grubby fingers. It was the only thing that survived from his childhood, and he wasn't going to lose it now.

"Bernie, come on, we don't have a lot of time."

He stuffed the ring in his pocket, then joined Bertie in the hallway. They left and Bernie locked the door behind them.

"Why bother to lock it?" Bertie asked.

"I always do it, and besides, we don't want anybody to wander in, not today."

"Good thought," she said. She opened the rear doors of the van and rummaged around in the gear stowed inside. "Just wanted to check, make sure we have everything, because we won't be coming back here. If all goes well, this should be a nice camping trip. When we come back all our problems will be over."

They took their seats and buckled their seat belts. Bertie inserted the ignition key but didn't turn it.

"What are you waiting for?" Bernie asked.

"Did you remember to leave the door open between the kitchen and the garage?"

"No, that shouldn't make any difference," he said.

"If you want to make sure we get rid of your truck, you'd better let the gas leak into the garage."

"I have to go back inside," he said.

"Yes but make it quick and hold your nose."

He should have remembered that damned door to the garage because often as not it got stuck, just as it was now as he tried to open it. It took both hands on the doorknob and one foot against the door frame to pry it open, meanwhile, he'd had to take a couple of breaths. He was coughing vigorously by the time he got back to the van. "I need a minute," he said. "It really stinks in there."

"That's why we have to get out of here," she said. "Just get in and open your window."

Once Bernie was inside and buckled up, still coughing, she turned the ignition key. The engine sputtered, coughed a couple of times, like Bernie, then died, unlike Bernie.

"Houston, we have a problem," Bernie said lightly but with a touch of concern.

"Not funny." Bertie tried again without success. "She's balky sometimes."

"This is not a good time for balky. Try it again," Bernie said with more anxiety creeping into his voice.

More coughing, more sputtering, but no forward motion. "Just be patient. It will start. I'm sure of it."

"Try again," he said.

"You have to wait for a minute," she said. "Sometimes the carburetor floods. Rushing just makes it worse."

Bernie took off his seat belt. "Oh, God, please start, please, please, please."

"Will you just settle down? You're not helping things by acting crazy."

"Bertie, it's almost nine-thirty, and we're sitting on a time bomb here." Hysteria crept into his voice. "If it doesn't start up this time, I'm going to start running." He'd decided years ago that, when his time on earth was over, he'd opt for cremation rather than burial, but that would only take place after he was dead, of course. Now he stood a good chance of being incinerated alive.

"You will do no such thing." She tried again…nothing.

Bernie opened his door, ready to dash if he had to.

"Don't you dare get out of the van," she said with vehemence.

One more try, and the engine started up.

Bernie went into a prayer pose, hands clasped in front of his face. "Thank you, thank you."

"I told you all you had to do was be patient. You got all upset for nothing."

Maybe, but Bernie could tell from Bertie's voice that he wasn't the only antsy person in the van. "Okay, burn rubber, get us out of here," he said.

"I'm not going to burn rubber. That would attract the attention of the neighbors. Use your head, will you?"

So, they proceeded down Mulberry Street at a leisurely pace, but they were barely to the end of the street when the blast jolted their van as if they'd run over a curb while a white light filled the cab. Then debris rained down on the roof like someone was pelting them with stones. By this time they were clinging to one another, wondering what would come next, another fireball? Even bigger than the first? Only when the clatter of falling objects stopped did they release one another and venture out of the van.

"Holy shit," Bernie said looking back at the carnage. "That could have been us."

Bertie latched onto him again. She was shaking and crying, and Bernie was shaking just as violently.

A sizable metal sheet had landed on the other side of the road. "What on earth is that?" Bertie asked.

"I think that's the door to my truck." When he looked back at the place where he used to live, there was no house. Only the walls of the foundation survived the blast. What used to be his basement was filled with rubble, and the remains of his former home lay scattered about the neighborhood like so much confetti. The far wall of Ms. Grosbeak's house was still standing and smoldering, but everything else was simply gone.

"Will you look at that." Bertie stood there, eyes wide and unbelieving, mouth agape.

"When you said burn it down, you really meant it."

"Not like this, I didn't, and don't ever, ever mention again what I just did. Just forget that it ever happened." She gripped his shoulders and pushed her face up close to his.

"No worry, I'm just as responsible as you are," he said.

They stepped away from the van to get a better look at the street. Bernie's and Ms. Grosbeak's lots were stripped so clean it looked as if they'd been swept, while the rest of the neighborhood was littered with everything that hadn't been consumed in the fireball. Most of the windows on the street side of the three houses closest to Bernie's were blown out and a small fire burned on the roof of one.

"God, I hope no one was hurt," Bertie said. "I can't stop shaking."

"It's okay, you didn't mean it." Which for Bernie pretty much wiped the slate clean. If there were unintended consequences, so be it. They'd accomplished their goal just as they'd planned, and who could blame them for doing something that had to be done?

Soon the other residents staggered out onto their lawns, turning in circles, apparently neither understanding nor exactly believing what had just happened. Some pointed to their broken windows, some sobbed openly. A few hugged their neighbors, maybe for the first time ever.

"Should we make a run for it?" Bernie asked.

"No, of course not. Someone might have seen us drive by. It would look weird if we left now. Besides, I want to see what happened. Gas fires are usually pretty intense, but I didn't expect this. I guess I must have made a mistake with the timer."

It still seemed incredible to Bernie that so much damage had been done so quickly. There was hardly anything left standing to indicate that two houses had been there just a few moments earlier. The charred remains of his truck, minus one door, blown into the street, was about the only identifiable structure left.

"Wonder where Ms. Grosbeak is?" Bernie asked.

"All over the place." Bertie looked up and down the street as if expecting to find traces of Bernie's former neighbor.

Bernie cringed when he considered that if he and Bernie had left a little later, they might have joined Ms. Grosbeak, all over the place.

Police and fire department vehicles clogged the narrow street within minutes. One officer ordered Bernie to drive their van past the corner and park it there. Then the officer drove down the street announcing a temporary evacuation order until they'd determined it was safe for residents to return to their homes. Most of the occupants of Mulberry Street, about fifteen of them, clustered at the end of the street. Bernie stood close enough to hear their conversations, although he knew none of their names, never being the neighborly type himself.

"Sounded like a bomb went off." This from a woman in a yellow housecoat, her hair in curlers. Several others voiced their agreement.

"Was anyone inside?" asked a short, hefty man wearing suspenders over a stained T-shirt.

"I lived in the last house," Bernie said. "Ms. Grosbeak lived next door to me. I don't know if she was home or not."

The other residents took a few steps back, as if Bernie had suddenly become radioactive. Did they blame him for the blast? The wayward looks he drew from the small crowd suggested they thought he might have something to do with it. He was, after all, conveniently absent when the explosion occurred.

A young female firefighter whose bulky uniform appeared to swallow her up, approached the group. "Do any of you know who lived in the houses that were destroyed?"

Bernie stepped forward once again. "I lived in the house at the end of the street. My name is Bernie Mitchell."

"How about the next house?" she asked.

"Ms. Grosbeak, an elderly lady, lived next door. I don't know if she was home or not." Bernie handled all of her questions, sparing Bertie as much as possible.

"How long had you been out of the house when the explosion occurred?"

"We'd just left. We were going camping." He nodded at Bertie.

"Did you remember to turn off the gas?"

"Absolutely, checked it twice, just like always. I don't know about Ms. Grosbeak, though. She was kind of forgetful sometimes."

"And there was just the lady living alone next door?"

"Her nephew lived with her for a while, but he left. I don't think they got along."

"I heard she threw him out, caught him stealing money from her purse." This again from the woman in the yellow housecoat.

"Do you know the nephew's name?" asked the firefighter.

Bernie shook his head, glad that the focus seemed to have shifted to Ms. Grosbeak's nephew.

"Where can we reach you if we have more questions? I expect that the fire marshal will want to talk to you."

Bernie gave her his cell phone number. He had no fear of the fire marshal, just another authority figure to be got around, and he'd had plenty of practice.

After a few more questions, the young firefighter stepped back to address the group. "We'll finish up our investigation, then you can return to your homes. It'll probably be a couple of hours. We have to make sure there's no leak."

No leak, Bernie thought, just Bertie. His blind faith in her technical expertise was shaken a bit by the premature blast, but he couldn't argue with the results, everything gone, right down to the foundations, and of Ms. Grosbeak, not a trace. The Luminol threat was erased permanently along with his nosy neighbor.

Bertie handed over her car keys. "You better drive. I'm still shaky."

They drove back to Bertie's house to unload their camping gear, and Bertie fixed them a light lunch. An hour later they drove back by Mulberry Street, but the lane was even more clogged than before. In addition to the remaining official vehicles there were TV camera crews and so many gawkers they were stumbling over one another. After a few moments during which Bernie experienced deep pangs of loss—it had been, after all, the only house he'd ever owned—he and Bertie left. It would all be there tomorrow, what was left of it.

"Well, this camping trip is not going to happen," Bertie said. "Let's just go back to my place, unpack and watch it all on TV."

The explosion was the biggest item on the local coverage. The reporters were on it from all angles. "There was only one fatality. The name of the victim is being withheld pending notification of family." Several TV types made that same announcement as if they were reading from the same script.

One of the newscasters stuck her microphone into the face of the same smallish firefighter Bernie had seen earlier. "It appears to have been caused by an accidental gas leak, but the fire marshal is completing her investigation. When she's done she can give you a full report," she said.

Since his house fire had gotten prime coverage on the evening news, Bernie's insurance agent seemed as if he was ready and waiting for his call the next day. "Ordinarily we send someone out to assess the damage, but I saw it all on TV. There was nothing left. Thank God you weren't inside."

"Yes, thank God," Bernie said.

The process went much more smoothly than he expected, and soon Bernie had a fat check and a rental car.

While bits and pieces were being sorted out, Bertie,

ever resourceful, had checked property records and discovered that Ms. Grosbeak's house was actually a rental. She suggested Bernie put in an offer. "You'd own all three lots then. You'd be a real estate mogul, and then nobody could ever go digging around in there. I know you have some concerns about what they might find."

Yeah, he had concerns, and some regrets too. He regretted that he hadn't kept some sort of record of where he'd put remains and how many, but given the spontaneous nature of his homicidal acts, systematic documentation was next to impossible. He guessed more than two and less than ten, not counting, of course, those he'd dropped into the ravine. And knowing some specific locations would be helpful too because even if he owned all three lots, he couldn't very well dig up the entire area searching for bones, could he?

But it was all over and done with now. They'd done what had to be done, and they deserved a reward. "Well, since we can't go camping, how about some bowling instead?" Bernie asked.

Chapter Twelve

The likelihood of Bernie and Bertie choosing to cohabit would seem remote considering the participants, Bernie because he didn't like people in general, and Bertie because she was, well...Bertie. Their very sameness would seem to rule out any kind of romantic affinity between them, since, in the universe as it then existed, opposites attracted, but likes repelled.

This sameness was apparent on their first official night together when Bernie emerged from the bathroom wearing his usual light blue cotton PJs with dark blue piping, only to find Bertie decked out in identical sleepwear, right down to the dark blue B monogram over the pocket. The only difference being that Bernie's B was expressed in Algerian script and Bertie's in Britannic Bold.

"We'll have to change something here," Bertie said when she finally stopped laughing.

"How about stripes and solids?" Bernie said. "I call dibs on solids, unless you want them."

"That's good," Bertie said. "I'll go shopping tomorrow." She didn't need to add that sizes wouldn't be an issue, given their similar body shapes. She gave him a chaste kiss on the cheek, and they both adjourned to their single beds on opposite sides of the room, the same arrangement Bernie had in his own bedroom before the contents were incinerated. They had already had *the talk* about sex, and both agreed that the twin bed system would work best for them.

****

"Have you thought any more about Ms. Grosbeak's lot?" Bertie asked as she pulled her chair closer to the kitchen table. Since Bernie got home a couple of hours before she did, he usually prepared dinner, and, surprising both of them, did a pretty good job of it.

The owner, the same Mr. Beeson who'd sold Bernie the lot beside Ms. Grosbeak, seemed all too happy to be rid of it. Apparently the recent history of exploding houses killed off any resale value, and Bernie, as the only interested customer, bought it on the spot. "I still don't know what to do with it, especially all three lots together." He pulled a casserole out of the oven and set it on top of the stove to cool.

"Whatever that is, it smells great," Bertie said.

"My famous tuna noodle dish," he said.

They were well into the casserole when Bernie sat back in his chair. "What about this idea for the lots, what if we cleared it off and planted a big garden, you know, organic vegetables and such?"

Bertie gasped, inhaled some of the water she was sipping, and began to cough.

Bernie pounded her on the back, but it took several long moments before she could breathe normally.

"I was afraid I was going to lose you there," he said. "What happened?"

"Where on earth did that come from?" she asked, still coughing.

"It just popped into my head, really. It's the first time I've thought of it."

"But, organic vegetables?" she said. "You want to

grow organic vegetables in a graveyard?"

"Why not? Technically it's not actually a graveyard. I mean, yes, there are a few bodies buried there, but no headstones or anything like that. Besides, I'll plow it up myself and pick out all the bones."

"How are you going to plow all that up? You'll need a tractor or something big."

"Yeah, I'll buy one. A used tractor shouldn't cost much."

"You can drive a tractor?" She looked more and more incredulous.

"Sure, I was driving a tractor at the commune when I was just a kid. Most of the men were too stoned out of their minds to plow a straight line, so I learned to do it as soon as I was big enough to reach the pedals. And there was a guy—he only hung around for one summer—who was up on organic gardening techniques, and I learned some stuff from him."

"I wonder what he'd say if he knew you were planting on top of bodies you'd buried."

"All the body stuff will be gone before I start planting. Nobody need ever know about all that. Maybe when our crops come in, we can open a little farmer's market. And what we don't sell, we can freeze for ourselves, since we have lots of room in the freezer now that Dr. Carruthers is gone."

****

Digging out the brick foundations of Bernie's and Ms. Grosbeak's house required two weeks, some heavy equipment, and three guys with a big truck. All the while, Bernie stood by wringing his hands, fearful that the next scoop of bricks and dirt might also include a human skull or two. But his luck held, and no incriminating boney remains turned up. The same crew took down the chain-link fence Bernie had installed around the vacant lot he'd purchased earlier, leaving him with an open plot of land the size of a football field.

"All cleaned up and no bones," he told Bertie that night at dinner.

"Great, I know you were worried about that. Now I guess you're ready to get started on your grand plan. But what about the neighbors? Have you thought about how they'll take living across from an organic farm?"

"Hadn't considered it," he said. "They'd probably rather look over at a vegetable garden than a big patch of weeds. Besides, I can give them some fresh veggies when then crops come in. That should keep them happy."

Bernie had always regarded his commune upbringing as "the wasted years," but now he reconsidered. Perhaps his participation in the communal gardening effort, slipshod as it was, made a more lasting impression than he thought. Now he was experiencing a revival of an almost primal urge he hadn't felt for a long time, if ever; he wanted to dig and plant, to sow and reap.

But first he had to get rid of bones he knew still lurked deep in the vacant lot, and for that he'd need a tractor.

Like many projects that began with a kernel of an idea, then quickly spread tentacles into other areas, growing, metastasizing, so Bernie's market concept took off at a gallop. "Corn, beans, peas, tomatoes, broccoli, zucchini, lettuce," he'd rambled on and on when Bertie asked for specifics about his crop proposals. "And pumpkins and squash for the fall."

"Calm down, Bernie," she said, not unkindly. Perhaps she wondered what genie had escaped from its bottle to fill his head with such ideas. "To begin with, there's just the two of us, and we both have full-time jobs. It's going to take a lot of work to tend to crops like that."

The grim face of reality cast a jaundiced eye on his dream, bringing second thoughts that he entertained for a moment, then dismissed. "I'll need a tractor and some cultivating attachments. I can get a lot done in the evenings after work, and there's always the weekends." His recollection from commune farming was that the actual human labor expended was minimal, and the group depended on natural processes to bring forth a bountiful harvest with the investment of very little true sweat equity, which was always in short supply at the commune. Bernie's garden would be different.

Bertie's skepticism seemed to increase even as Bernie's plans continued to evolve bigger and bigger before their eyes. "I see you're determined to go through with this," she said after their third or fourth discussion.

But Bernie was still way ahead of her. "And we'll need a shed for our tractor and tools. And some sort of stand for the vegetables we'll be selling."

"And who exactly is going to be selling these vegetables?" Bertie asked.

Just another detail that had never proven problematic at the commune where there was always a number of adults doing nothing at all, but coaxing any of them to run the vegetable kiosk was a daily chore. So, the task fell to Bernie and the other kids. But Bertie was right as usual. For a garden as large as Bernie planned, there would be a small problem. With both of them working, there would be a labor shortage.

"Maybe I can convince Dr. Doolittle it would be therapeutic for me, you know, help me reconcile with my past. And it could help with my depression, too. He could make it like a medical recommendation."

"Slow down, Bernie, it's just a garden. You're getting way ahead of yourself."

But now that he'd started, Bernie was not to be deterred. "I wonder if they award grants for this kind of endeavor. Organic gardening therapy for depression…sounds like something some government agency should fund. I'll ask Dr. Doolittle."

Bertie laughed and wrapped her arms around his neck. "My guy is a genius," she said.

Bernie hoped that marked an end to the occasional reticence she'd shown about a project that he considered to be theirs rather than just his.

****

It was a carefully crafted message, most of it factual, that he prepared for Dr. Doolittle, one of severe depression brought on by his disturbing memories of life in the commune and all that came after, exacerbated by the recent gas explosion that very nearly took his life.

"I was doing okay on the ECT program until the big bang. The thought that I might have been blown to bits made my depression a lot worse." He drew his arms around him as if trying to fend off the blast.

"My heavens, Bernie, that must have been terrifying. Thank goodness you weren't injured. How did it happen?" The therapist's eyebrows arched up into little peaks.

"Gas leak, the fire marshal said. She said I was lucky to be alive. If I'd been in the house I would be gone too. As it was, my home was destroyed and most of my stuff. I've had to move in with a friend."

"It's easy to see how that upset you. I wonder if we should add a medication to your regimen, at least, until you get over the shock."

"Well, somehow, a near miss like that got me to thinking about gardening. I did some of it as a kid, and the more I thought about it, the better I felt. I'd really like to try it, see if it helps my depression."

The good doctor stroked his beard for a moment, nodded as if in agreement. "I can see this new avenue might have a very positive effect on you," he said. "I'll do whatever I can do to help."

"I feel like I've been given a second chance," Bernie said. And this was where he needed Dr. Doolittle's assistance.

As much as Bernie wanted to pursue this new therapeutic avenue, he wanted to keep his salary and benefits from his current job at the Post Office, where, by means of an arbitrary and arcane set of rules, he was required to be on site and actively performing work tasks to receive that same salary and benefits package, even though doing so jeopardized his health. Surely Dr. Doolittle could help formulate a new work schedule for Bernie that would allow him to pursue his new passion, and along with it, enforce compliance by the Post Office, all in the name of mental health.

Bernie left that therapeutic session feeling very, very good, so good that he walked right past his scheduled ECT appointment without giving it a thought. Now it seemed as though a magical door had opened onto a future he could live with and be happy, and that future was organic farming.

****

In his agreement with Dr. Doolittle, Bernie returned to the state hospital the following week to begin a series of before-and-after tests of his cognitive ability and emotional status, all to assess the therapeutic effectiveness, or lack of it, of a summer of organic farming.

For the months of June through September, Bernie would work half-days at the Post Office without a reduction in his salary. His supervisor was not at all happy with the settlement, but Dr. Doolittle's letter which included a rather liberal interpretation of sections of the Americans with Disabilities Act must have convinced her that resistance was futile.

"You might just have saved my life," Bernie said to Dr. Doolittle, a phrase he had used several times with Dr. Peele, always effectively, but never with Dr. Carruthers because she'd spoken a different language before and now, of course, did not speak at all.

"Glad to help," Dr. Doolittle said. "I'm eager to see how this works out for you."

Bernie bought a tractor.

And a shed.

The tractor was a five-year-old Farmall—practically new in tractor years—that came with enough attachments to cultivate a plot several times the size of Bernie's. "Just right," he said.

The shed, a pre-fab model erected right on site on top of a newly laid concrete floor, was initially intended for storage of tools, but by the time Bernie was finished, it was fully wired for light and heat, and had hot and cold running water and a toilet. Then he added a microwave oven and brought Bertie over to inspect his new facility.

She stalked around the shed, scowling. "You said before this was just a place to store your tools. Is there something you're not telling me?" she asked, her nose just inches from his. "Are you planning to move in here?"

"No, of course not. It's just a lot more convenient like this. Everything I need to work is close at hand." How could she not see the perfect logic in his plan?

Bernie was not familiar with the concept of the man cave, that home-away-from-home, that manly shelter-from-the-storm, nor was he aware of the trouble it could bring down on him until he apparently crossed over the line by installing a small refrigerator alongside his microwave oven. By then the utility shed had doubled in size, and while begun in all innocence, could never again be regarded as a place for the storage of tools.

Bernie felt quite pleased with himself; why, he could work for hours and hours in a self-contained environment where most of his needs were close at hand. He had a microwave for hot snacks and a refrigerator for cold beverages and a bathroom to complete the cycle.

But Bertie did not seem to share his enthusiasm. In fact, the look she gave him when he returned from an afternoon at his small farm made him wish he knew where she kept her ice pick.

He wasn't sure exactly what he'd done to provoke her, only that the situation on the home front had become tenuous. There was an edge in her speech that hadn't been there before. Those little touches and hugs they'd shared before were few and far between now. When he posed the unfortunate question, "Is something wrong?" He got the answer he should have expected but didn't.

"Nothing." Then she went into the bedroom and closed the door.

Perhaps she regarded the whole idea of organic gardening as frivolous, just a passing fancy, so to prove to her that his intentions were serious, he began plowing in earnest.

He began work in the formerly vacant lot on the other side of what was before Ms. Grosbeak's residence. Here was where he expected to encounter any remains he'd left lying about from earlier adventures. He paid special attention to several sites where the grass and weeds grew more luxuriantly than in other spots, and his suspicions proved correct; from the bones he found, he concluded that those areas had received an extra dose of plant food of the true organic variety. Had they wasted Dr. Carruthers's potential contribution to his gardening effort, just floating her down the river that way? Probably not, decomposition would take some time, and he was already well into his plowing season.

Over the space of an afternoon, he recovered three skulls, an assortment of ribs, other small bones, and five femurs, which he bagged up awaiting a trip to the ravine. He looked in vain for the missing femur—it had to be there somewhere. He certainly would have remembered any of his victims missing a leg.

****

By the first week of June, he had all the sod broken up and tilled and sections laid out in perfectly straight rows. It was time to plant. He brought Bertie over to view his handiwork.

Her mood seemed to have warmed with the weather. "I can help you with the planting, but you'll have to show me how to do it."

"Not complicated at all," he said. "It's a lot easier than bowling."

Working from a diagram he'd carefully laid out over several evenings, they had, by the middle of the following week, completed most of the task. Tired but elated, that peculiar form of exhilaration that came from working with the soil, they stood arm in arm watching the sun set over their labors. The rest was up to Mother Nature.

"I was wondering," Bertie said as they walked back to the shed, "what exactly does organic farming mean?"

"I don't know. The guy at the commune used to say it meant whatever you wanted it to mean. So, we're just as organic as anybody else, probably more." But he still wondered about the missing femur.

****

Bernie Mitchell, the gentleman organic farmer, part-time postal worker, was becoming a far different man than Bernie the reclusive full-time mail sorter. Something more fundamental was afoot, wasn't it? The game was changing. Earlier on he'd have attributed such possibilities to his association with Bertie, but somehow this new process seemed altogether separate from her. He felt it most acutely while driving his tractor across his field, opening up the earth to the possibility of new growth.

Something in this basic process, one repeated by his forebears all the way back to the split between hunters and gatherers, now resonated with him. Some common chord was struck.

No, Bernie didn't know what it was, only that it was real and he felt it. Whatever it might be, it caused him to do strange things; he whistled while he worked. Sometimes he sang. Old Bernie seldom whistled and almost never sang. Old Bernie would never have climbed down from his tractor to move the slow-moving terrapin out of the way so it wouldn't be crushed beneath his wheels. Yeah, the times they were a'changing.

True, his bowling game suffered because there was less time for practice, but his mood improved to the point that he asked Dr. Doolittle if they might put his ECT program on hold for the time being, maybe the entire summer.

"Quit cold turkey? Are you sure?" Dr. Doolittle had asked.

"I'd like to try," Bernie said. "If it doesn't work out, we can always start up again, right?"

"Of course, I'm delighted that you're having such an excellent response to your organic gardening hobby." Doolittle seemed to latch onto the organic label as he scribbled notes in the file on his desk. "Next month I'd like to repeat some of the tests you took before we began all of this. Maybe this is the kind of program we should begin on a larger scale. Therapeutic organic gardening...I like the sound of that, something we might do right here on the hospital grounds."

"No problem." Bernie took notice and liked that Doolittle had included himself in the equation. Taking ownership should make him more amenable to suggestions Bernie might have as they got farther along in *their* project. And who knew, perhaps in time, Bernie might become a consultant in organic gardening at the state hospital, giving some of those hospitalized depressives the benefit of his experience. A whole new career track? Stranger things had happened...probably.

Best of all, Bertie appeared to have come on board without further reservations. She often referred to him now as "my new Bernie." Life was good.

****

Then the missing femur turned up. Bernie found it leaning against the door of his shed with a note attached. The handwriting was so poor it was barely legible, but he got the message: *Thought you might be looking for this. I have others. I'll be in touch. Have your wallet ready. Nathan Grosbeak—Aunt Ginny's nephew.*

Bertie looked angry enough to chew nails when he showed her the note. "Nathan Grosbeak? You know him?" she asked.

"I saw him a couple of times."

"Is he dumb enough to sign his name to a note like this?" she asked.

"Yeah, I'd have to say he's just about that dumb." Bernie edged away from Bertie. When she got this angry, anything could happen.

"But he's found bones," she said. "He could cause us trouble."

"Honestly, I don't think he's smart enough."

"You'd better be right," she said.

That night, Bernie had a nightmare. Instead of plants growing in his garden, there were bones, bones

210

sticking up everywhere, and at the end of each row sat a skull, laughing at him.

The next morning at breakfast, when the dishes were cleared away, he and Bertie had a council of war. "I'll check my camera," she said.

"What camera?"

"The one I installed above the door to your shed."

"Why did you put a camera on my shed?" he asked.

"In case there's ever a break-in," she said. "Thieves go for small buildings set off by themselves. There should be some visual record of whoever left the bone."

Most of the footage from the camera was Bernie coming and going with a big smile on his face, no surprise there, except for the smile, but then the bone thief appeared, and there he was, red-handed, leaving the bone against the door. "That's him," Bernie said. "That's Ms. Grosbeak's nephew."

"Nathan Grosbeak." Little furrows formed across Bertie's forehead, and she pushed the corners of her eyes up with her forefingers.

Bernie knew this look. Behind it lay deep, dark thoughts. Somebody was in big trouble. Bernie almost felt sorry for the poor bastard. If he had any idea what he was facing, he'd probably jump in front of a truck.

Bernie went right on tending his garden as if nothing had happened, knowing that Bertie was on the job. Two days later, again at breakfast, she opened a folder at the table and removed some pages. "Here's where he lives, here's where he works, here's his car, here's his dog. He's usually gone during the day, so that should be a good time to go over to his house and have a look around." She made it all sound so simple, as if they were planning to visit a friend.

****

Nathan's Grosbeak's house had probably been a hovel in its better days and had gone downhill since. Both of the front windows were broken, and the front steps looked as if they wouldn't support the weight of a toddler, much less an adult. It looked like a place that should be deserted, even if it wasn't. Apparently Nathan hadn't expected such rapid and effective pursuit when he'd dropped off the femur, but then, he'd never met Bertie, had he?

Breaking in was almost too easy given the flimsy state of the structure. Bernie wondered why the nephew even bothered to lock the doors. He was rather proud of himself when he spotted a camera above the door. "Why in hell does he have a camera up there? Who would ever want to break in here?"

"Cheapest model you can buy," Bertie said. "Don't worry about it. They never work."

They divided up to conquer. Bertie headed toward the kitchen, and Bernie, toward the bedroom. As soon as he entered the bedroom, Nathan's small dog, confined in its crate, began barking like crazy. The aroma in the confined space suggested the old axiom about pets not pooping where they slept was not altogether accurate. But maybe it wasn't fair to blame it all on the dog. There was Nathan to consider as well. Either way, dog and crate were about to leave the premises.

"Good job," Bertie said when Bernie emerged carrying the crate.

She left a note tacked inside the front door.

Leave all bones in a plastic garbage bag by the shed. Otherwise, Fido will be sent back to you stuffed and mounted.

"Maybe knowing we can get to his dog will scare him off. If not, I'll take care of him," Bertie said.

The next morning, a bag of bones including two more skulls Bernie hadn't counted on, sat by the shed door. Bernie left crate and dog by the edge of the garden. Bertie seemed a bit disappointed they'd let the guy off so easily, but the new, benevolent Bernie was in more of a live-and-let-live mood these days. So, Nathan and Nathan's dog escaped a fate that surely would have given the nephew night terrors, had he known how close he had come to a firsthand experience of becoming a bone donor himself.

Chapter Thirteen

"Isn't this beautiful?" Bernie asked as he and Bertie walked hand-in-hand down the garden rows where green life forms, soon to be edible and sustaining, poked through the ground all around them. "We did this, you know, you and me."

"With a little help from Mother Nature," Bertie said.

"True enough, but without all the planning and work we put in, this entire area could just as easily have become a field of weeds…and bones."

They reached the end of the row and turned to look back over the green expanse.

"You're loving this aren't you?" Bertie said.

"You know it. Just standing here makes me feel happy."

"Don't go overboard on me," Bertie said. "I worry that you'll want to expand even more."

"No, this is enough, perfect, just as it is." Yes, love, joy, and no small amount of pride now filled the space around Bernie like a soft pink cloud. Wouldn't his former therapist, Dr. Bowman, be proud of him now, if she was still alive?

In the early months of his therapy with Dr. Bowman, before he'd been forced to kill her, she'd posed a troubling question to Bernie: "What would your ideal life be like? If you could do anything you wanted, what would it be?"

Bernie fumbled that one. He simply couldn't think of doing anything else at the time. He sorted mail, he had life's basic needs—food, shelter, good health—what else was there?

His answer then must have disappointed Dr. Bowman too. "Really?" she'd asked. "That's all?"

Now he knew what he hadn't known back then. As he stood beside his little farm on a warm evening in early July, Bertie by his side, he knew the real answer to that question. If he'd known the answer back then, Dr. Bowman would still be alive, but that was beside the point. What he hadn't known about then but felt so strongly now was love and joy.

****

"Bernie, this is too much. We're drowning in vegetables." They stood alongside bushel baskets of peas, baskets of beans, even a few early squash, and cucumbers.

By late July, Bernie's work shifted into harvest mode, because the plants were on their own schedules, not his. There were beans and peas to be picked, then squash and cucumbers. Soon they were, as Bertie said, awash in vegetables. He'd always hoped for a bountiful harvest—what real organic farmer did not?—but not quite so bountiful as the one that now kept Bertie and himself covered in green. It was time for the second phase of the master plan. "Maybe we can sell some of it," he said.

He ordered a small three-sided shed with a broad shelf on the open side for display of baskets of their organic vegetables, as indicated by the hand-painted sign he'd had Bertie draw out. Then he and Bertie set up what he considered to be an attractive array of vegetables before he took his seat at the stand. He'd taken a bag full of loose change and dollar bills in preparation for a thriving business.

But there was little traffic on the dead-end street and few takers for their organic produce. Bernie was ever so disappointed. As twilight crept in, he loaded the baskets back onto the cart that he pulled behind his tractor and headed back toward the shed. The business side of their venture was a bust…so far.

"How'd it go?" Bertie asked as he plopped onto the sofa.

"Not so good, not even one customer."

"So, you'll try again tomorrow, right?"

And he did, the next day and the day after that and so on, with the same result…no sales.

Far from a total loss, they feasted throughout the late summer months on the bounty from their field. Bertie succeeded in stashing away a winter's supply in the freezer, and their new diet, almost vegan, helped them both lose weight. Bernie could have been even more successful in the weight loss area were it not for his addiction to blueberry pancakes.

****

"Honestly, Bernie, you've been working on that vegetable basket for the past half hour. What's the big deal?" Bertie stood beside him on the porch shaking her head as if she thought he might have lost his marbles.

"I want it to look good. I put the beans and peas on the bottom, the corn on top of that, then the zucchini and cucumbers, and lettuce and tomatoes on top. Each layer is separated by Styrofoam, neat, huh?"

"All you need is a red ribbon. It looks like

something you'd enter in a county fair."

"Maybe I will, not this one, though, this one is for my doctor. I have to go back to the state hospital for more testing, and I have to convince him that this gardening thing is doing me some good. That way he'll keep the pressure on the Post Office to keep me on part time with full time benefits. It's worth the effort, believe me."

Later that day when he presented his trophy to Dr. Doolittle, the response was all he could wish for. The doctor's eyes looked like big circles, even behind his glasses, and his smile went ear to ear. "My word, Bernie, what is all this?"

"Just some stuff from our garden. Thought you might enjoy some fresh veggies."

The doc eagerly rummaged through the basket, upsetting Bernie's careful preparation, but Bernie didn't mind. Dr. Doolittle's enthusiasm made up for all. "Why, there's all sorts of beautiful vegetables in here, a veritable cornucopia of succulent produce."

"A what?" Bernie asked.

"Cornucopia, it means horn of plenty," Dr. Doolittle said.

"Whatever, I just hope you enjoy it."

"For sure, and there's so much here, I'll share it with all the staff, too. When you mentioned gardening, I never dreamed you would be doing it on such a large scale. You won't mind if we take a few photos, will you?"

He had his receptionist take several of a smiling doctor and his smiling patient, then added a few of the staff in too. Soon, staff from the other offices, including some of the doctors, came by to marvel at Bernie's success. Bernie smiled so much his facial muscles became fatigued.

"We'll need to repeat the tests we did earlier," Dr. Doolittle said after the crowd had dissipated. "We both know how the results will be, but I have to have it down on paper for it to be official."

"No problem," Bernie said.

Bernie didn't have to fudge the answers on his mood analysis exam; he was a happy guy. And a happy Bernie made Dr. Doolittle happy also. "I don't know when I've seen a more dramatic about-face," said the beaming doctor. "The real trick now will be sustaining all the gains you've made through the winter months. I want you to know that I've discussed your progress with the staff here, and we might very well ask you to help set up a program here next season."

Bernie Mitchell, mental health consultant…what next? But his inner glow dimmed a few notches as he considered the inevitable onset of winter with shorter days and longer nights. Whatever did real farmers do when their fields lay fallow and plowing, planting, sowing, and reaping no longer filled their days?

Later that afternoon he returned home like a conquering hero. "You should have been there," he told Bertie as they prepared dinner. "I've never seen people get so excited over vegetables."

"Too bad some of the local folks couldn't get that excited too. Maybe they could have bought some of it. We're up to our elbows in squash, and there's more coming in ever day."

"The doc said something that started me thinking," Bernie said. "What do organic farmers do in the winter when the gardening is over? Any ideas?"

"I'm sure you'll think of something."

The question continued to ping around in Bernie's head, because it aroused some basic concerns he had about himself. At the moment, Bernie Mitchell was a happy guy, an unusual state for him, and one he much preferred to the Bernie of old. He'd do all he could to make this a permanent change, but he wasn't sure exactly which way to turn. A potential answer came to him the next night after a dinner of corn, green beans, and brown rice. "Chickens," he said rather loudly. The pronouncement surprised him almost as much as it did Bertie.

Bertie dropped the serving spoon spreading rice across the table.

"I can raise chickens. They'll provide us with eggs, and occasionally, Sunday dinner. And chicken poop will be great fertilizer for the garden, organic, too. The guy back at the commune told me that years ago. 'Nothing like chicken poop,' he always said."

"Where will you keep them?" she asked. "You can't keep them here. The neighbors will raise hell if you keep chickens in the yard." It was clear from Bertie's expression that she would be one of the major hell raisers herself.

"I'll keep them over at the garden, put in some new fencing, buy a little shed and convert it into a coop with a place to lay eggs. Organic vegetables and eggs for sale. How does that sound to you?" he asked.

"Like you're planning to start up your own commune. You're not planning to start a new commune, are you, Bernie?"

"If you don't think chickens are a good idea, I won't do it. Mostly I'm just looking for a way to stay busy during the winter." But down deep, the more he thought about chickens, the better he liked the idea.

"No, go ahead, and while you're at it, get a cow. We can use the milk, and I hear cow poop makes really good fertilizer too, but you're going to have to shovel it up yourself, same goes for the chicken poop."

Before he could respond, she left the table, leaving behind a confused and dejected organic farmer. It was their first cross exchange in a long time. Even his meltdown when she was dissecting Dr. Carruthers hadn't provoked anything nearly so sharp.

Bernie's default reaction when faced with unpleasantry that he couldn't solve with his axe, was to retreat inside his own protective shell, the one he'd built up over many years. But he didn't want to go back inside. He'd seen a better way, and that way was Bertie and his new life. Now, if only he could find a way to have Bertie and organic farming and chickens too.

****

"Beans, corn, and peas, every night it's beans, corn, and peas." Bertie slammed a pot on the stove. "We have a freezer full of the stuff. It will take all year to eat it. Meanwhile, I'm sick of these vegetables. It's all raising hell with my IBS."

"IBS?"

"My irritable bowel syndrome. I'm sure I mentioned that before. I'm going out for Chinese. You coming?"

"Yeah, I guess so." He'd almost said, "If we had some chickens...." but that would have caused her to boil over for sure. He hadn't said anything more about chickens since that fateful night when, in a fit of temper, she told him what would happen to any and all chickens he brought around. And for all he knew, might happen to him as well.

The long winter nights had accentuated their differences. No longer were they two exact halves of a whole. Bernie thrived on routine, a bit of reading followed by dinner—beans, corn, and peas, nothing wrong with that—and then a couple of hours working on his model airplanes.

His partner had different needs. She wanted, he was surprised to learn after all these months, variety, some excitement, both things that gave Bernie a splitting headache.

Maybe things would have been different if their Organic Farmers' Market hadn't been a washout, but there was no reason to believe it would improve the following year. The sulfur odor that sometimes rose out of the ravine at the end of the lot and swept across the garden made any potential customers run for cover.

"But it's all organic," Bernie had protested more than once.

"Smells like a waste treatment plant." Yeah, he'd heard that several times. Still, he would be happy raising vegetables for what he now considered his little family, except part of that family was in full revolt and would not look favorably on a new harvest the coming summer. It had become a time of slamming doors, and Bernie didn't know what to do.

****

Bertie, always ahead of the curve, came up with a few thoughts of her own. "Did you ever rob a bank, Bernie?" This after a dinner of beans, peas and corn…what else?

"What? Of course not, I work for the Post Office.

I'm a federal employee. We don't rob anybody." Where in hell had this come from? Rob a bank? What a crazy idea, but that was probably it, right? Bertie floating something off-the-wall just to get a rise out of him. He kept on washing the dinner dishes.

"That doesn't mean you still can't have a little fun."

"Fun? When did robbing banks become fun? It sounds dangerous." Now Bernie was getting just a bit anxious. He couldn't quite get his head around this one. Was she making a real suggestion, or just winding him up?

"Just one bank, and a small one at that. Come on, live a little," she said.

"We'll get caught," he said. "Bank robbers always get caught."

"I've got it all figured out."

"That's what scares me." His complete faith in Bertie's planning capability had taken a hit when her attempts at burning down his blood-streaked house came within a hair of burning up both of them as well.

"It'll be a piece of cake. Brockton is about thirty miles east of here. I've been scouting it out. The local bank is almost deserted from one to two every Thursday. That would be the best time."

Clearly, her plans were in an advanced stage, and Bernie, unless he could come up with a plausible objection, would be part of the project. "They have cameras. All banks have cameras these days."

"We'll wear monkey masks. No one will recognize us."

"Fingerprints." He was becoming desperate.

"Gloves," she said.

"Somebody will recognize the car."

"I have a set of license plates I stole off a car at the market." She had an answer for everything.

"What about weapons?" You can't just walk in and say, 'give me the money.' You have to have guns."

"Got 'em," she said. She produced a cloth bag from which she withdrew a pair of nine mm semiautomatics.

"I've never fired a handgun." Bernie eased away from her. Homicide with an axe was one thing but shooting someone sounded far too violent, noisy too.

"No problem," she said smiling. "Just point it at the door and pull the trigger. You can't very well miss the door."

"I don't want to shoot the door. I don't want to shoot anything." He dropped the dishcloth on the counter and backed farther away as she pushed the gun toward him.

"Okay, then, I'll do it. Put your fingers in your ears. This could be loud." She spread her feet out shoulder-width, held the weapon in both hands, then pulled the trigger. A silent stream of water splashed against the glass window in the door. She turned to Bernie, a huge smile on her face. "Pretty clever, huh? No deadly weapons. No chance of anybody getting shot."

"The guards won't be using water pistols." Yeah, it was clever enough, until they came up against somebody with real guns, and, as much as he disliked the idea of shooting someone else, the possibility of getting shot himself was a real turn-off.

"We just have to scare them, make them think we'll shoot them if they don't cooperate."

"Tell me again why we're doing this. Do we need

money?"

"No, we don't need money. It's just something to do, you know, for a laugh."

For Bernie, phrases such as "low profile" and "no drama" described his ideal life, and the quiet routine of an organic gentleman farmer was a grand prize. The very idea of a bank robbery for a laugh seemed downright crazy. But Bertie seemed well beyond the planning stages and was ready to carry it out.

Bernie's participation was a foregone conclusion. Of course, he could refuse, but, as there was already a bit of tension in the house over his organic gardening plans, he didn't want to risk any escalation. An angry Bertie was a truly frightening prospect, far worse than participating in a bank robbery.

But first, they would rehearse with Bertie directing. "You wear the black raincoat, and I'll wear the tan one. We wear baseball caps to partially cover our faces until we're past the door of the bank, then we put on the monkey masks. We approach from opposite sides of the street, so people won't connect us right off. Do I need to go over that again?"

"No, I got it."

And right there in the living room, she set up chairs to mark the door of the bank. They approached from opposite sides, passed through, doffed their caps, and put on the monkey masks. Bernie managed to get his on backward.

"See," Bertie said. "This is why we practice."

He replaced his mask, this time with the eye holes in front.

"You're taking too long. It has to go on quickly before anyone sees your face. Try it again."

Repetition just made things worse. Bernie began to sweat, making the mask harder to pull over his face. "I need a bigger mask," he said.

"They only come in one size."

"I can't breathe." Indeed, having his airways blocked off by a rubber mask was very uncomfortable.

"You'll only have it on for a minute or two. Surely you can manage that." Her voice became less and less cheerful.

"What if I pass out?"

"I'll have to leave you behind. You're too heavy to carry," she said.

"You're kidding, right?"

"Maybe."

The following evening, halfway through their final dress rehearsal, Bertie held up her arms. "Latex gloves, I forgot the damned gloves. I left them in the van."

"We can put them on when we get there."

"No, we have to practice everything." She ran out the door and returned moments later with several pairs of latex gloves. "Take off your mask, put on your gloves, and see if you can get your mask on wearing gloves."

Not going to happen. "These gloves don't fit." Bernie's own supply of extra-large latex gloves that he usually bought in bulk for emergencies were all destroyed when his house exploded. He had not yet taken time to replenish his stores because his rage-inspired homicidal actions had become so infrequent.

"Bernie, you're acting like a child."

"Honest, they're too small, see?" He held up one hand with a glove that wouldn't pass the first knuckle of his fingers.

"Wear your own winter gloves then. It's February, nobody will notice. Okay, we're inside the bank, wearing our masks. You go over to the guard and say, 'Hands up.' Show him your gun but don't let him get a close look at it. And for heaven's sakes, don't pull the trigger. He's not going to be impressed if you squirt him."

"I got it," Bernie said with more enthusiasm than he really felt.

"As soon as I get the money, we run for it. Drop the water pistols on the floor on the way out."

"The masks?"

"Take them off, but don't leave them behind, DNA, you know."

****

Even with all the preparation and rehearsal, it still seemed unreal to Bernie as they drove slowly down the main street of Brockton, identifiable as Main Street only by the sign at the corner. Any minute now he expected Bertie to burst out laughing and say, "It was all a big joke. There is no robbery." But there was no laughter. She was pure concentration.

The Bank of Brockton was a large imposing building that dwarfed the two shops on either side of it. The glass doors in front, complete with iron bars running vertically top to bottom, were at least eight feet tall.

"I thought you said it was a small bank," Bernie said.

"It just looks big from the outside. Don't worry."

Bernie's grip on the steering wheel was becoming more and more vicelike, and he wondered if he'd be able to let go when it was time to exit the van and begin robbing the bank.

"We'll come up this street when we leave. There's no traffic light and no stop sign," she said. "Are you paying attention, Bernie?"

"Oh, yes." Nothing like the possibility of apprehension by the police and a jail sentence to hold a guy's interest.

"Park over there so nobody can block us in."

Nerves had begun to take hold of Bernie as he still held out hope for a cancellation, saved by the bell, but then Bertie said "Showtime, final check, monkey masks, gloves, guns. Ready?"

"What about the bag for the money?" Maybe she'd forgotten? No bag, no money, no robbery, right?

She pulled a flimsy plastic shopping bag from her pocket. "Got it," she said. "Let's get to work."

They set off down the street in opposite directions, Bernie's knees knocking so loudly they must have been audible. They would circle the block on foot and meet back at ground zero, the door to the bank. Was Bertie equally nervous? More importantly, were they having fun yet?

Bertie, even though she had farther to walk, was waiting for Bernie in front of the bank. "I thought you chickened out," she said.

He shook his head. "I'm here."

The light breeze blew open the flap of Bernie's coat revealing the axe he'd slipped into the inside pocket. He jerked it shut, but too late, she'd seen.

"You brought your axe? You brought an axe to a bank robbery?"

"Just in case," he said. "Besides, you brought your icepick. I can see the handle in your pocket."

227

"I just hope we don't have to use them. Okay, monkey masks and guns. Let's go."

The security guard was reading the newspaper and must not have noticed Bernie until they were only a couple of feet apart. Bernie made sure the guard got a glimpse, and only a glimpse, of his gun before he said "Hands up. This is a robbery."

The guard was either too stunned by Bernie's demand or frightened by the voice coming from the hideous monkey mask to comply, so Bernie had to say it again. The man dropped his paper and raised his hands. "Please, don't shoot," he said.

Bertie now had the undivided attention of the single teller on duty, a blue-haired senior citizen who did not appear ready to yield up the funds of the residents of Brockton without a fight. "Put the money in the bag, or so help me, I'll blow your fucking head off and kick it around the floor like a football."

Bernie was just as shocked as the teller. He'd never heard Bertie use that kind of language before, but it worked, and Bertie walked away from the window with a shopping bag full of cash. "Let's go," she said.

They dropped the water pistols on the floor, and, as soon as they were past the door, pulled off the monkey masks. Bernie started running, but Bertie paused to rip open the bag, spilling the cash all over the sidewalk and laughing as the breeze blew much of it into the street.

She caught up with Bernie at the truck. Both were panting as they climbed inside. "Turn left at the corner and drive slow. We don't want a speeding ticket," she said.

"Why didn't you tell me you were going to throw away the money?" he asked.

"If I'd told you, you wouldn't have come along, would you?"

"No, because it doesn't make sense stealing something just to throw it away." Not that it made a lot of sense robbing banks in the first place.

"I told you all along, it was just for fun."

He was so glad it was finally over, but still pissed at Bertie for putting them through such a risky endeavor "just for fun." Why had he let her talk him into something so crazy? Was she losing it? Was he?

As soon as they arrived home, Bertie parked herself in front of the TV and began flipping through the news programs, while Bernie paced about the room, pondering this new twist in his relationship with the woman around whom his personal planet now orbited. Bank robbery for fun? What would she come up with next? This would require some deep consideration.

About forty minutes later, Bertie sang out, "It's us. We're famous. Come and see."

"Breaking news about the Brockton Bank, a robbery attempt was foiled this afternoon when one of the robbers dropped the bag of loot. The clumsy culprits are still at large, but the money was recovered thanks to the courageous pursuit by the security guard, Harold Smithson."

"Clumsy culprits? That's a big fat lie," Bertie said. "I didn't drop the bag. I tore it in half. And that security guard never got off his ass. I've a good mind to call them and tell them what really happened."

"No, definitely not, do not do that," Bernie said.

Bertie changed channels. "Pranksters held up the Brockton Bank this afternoon using water pistols. They threw the money aside as they fled. It is not clear what their motive might be, perhaps a protest of some sort, but definitely not robbery."

"Pranksters, they called us pranksters." Bertie seemed even more outraged now. "Somebody needs to set them straight."

"Promise me you will not make any calls," Bernie said.

"Okay, but I'm really pissed over how they botched the story."

The next few days were agonizing as Bernie waited for the knock on the door that would signal the arrival of the Brockton PD, guns drawn, announcing, "You're under arrest for bank robbery."

But the knock never came. Some two weeks after the prank/robbery, Bertie announced that the coast was probably clear. "If they knew anything, they'd have come for us by now."

As Bernie turned to walk away, she grabbed his arm. "Look me in the eye and tell me you didn't get a kick out of our little caper."

"Maybe a little, but I don't want to do it again." But it was just a matter of time before she came up with another idea for excitement, he was sure.

Chapter Fourteen

Two uneventful months followed, a time of no stabbing with icepicks, no bashing with axes, and no bank robberies, a time of quiet contemplation when Bernie gave thought to his upcoming spring planting season. He'd abandoned his idea of chickens in view of Bertie's resistance.

As the days began to lengthen, his desire to fire up his tractor and begin tilling the soil grew ever stronger. But the decisions he made now would be his and his alone, because Bertie's interest seemed lukewarm at best and occasionally hostile.

But real organic farmers were not to be deterred by details. Real organic farmers did what had to be done, right on schedule, and Bernie would prove himself a worthy member of that tradition. Besides, what else was he going to do? As proof of his commitment, he bought himself some real farmer togs, a straw hat, denim overalls, a denim work shirt, and a pair of steel-toed boots. The boots were a bit over the top, but he liked the feel of them when he kicked things.

Bernie entered a deep meditative state as he drove back and forth across his lot, turning over sod, releasing the rich loamy aroma of earth that had lain undisturbed for months and occasionally releasing a less pleasant aroma left over from his homicidal days.

Bernie would not have been surprised to see his

dream people floating around, disturbing this pastoral setting, but none came. In fact, it had been weeks since he'd seen any at all. Was the role of gentleman organic farmer having such a profound effect he might forego further ECT sessions permanently? What would Dr. Doolittle say about that? Would he really bring Bernie on staff as a mental health consultant?

True, Bernie hadn't swung his axe in many months. The automatic urge seemed to have receded. Hearing those provocative phrases from the 60s, and he'd heard a few, failed to provoke that old rage reaction anymore.

Even though Bertie was not exactly a member of the organic farming fan club, he was sure she couldn't help sharing his joy over the therapeutic effects of his gardening program, and he particularly wanted her to see his new official farming togs, so, as soon as he'd finished his plowing, he ran back to the house to tell her. He found her perched on the sofa in front of the TV, a broad smile on her face.

"That's him," she said as a photo of a fiftyish, rather distinguished-looking male posed in a jacket and tie, appeared on the screen. "It took three years, but I finally got him."

Bernie's knees turned into pulpy globs of silly putty, and his legs seemed to have no further interest in supporting him. He latched onto the back of the sofa, only to realize that his arms had joined the rebellion and were no longer under his control either. He collapsed into an unhappy heap.

"Bernie, what's wrong with you? You're missing everything."

"Must have slipped," he said. He felt, he supposed,

like an infant must feel attempting its first steps. Pulling on the edge of the sofa, he hoisted himself into a kneeling position and crawled around to the front of the sofa.

"What on earth are you doing?" Bertie asked.

"Just thought I'd sit on the floor for a minute."

"Sit wherever you like, just don't block the TV. They're getting to the good part." She hadn't said one word about his new farming outfit.

A blonde with a beehive on her head and a microphone in her hand said, "The police thought Mr. Barton might have died of a heart attack until they found a small wound in the back of his neck. Officer, would you tell us what you discovered?"

The blonde started to hand the microphone to the officer who grabbed her by the shoulders and spun her around. He pointed to the back of her neck, a spot just below the hairline. "There was a spot of blood right here, like something small might have been stuck into his neck."

The blonde struggled and tried to turn back facing the camera, but the officer held her fast, his finger pressing into her neck. "My guess would be an ice pick," he said.

Bernie remained sitting because he knew he couldn't get up if he tried.

"He just got out of jail two months ago," Bertie said. "I've been waiting for him. I'm gonna get a beer. You want one?"

"No thanks." He knew immediately that this was Bertie's latest kill, but he couldn't understand why it affected him so strongly. As the old saying went, it wasn't her first rodeo, his either. Why, then, was he sitting on the floor, confused and stuporous?

"What the TV people didn't say was that he's destroyed three families over the past ten years. The last one was a new mom and dad driving home from the hospital with their newborn. Killed them all, and the bastard walked away without a scratch, drunk as usual. They put him away for six months, but that wasn't nearly enough. So, I finished the job." She took a long swig from her beer. "Hey, we should be celebrating. Aren't you happy for me?" Bertie couldn't appear more pleased if she'd suddenly discovered a cure for cancer.

Happy? Celebrating? Bernie had come into the room to share some life-changing information, but Bertie's revelation crushed his own. It took a moment before he came upon the word that best described his feelings…deflation, complete and total deflation. The air had been sucked right out of his balloon. "You left him there, sitting in his car."

"Yeah, I wanted them to find him. I wanted them to see what should have been done years ago. Now maybe they'll try harder to keep drunks off the road."

They couldn't have been farther apart at that moment if they'd been on different continents. Bertie was at a pinnacle, a place of elation, while deflated Bernie was sinking into an abyss of depression. Bertie twirled in sunlight; Bernie couldn't see his hand in front of his face.

Even in the depths of his worst clinical depression, things had never been this bad. He lay down on the floor, curled into a ball, and didn't understand how he'd got there.

"Sometimes it gets to you," Bertie said. "I've been there too. It gets better."

Bernie had his doubts.

Indeed, one might say he never recovered from that incident. The very thought of more killing, which had been an almost casual occurrence before, nothing to get excited about, became abhorrent, not because of the dream people—they never came back—but because some internal switch in Bernie's psyche had flipped, and he wasn't the same man as before. There was a better way, and he'd seen it, and he couldn't forget it.

****

After the killing, Bernie and his doppelganger came to occupy separate spaces. No longer two halves of a whole, they spun in different orbits. Her time was now taken up with some mysterious activity at her desk in the bedroom with the door closed. Sometimes she was away during the evenings but never told him where or why.

Bernie took refuge in his garden, becoming a full-time plowman. He still maintained his part-time position at the Post Office, with full pay and benefits, of course, but his heart, what was left of it, belonged to his tractor. His became the most thoroughly tilled plot of land in southwestern Oregon.

But as he checked off the calendar days in June, he realized that, once again, he had gone far overboard with his planting efforts. Bertie would not be pleased.

By late June, he gazed out over a tidal wave of green, amorphous now, it would soon define itself as peas, beans, corn, tomatoes, etc., all organic, of course. Whatever would he do with all of it?

"Why don't you just give it away?" Bertie suggested. "There are church groups that set up food banks for homeless people, stuff like that. They'd be glad to get your extra vegetables."

The idea of cozying up to a church group did not fill Bernie's heart with joy, a reaction left over from one of his early foster families, the Winkles, who force-fed him their religious code, no exceptions permitted. If religious fervor turned out rigid, narrow, and generally unpleasant folks like the Winkles, Bernie wanted no part of it, but they couldn't all be like that, could they?

"Which church?" he asked.

"There's a Baptist church just a couple of streets over. I've met the preacher, seems like a nice guy," Bertie said.

"Where did you meet a preacher?" he asked, knowing that Bertie was no more a churchgoer than he was himself.

"He came into the market one afternoon, nice fellow, very chatty. I wish I'd thought then about the vegetables, but I didn't know you'd be planting such a bumper crop again."

Could this make a difference, he wondered? Could this help him get his life back on track? Combining efforts with a church, even considering such an idea—and he was considering it—set up a push-pull, to-and-fro response in Bernie's head, because such a thought usually pushed all his buttons the wrong way. But that would have been the response of the Bernie of old, not the new Bernie Mitchell Gentleman Organic Farmer Philanthropist. The new Bernie, less daunted by the prospect of new faces, new commitments, and most difficult of all, new small talk, took Bertie's advice and drove straightaway to the preacher's house where he found the man of God mowing his front lawn.

New Bernie with but nascent social skills got out of

his car smiling, hand extended, and walked over to where the preacher stood sweating in the noonday sun. "Sorry to interrupt," Bernie said. "Guess I picked a bad time. Wouldn't mind doing a few laps with that mower for you if it would help out."

"Not at all, I could use a break." The young thirtyish man, slightly taller than Bernie, his height increased an inch or two by a head of dark, wavy hair, took Bernie's hand in a firm grip. "Mark Shawcross, why don't we sit over here in the shade?"

Bernie followed along behind him and took the folding chair he was offered. "I won't keep you long," he said. "I just wanted to mention, I live less than a mile away, and I've put in a big garden over off Mulberry Street. Last year I had more vegetables than I knew what to do with, and this year it'll be even bigger. I wondered whether your congregation could use some of them."

"Oh, yes, I'm sure, but we couldn't pay much."

"I'm not trying to sell them," Bernie said. "What I enjoy is the plowing and planting, the gardening part. But I planted way too much. My sister and I ate vegetables last year until we were sick of them, and she has a bowel problem anyway, so too many vegetables really upset her." It was a bit more information than he'd intended to divulge, but Shawcross, with his frank, open gaze seemed to invite such disclosure.

The preacher folded his hands in his lap as if he was contemplating a prayer. "This almost makes me want to say, the Lord works in mysterious ways. We've been trying to start up a little food bank the past couple of years, but we've never had enough produce to really get it going. Your extra vegetables might just be what we need."

"Good, I have a little vegetable stand you can have too. I thought about setting up a small market myself, but it never worked out. Maybe you'll have better luck."

"Times like this I like to offer up a little prayer of thanks, Mr. Mitchell. Do you mind?"

"Be my guest," Bernie said. He couldn't remember the last time he'd sat through a prayer voluntarily, but now it seemed like the right thing to do.

Preacher Shawcross was both succinct and heartfelt in his words, leaving Bernie with a warm but unfamiliar glow. He felt as though something significant had happened, but he wasn't sure what it was.

"May I ask about your church affiliation?" the Reverend Shawcross said.

Should he get up and run away now? No, instead, Bernie squirmed a bit like he'd come up a few dollars short on his dinner check. Ordinarily he would have lied when asked such a question, sort of like confessing to an insurance salesman you didn't have a policy. The salesman would then latch on like a remora to a shark until you bought something or hit him with your axe. But Bernie wasn't about to bash the Reverend Shawcross. This new Bernie was open to new things, a nuclear change if ever there was one. "We don't have one," he said, looking down at his feet.

"Would you like to hear about our church?"

"I would." The words tumbled out of him, unchecked and unprepared.

So ended a momentous and pivotal afternoon in the life of Bernie Mitchell. He had listened intently to the Reverend's pitch, delivered it seemed with both passion and sincerity. Before Bernie left, he'd committed himself to attending services the next Sunday morning.

A small problem remained—what would he tell Bertie? She couldn't very well come down on him with both feet, since the church idea was hers to begin with, but more and more his usually predictable housemate was becoming unpredictable, and he never knew quite what to expect.

****

On one occasion during the first months of his therapy with Dr. Bowman, she'd asked him about his friends…how many, what kind, work, social, whatever, and recreational preferences—her words. Bernie, up to the task, rattled off a series of names of people he'd never met and activities in which he'd never participated. Dr. Bowman seemed pleased with his wide range of social contacts, fictional, of course, but how was she to know? And that was the name of the game back then, keeping his therapist happy.

Fabricated friends were the variety Bernie favored. He didn't have to talk to them, never had to meet them for drinks or whatever. They never asked for favors, never wanted to borrow his car. And the pals he'd made up never extended beyond the limits of his own imagination.

But there was change in the wind now, change beginning with Bernie's first visit to Mark Shawcross's Baptist Church. Bernie had driven by the church the Saturday before the promised Sunday services to check it out. He had an aversion to large, imposing buildings, and stained-glass windows gave him a headache. But the Baptist Church proved to be a modest building, just slightly larger than some of the surrounding houses, distinguished in part by its gleaming white steeple that seemed to draw in the June sunlight so that it glowed, or so it appeared to Bernie.

His Sunday morning plan was to arrive late and leave early to limit the damage, but he blew it when he discovered he'd misread the sign placed out on the front lawn and got there almost an hour before services started...a tragic mistake. Unless he could pull a fainting spell or fake a heart attack, he might be forced to mingle and chat for an hour, something far beyond his physical limits.

Facing a near-death experience, he decided to run for it. He could always say he'd forgotten to feed the cat, turn off the stove, something, anything. But the fates had conspired against him because before he could get his car turned around, Mark Shawcross trotted alongside.

"Bernie, I'm so glad you made it. Come on and meet some of our people."

Yeah, sure, come on in and we'll probably talk you to death in about fifteen minutes. But if you die, no problem. We have a graveyard right out back.

But Shawcross's smile was so warm and hopeful, Bernie couldn't resist. Well, maybe for a few minutes, then he could faint, or die.

Bernie met people. They all seemed so glad he was there. They shook his hand, patted his back. A few of the older ladies hugged him. "Welcome, welcome, we're so glad you're here." How many times did he hear that refrain?

"I've already told them about your vegetable garden," Shawcross said. "They're really excited about it. We have some real enthusiastic gardeners here, and they'd love to help you out with weeding and things like that."

Bernie, if not the most private, even secretive person on the planet, found himself caught up in the moment. He stayed through the entire service in spite of feeling, as the saying goes, nervous as a whore in church. He stayed afterward for more meeting and greeting. He stayed for the lunch on the lawn that the church ladies seemed to have conjured up out of thin air. He had no time to invent a past history for himself to deal with the questions he should have known would come, so he stuck with the basic facts: his parents died in a fire, he was an orphan, he'd worked at the Post Office forever, he lived with his sister, Bertie. That was all anybody needed to know.

The big shock of the early afternoon came when the entire group, Bernie included, took a stroll through the little graveyard in back of the church.

"We do this a couple of times each month." Shawcross walked beside Bernie, his hand on Bernie's shoulder. "Just to remember those who have gone before."

The whole idea seemed strange to Bernie who had undergone so many ECT sessions just to forget those who had gone before. Now here were folks wandering among the graves, leaving clutches of spring flowers, holding their memories close. Of course, Bernie had different memories, most of which he didn't want to recall; the ghosts who came back to haunt him had attained their ghostly state by his own hand and seemed very unhappy about that fact.

Shawcross must have sensed Bernie's disquiet, if not the source. His hand tightened on Bernie's shoulder.

"You don't particularly like graveyards, do you?"

Bernie shook his head, fearing that his voice might give something away, something that should remain hidden.

"If you ever want to talk about it, you know where I am." Shawcross gave him a pat and walked on, leaving Bernie with his jumble of thoughts.

Sometime later in the early afternoon, a confused Bernie drove home to find Bertie waiting outside at their small round picnic table with a pitcher of lemonade. By that point in the day, Bernie had consumed enough lemonade to last him for the next few years.

"You survived, I see," she said. "Must not have been too bad if you stayed so long."

"It was okay," he said. "The people were nice enough, and Mark Shawcross seems like the genuine article."

"What do you mean by that?"

"He seems like a true believer, and he's more than just talk. He seems to try to put his faith to work." Bernie was more than a little shocked at what was coming out of his mouth, and he could only imagine what Bertie might think.

"Oh, ho, sounds like he really got inside your head. Do I need to worry?"

"Nothing of the sort. The good news is they'll take the vegetables. They'll help out with the weeding and harvesting, so there won't be so much for us to do."

"Hallelujah," she said, raising her glass to the heavens. "My IBS thanks them. I couldn't make it through another summer like the last one."

"You might think about attending church with me

next Sunday, and there's a Bible study group Wednesday evening. I think I'll go to that. You can come too, if you want."

She shot him a long, questioning look, like he'd just asked if she'd like to jump off a bridge, or maybe rob a bank.

"It's okay," he said. "They're just regular people. That's kind of how I'd like us to be, regular people."

"We aren't regular people, Bernie. We never will be. We're better than that. We do what has to be done. I might go to church with you, though. It might be fun to meet some new people, but don't get the idea that makes us regular folks. That's not going to happen. I'll leave the lemonade out here for you. I have work to do inside."

Once again, the air escaped from Bernie's balloon, leaving him deflated—not depressed, exactly—truly deflated. With the outrushing air that had supported him went the feeling of hope that he'd discovered that afternoon at the church. Yeah, Bernie Mitchell, whose best-case scenario had usually been just getting through the day, had experienced what he could only describe as hope, hope that what was to come might be better than what had been.

Maybe if he hadn't had that glimpse of a different kind of life, he could return to the status quo, Bernie Mitchell, freak, always had been, always would be, no questions asked. But it was too late, wasn't it? He'd seen, and he couldn't very well pretend he hadn't. The genie was out of the bottle, the toothpaste was out of the tube, etc., and it wasn't going back. He'd always thought he was the smartest guy in the room, but what if all along, he'd been the chump?

Chapter Fifteen

"Bernie, welcome, I'm so glad you made it." Mark Shawcross held open the side door to the church with his left hand and extended his right to Bernie, greeting him like a long lost friend.

But a Bible study group, what was he, Bernie Mitchell, doing there? It wasn't the religious bit. Bernie had his own ideas about that, the afterlife, in particular. He'd seen the dream people, and the other side didn't look like a fun place to be.

No, here and now was as far as Bernie could see or wanted to. If Mark Shawcross had some new tricks up his sleeve, something that might fill the gaps in Bernie's life, bring them on. He was willing to give it a good listen if nothing else.

Mark pressed a Bible into Bernie's hands. "This one will be yours to keep," he said. That addition doubled the size of Bernie's personal library. He stared at it for a moment, wondering whether it might burst into flames considering the lethal transgressions of the hands that now held it.

Mark must have picked up on Bernie's angst. "No pressure," he said. "Come on, let's go inside, and meet the members. You probably remember some of them from the Sunday service." He led Bernie down a short hallway and through an open door. "Folks, this is Bernie Mitchell. He'll be joining us tonight."

Suddenly there were about fifteen heads, all turned his way, an event that usually would send Bernie running for the nearest exit. Nothing good could come of this. But the faces in front of him were all smiling, not just little smiles but full-bore welcoming smiles. Smiles that said, "Come on in, we're glad to see you." And that's just what he heard, over and over. He couldn't remember ever being greeted, patted or hugged so vigorously as he'd been since he joined Shawcross's flock. There had to be a catch.

"Mr. Mitchell, come and sit by me. I'm Agnes Montgomery." No handshake this time. He got another warm hug instead. Agnes was like the pleasantly plump quintessential grandmother everyone, including Bernie, wished they had. Squeezing her, which he did with some enthusiasm, was like squeezing warm cookie dough. She smelled of cooking spices.

"Please, call me Bernie. Nobody calls me Mr. Mitchell unless I've done something wrong."

Her whole body shook when she laughed. "You don't have to worry about that around here. Mark has told us so much about you and your wonderful garden. We're all excited about it."

"I'm just glad you can make use of some of the stuff. I got carried away again this year, planted way too much."

Soon they were all seated in a circle in a small room with all the windows open and a refreshing breeze flowing through. Instead of the acute anxiety attack he would usually experience in such a gathering, Bernie felt comfortable, like he was where he should be doing what he should be doing.

"The format for the session is pretty open-ended,"

Mark said. "The Bible is a very old book, but in many ways it's timeless and still speaks to us." Mark wrote a quotation on the green chalkboard up front, then invited members of the group to express their own interpretations or how they might see its application in their own lives.

"A merry heart does good like a medicine; but a broken spirit dries the bones."

Proverbs 17:22.

This group, Bernie guessed, must have very strong bones indeed, because their spirits seemed anything but broken. About his own bones, he was less sanguine. But appearances could be deceiving and smiles in the present did not mean absence of sorrows in the past, he learned, as he listened to the brief testimonials offered up from the group.

They told stories of loss, the deaths of friends, family, financial losses. Bernie guessed that many, if not most of these stories had been heard before, but this wasn't about new material, it was about sharing, and it seemed to work. Somehow they'd chosen to greet the present and the future as well with the hopeful countenance of the type Bernie would like to have present on his own face. How did they do it? What was the big secret?

Okay, he got the happy heart, happy face connection, but how to make the big jump? How to get there? After all, he had a closet full of malignant dream people who, although he hadn't seen them in months, were doubtless waiting for the right moment to pounce on him.

As the hour drew to a close, with no plan and no intention, Bernie took a giant step…he spoke up.

"Being the new guy is a little scary," he said.

But Agnes reached across and took his hand, and he got a pat on the shoulder from the guy on the other side.

"Just do what you're comfortable sharing, Bernie," Mark said. "We were all the new guy here at one time or another."

"I was an orphan because my parents died in a fire when I was seven." Maybe he should have divulged the circumstances of his parents' deaths, but he couldn't bring himself to do it, not yet. "I went through some foster homes and finally wound up in an orphanage in…I was there for about eight years. I did odd jobs for a while before I got the job at the Post Office. It's been really hard to trust anybody or open up to anybody except my sister, but I feel comfortable here. Thank you."

It was a brief story, a baby step, and he'd left out major chunks of his own history. He certainly couldn't stand up and confess his homicidal misdeeds—he'd concealed those even from his therapists—but what he'd done was, for Bernie Mitchell, seismic. He'd put himself out there, before people he barely knew, and he'd begun to sweat.

But this wasn't a critical audience. This group was all about aiding and abetting. They wanted Bernie to smile. They wanted his heart to be happy. Bernie had a new cheering section, and they gave him a little round of applause.

"Thank you, Bernie. It's a hard thing, scary too, to stand up in a group and tell about your life story. We're all grateful that you've shared yours with us," Mark said.

As they filed out into the late evening air, the handshake he gave Mark Shawcross was so forceful the good pastor winced. "Sorry," Bernie said. "I got carried away."

"No problem," Mark said. "I'll take that any day."

The euphoria that enveloped him at the church lasted until he entered the house he shared with Bertie. No warm friendly greeting there. The bedroom light shone beneath the door, and he assumed Bertie was working away at whatever was keeping her so busy these recent months. Since she'd displayed expertise in so many areas, the possibilities for her project were vast, so he resigned himself to not knowing until she was ready to show him.

****

Later in the week, when he noticed the weeds around his tomato plants were getting taller than the plants themselves, Bernie grabbed a hoe from the shed and started in on his least favorite gardening chore. He'd chopped and hacked long enough to cause a bead of sweat to trickle the length of his nose when Mark Shawcross drove up with four men in the back of his truck. They dismounted, bearing an assortment of gardening tools, hoes, rakes, and shovels.

"Looks like you've been hard at work," Mark said. "These fellows wanted to come over and lend a hand. Sorry I didn't call first."

"You've come at just the right time," Bernie said. "These weeds got ahead of me again." He'd wondered earlier whether the offers of assistance from the church group might go no further than lots of free advice, but these men looked ready to work. Mark introduced his crew, a couple of whom Bernie recognized from the

Bible study group.

They attacked as a team; the weeds never stood a chance. And these fellows were not silent workers, oh no, they laughed, they joked, sometimes they even sang, and Bernie Mitchell, wonder of wonders, joined right in. It just seemed like the right thing to do. Boy-oh-boy, if Dr. Doolittle could see him now.

In no time at all, the weedy invaders were vanquished, leaving the field to the produce-producers.

"That looks one hundred percent better," Bernie said as he wiped away the sweat from his brow with his shirt sleeve."

When it was over, and the dust was settled, the tools stowed back in the truck, the now sweaty men, gathered around Bernie, shaking his hand, thanking him for letting them help out. This was, perhaps, strange behavior, but it left Bernie with a warm, internal glow. Best of all, Bernie had enjoyed the battle. Slowly but surely, solitary Bernie was become sociable Bernie, in spite of himself.

****

"How do you like the new picnic table?" Bernie stood alongside the eight-foot redwood table, complete with benches, that he'd had placed alongside the garden.

"Tell me again why we need a picnic table," Bertie said.

"Some of the folks from church come over to work in the garden, usually on Thursday, and sometimes a few of the ladies come over too. They bring lemonade and snacks. You should come out and join us. They're a really nice group."

"Ladies, you say?" Bertie's right eyebrow arched,

and this usually meant trouble.

"Yeah, some of the fellows bring over their wives. I really wish you'd come too."

"You're becoming quite the church mouse," she said. "I never would have guessed. At least you're outdoors and active. That part sounds good. Anyway, Thursday is a workday for me, but you enjoy your new friends." She didn't sound as though she was completely on board with the idea, but maybe he could convince her over time that his intentions were totally for the best.

He'd planned his garden ever so carefully; all that followed just happened naturally. Like the earth yielding up a harvest, it also brought forth new friends and fellowship the likes of which Bernie had never imagined.

People came. Of course, the official motive was to help out with the gardening chores, but they came bearing gifts of food that often filled Bernie's eight-foot table, so he had to buy extra folding chairs to seat everyone. In no time at all, Bernie had gone from bystander to participant to host. He found himself caught up in things he would never have permitted before. Except for cuddling with Bertie, which happened less and less frequently of late, the old Bernie avoided physical contact with his fellow man, unless he was forced into it unavoidably by circumstances that usually turned out very badly for someone. But now he both received and gave pats and hugs and touches freely and without a second thought. He even indulged in that set-your-hair-on-fire activity…small talk.

The only way life could possibly be better would be if he could include Bertie in his new circle of friends, but she seemed preoccupied these days. Except for meals, he saw little of her. "You have your things, and I have mine," she said. But what her things might be, he had no idea.

****

If Bernie needed any further validation of the about-face his life had taken, he received it whenever he drove back to the state hospital for his follow-up visits. "You're like a new man," Dr. Doolittle said. "And your last ECT was over two months ago. What's your secret? Is it all about the gardening?"

These sessions were no longer about prying into the dark recesses of Bernie's life trying to tease out the causes of his depression, because depression was no longer an issue. Now they both…Bernie and the good doctor…lapsed into a mood of self-congratulation. Bernie's apparently complete turn-around reflected well on both of them.

"I do enjoy the gardening, and some of the people from the church come by to help out. They're nice too." Although not the most introspective of men, Bernie had sufficient insight to realize that none of what he'd described was exactly earthshaking. He was simply doing normal things that normal people did.

"I've started writing up a brief clinical report about your success, you know, an alternative to the usual medical approach for depression. I'll let you read it over when I'm finished," Doolittle said.

"Happy to help any way I can," Bernie said. Sure, why not spread the joy around a bit, put smiles on a few faces that hadn't had smiles for a long time. The idea of giving back appealed to him in ways he'd never imagined. The Bernie Mitchell who left Dr. Doolittle's office floated along on a new wave of euphoria. Instead of the doctor helping him, Bernie was helping the doctor.

Bertie's earlier admonition that the two of them were not regular folks and never would be did not seem so iron-clad as when he'd first heard it, so he added his own corollary: "Regular is as regular does," and, for the moment, he was doing regular. If Bertie's own path diverged from his, and, of late that seemed to be the case, he'd just have to live with it, she would too.

****

By mid-August, when his vegetable garden was yielding up its bounty and the church congregation members were in full harvest mode, Bernie felt he'd found his true calling, some of it, anyway. So far, Bertie had remained absent from his agricultural world and church activities, but he still wanted to draw her in, make her a part of it, share the joy.

On his return home one particularly warm August evening, after he and his new helpers had harvested two bushel baskets of beans, all of which he gave to the church group, a fatigued and elated Bernie envisioned a cozy sit-down, just he and Bertie, to resolve some of the differences that had grown between them and to begin making some long-range plans.

But Bertie must have been making plans of her own because no sooner had he settled in on the sofa than she marched into the living room, hands behind her back and a smile spread the width of her face. His own plans would have to wait, because this, he guessed, must be the day of the big reveal. Finally, he was going to learn the secret project she'd been working on in their bedroom for several months. True, he could have peeked earlier, but she'd find out for sure, and he both respected her privacy and feared her wrath.

She stopped a few feet from where he sat on the sofa. "Surprise, I have a publishing contract." She pushed a book into his hands. "This is an advance release copy. The real book won't be out for several more weeks. Check out the cover."

The title, *The Avengers*, was set off in bold red letters. Bernie's jaw dropped so far his chin bounced off his chest. There were two figures on the cover, one male, one female, the male holding a climbing axe similar to his own, the female, an ice pick. Bernie was glad he was sitting, otherwise he would have fallen for sure. Both of the figures on the cover had blonde hair, for which he was ever so thankful, but still, the disguise, if that's what it was, seemed very thin.

"You can read this one," Bertie said. "It's your story and my story and our story together. And it has a surprise ending, a Bonnie and Clyde sort of thing where we go out in a blaze of glory."

Bernie couldn't speak. He could barely breathe.

She sat beside him, put her arm around his shoulder. "I did it for us, Bernie. Down deep, I guess I always wanted to be famous. Haven't you?"

Not even close, for most of his life, Bernie's primary goal had been to remain invisible. Showing up on anyone's radar screen usually meant trouble, and the type of fame this book was likely to generate was definitely not on his bucket list.

"Some of it's made up," Bertie said. "Some of it's from my own records—I kept a diary—and a lot of it is from Dr. Carruthers' files on you. You might be surprised at some of it. When she interrogated you under Pentothal she got information that you probably didn't even know yourself. I am so glad we got to her when we did. She could have made so much trouble for us."

As if this book wouldn't make trouble enough?

She patted him a couple of times. If she meant to be reassuring, she missed by a mile. "I'll let you read for a while. I have to go shopping for dinner."

Bernie left the book on the cushion beside him, not daring to open it. He edged away from it, knowing his deepest, darkest secrets lay inside including, according to Bertie, the stuff Dr. Carruthers had pried out of him while he was sedated. The dream people were probably in there, along with other memories he didn't want revived, and, for certain, didn't want to become public knowledge.

"No!" He let loose a bellow that would easily be audible across the street. With the information in this book, she had dashed all his hopes, crushed his future, and seemed quite pleased about it. For as long as he'd known her, he'd considered Bertie his reality principle. Yeah, sometimes she was rather aggressive with her ice pick, and the bank robbery was over the top, but most of the time she seemed to have things under control.

Now this. He picked up the damned book. Might as well hang a big sign in the front yard. Beware, Killers Inside.

Why had she done it? If the pages held the details she'd indicated, it wouldn't take Sherlock Holmes to trace them back to their door. The cops would be lining up on their front porch in no time at all. And what the hell did she mean by a Bonnie and Clyde ending, going out in a blaze of glory? He didn't want to go out at all.

Of late, his life had definitely taken a turn for the better, and he wanted to be around to enjoy it.

Bernie got up and paced, circling the book at a distance like the dangerous item he knew it to be. When he could stand it no more, he opened the book near the end and read.

There, at last everything was in place. Getting the C4 set exactly right had taken weeks, often as not crawling along on her abdomen like some Middle Eastern terrorist, creeping past the areas covered by the motion sensor lights. The house was set off on a rocky promontory, away from other dwellings, but a chance exposure could spoil her whole project. Besides, she could take her time. Anticipation was part of the fun, wasn't it?

Now, Tuesday evening, all her planning and preparation had coalesced into a single point of readiness. The Andersons were both at home. Too bad they wouldn't be able to see the grand finale, but, being strewn over the Pacific Ocean along with their beautiful home, they would miss out on the fun.

The C4 packets were placed around the rear of the house, and, if her calculations were correct— demolition was an inexact science—the force of the blast should direct the debris out over the open water.

Each minute seemed like an eternity as she waited for the exact moment when the setting sun would be perfectly reflected in the ceiling-to-floor windows. It would be like a gigantic rainbow. Great art should be admired by others, and she had considered inviting her soul-mate to witness her creation, or, destruction as it were. But he might not appreciate the necessity of the action she was taking and its artistic merit, so she would be the sole observer. She would capture the event on film, however, so the grandeur of the moment would not be wasted.

One stray strand of purple cloud hung in an otherwise clear sky painted in glorious hues of gold. The moment was now. "Action," she said to herself. She turned on the camera and pressed the button on the detonator.

All six charges must have gone off at once because even at over one hundred yards from the site, a blinding cloud of sand whipped around her. The photo shoot was probably a total loss. When the dust settled, she crawled up onto her knees to check out her handiwork. Nothing but the remnants of a foundation remained. The threat had been neutralized, pulverized, blown away like the dust that covered her now.

She wished she'd worn a poncho, anything to shield her from the dirt that found its way into her nose, into her mouth, covered her so completely that she would probably remain invisible if she remained motionless. But she couldn't stay. Such a blast would attract a lot of attention, so she gathered up her camera and other gear and scurried back to her van, also covered in a layer of dirt. There was a crack in the front windshield. She climbed inside and drove away, never exceeding the speed limit by more than two miles an hour.

Bernie dropped the book on the coffee table. It was worse than he'd imagined, another episode of mass destruction. But what house was she writing about? Who were the Andersons? Why did they have to die? He closed the book and set it back on the sofa. There had to be some way out, but he couldn't see any. He sat there, dazed, lower than he'd ever been in his life.

Bertie came in through the back door, two plastic bags from the market in her hands. "What do you think of it?" she asked. "Do you like it?"

Bernie's mind was still a bit off kilter as he tried to process the new development that would, in the non-fiction world, knock his life completely off the rails and send the Andersons, whoever they were, into oblivion. All he could manage was a shrug.

"I'm fixing pasta for dinner. Why don't you work on the salad, and we can talk while we eat?"

She seemed so calm, so matter-of-fact about everything. Maybe it was all a big joke. That was it, had to be, Bertie's warped sense of humor taking center stage like a bank robbery with water pistols. His heart stopped racing, and his breathing, although not exactly normal yet, became less like a steam locomotive climbing a steep hill.

By the time they sat down to eat their pasta, the hopeful aura that had enveloped him for the past few days had returned. "You had me worried for a few minutes," he said. "That stuff about blowing up the house…." He forced a laugh.

Bertie's fork, laden with linguine, stopped halfway to her mouth and fell back onto her plate. "It's no joke, Bernie. I'm going to do it. Everything is already set. I have to do it before the book comes out, otherwise it doesn't make any sense."

Bernie saw his new world—the one where he was a regular guy doing regular things—get kicked aside, replaced by gloom and doom so thick he saw no way through it.

"You started reading near the end, didn't you? If

you started at the beginning you'd understand it better," she said, as if there were some explanation for the carnage she planned.

"Understand what? That you're going to blow up another house and some people named Anderson with it? Please, tell me this isn't so." A crushing weight pressed down on Bernie.

"That's why you have to start with the first page, then you'll see why it has to be done. There's no other way. And the people aren't really named Anderson. I made that up."

Dinner was effectively over before it began, so they cleared away the plates and headed for the living room sofa.

"See, the more I dug into Carruthers's files, the more I learned about what she was up to. I was wrong when I assumed the lady in the big house was just a friend. She was actually Dr. Bowman's sister. I got into her house one night and read some of her files that she had, and they were even worse than what I found in Carruthers's stuff. So, she had to go and her files along with her. It was the only way."

"But you haven't done it yet?"

"No, but everything is in place. I'm planning for this Friday. She's always home on Friday."

"How? Another gas leak?"

"No, this will be even bigger. I got some real C4 from somebody I used to work with. I can be a lot more precise about the timing. That way, you can come to watch, if you'd like."

"I don't think so. Look, Bertie, even if we get away with the explosion, the book will give us away for sure."

A word about the author…

Occupation: Physician (retired)
Undergrad. edu. Univ. of North Carolina, Chapel Hill, NC, MFA Old Dominion Univ., Norfolk, VA
http://www.mikeowens42.com

Thank you for purchasing
this publication of The Wild Rose Press, Inc.

For questions or more information
contact us at
info@thewildrosepress.com.

The Wild Rose Press, Inc.
www.thewildrosepress.com

"I'm not afraid of the cops. We've beaten them all these years, and we'll go right on beating them."

"Bertie, I'm begging you, don't publish the book, and don't blow up the house."

"I have to do it, and it has to take place just as I've described it, first the explosion, then the book release. It'll really be big, you'll see." Once again, she gave him that reassuring pat from which he drew no comfort whatever.

That night the dream people descended on him en masse. There were his parents in flames, his mother waving an accusatory finger at her wayward son, on and on they came, gory specters with battered heads. Ms. Grosbeak's charred image, barely recognizable, danced around his bed. He could almost hear her say, "They've got you now, Mitchell. Now you'll pay."

He got up the next morning feeling as if he'd have been better off not going to bed at all. Now, once again, he began to dread the prospect of nightfall, darkness which would open the gates of hell for Bernie Mitchell. ECT probably would not save him this time.

He drove over to his garden, usually a place of solace, even inspiration, but not today. He climbed aboard his tractor but didn't fire it up. Indeed, where could he go? Where could he hide?

Any hope for a future now required action, drastic action that would stop the onrushing train that threatened to crush him. Bertie was not home when he returned, so he went into the garage, retrieved his axe, and stashed it on the bottom shelf of his nightstand. If negotiations failed, he'd have no choice.

But there would be no negotiations, not tonight. He gave up waiting just after three a.m., and he was already in bed, feigning sleep when Bertie finally got home. She'd probably been putting the finishing touches on her preparations for blowing the Anderson house along with its inhabitants into the great beyond. For a moment or so he reconsidered the possibility that she might be bluffing. What if he invited himself to a ringside seat to watch the big blast? Would she laugh and say, "Just kidding?" But that thought lasted only for a short time. Bertie didn't bluff.

The dream people arrived soon after Bernie had bedded down, but this time they weren't swooping around like a swarm of angry hornets. They were all there, lined up shoulder to bloody shoulder along the wall, waiting like they knew what was going to happen.

Bernie waited too, for what he knew would come. When he thought about it, there could be only one ending, no substitutions allowed. The creaky board halfway between their beds alerted him to her presence, and he drew his axe alongside. The timing was so perfect, as if they'd practiced it many times, Bertie's downward thrust with her icepick, Bernie's arcing swing with his axe, the crunching sound as he crushed skull bone and the softer thump as her icepick penetrated his chest, then the silence that neither one of them would hear.